REC

MW00322953

RECEIVED DEC   - 2022

To Hope —

The Secret Heart

Marie Wells Coutu

Romans 5:2

W
Write Integrity Press

Marie Wells Coutu

Marie Wells Coutu

Write Integrity Press
The Secret Heart
© 2017 Marie Wells Coutu
ISBN-10: 1-944120-06-8
ISBN-13: 978-1-944120-06-1
E-book ISBN: 978-1-938092-93-0

All rights reserved. No part of this publication may be reproduced or transmitted in any form or by any means without written permission from the publisher.

This book is a work of fiction. Names, characters, places, and incidents are either products of the author's imagination or used fictitiously. Any similarity to actual people and/or events is purely coincidental.

Scripture quotations are from the ESV® Bible (The Holy Bible, English Standard Version®), copyright © 2001 by Crossway, a publishing ministry of Good News Publishers. Used by permission. All rights reserved.

Published by Write Integrity Press, 4475 Trinity Mills Road, PO Box 702852, Dallas, TX 75370
Find out more about the author, **Marie Wells Coutu,** at her website,
www.MarieWellsCoutu.com
www.WriteIntegrity.com
Printed in the United States of America.

Dedication

To the One who knows the innermost secrets of my heart,
and loves me anyway.

"Behold, you delight in truth in the inward being, and you teach
me wisdom in the secret heart."
Psalm 51:6, ESV

Chapter 1

The sun should not be shining. Not on this day.

From the front row of folding chairs, Shawna Wilson could see acres of manicured grass. The tent overhead and the chair covers matched the deep green turf. Flat stones marched across the ground in symmetry, each one reflecting the rays of the sun. In vases atop the markers, bouquets of spring flowers glistened in yellow and red and purple. Sparrows flitted about and robins chirped their annual "all is new" song.

But this day was not about new life.

Shawna sat numbly as the preacher read the Twenty-Third Psalm. *The valley of the shadow of death.* That's where she was. Again.

Maybe if she had stayed on those paths of righteousness he mentioned, she wouldn't be walking this road of grief. But it was too late to turn back.

She clinched her hands into fists and forced them to rest unmoving on her lap. Hunter reached over and gently covered both of her hands with one of his. She couldn't look at her husband now, so she focused on the row of trees at the end of the drive. Beyond the trees, cars sped along the divided highway, people shopped at the mall, and normal life continued.

Behind her, someone coughed. On Hunter's other side, his two young boys, Hunter Lynn and Cooper, squirmed. Thank goodness, their grandmother Mimi could keep them in line. Heaven knew Shawna couldn't handle a nine-year-old and seven-year-old, especially boys.

Her two older sisters sat somewhere behind her, their presence a comfort even if their persistent prayers had failed.

Two men in black suits and crisp white shirts rose and took their places at each end of the gaping black hole. One turned the crank, setting the contraption in motion. Metal scraped against metal as the shiny black coffin disappeared into the ground. The box was small. Too small.

A third man, the funeral director, gestured to her. Time to say good-bye. Hunter stood and grasped her arm. Shawna rose automatically from her chair, as if a puppet master were pulling her strings.

She lifted a perfect pink rose from the blanket of flowers that had covered the casket. Thorns pricked her fingers as she held the blossom to her nose and inhaled the rich fragrance, just as she had inhaled the sweet smell of her newborn two weeks ago.

"Goodbye, precious Hannah," she whispered, tossing the long-stemmed rose onto the sinking casket. Hunter copied her motion.

He squeezed her elbow, then tucked his hand against her back. "Ready?" he murmured.

No. She would never be ready. She could not walk away from her baby girl. She watched the box lowering deeper and deeper into the earth. She hoped Hannah Lea would not be afraid of the dark.

Only when the coffin was settled did she take her eyes off of it and nod. She turned and pressed against Hunter. He wrapped his arms around her, and she leaned her head on his sturdy shoulder. She took deep breaths, fighting the sobs that hovered below the surface. Crying wouldn't change reality. After a few moments, she allowed Hunter to guide her out from under the canopy, out of the section formed by low hedges.

Perhaps burying Hannah Lea in the middle of that cross-shaped area meant her baby was in the arms of Jesus, as Shawna's sisters assured her. But her spirit wondered whether there was any truth to the beliefs she'd held all her life.

She could hear rustling and low voices, a sign that the small crowd of mourners was following them to the line of black limousines waiting under the Bradford pear trees. As they walked down the steps to the drive, a light breeze picked up the sour odor of death from the fallen white blossoms and sprinkled it over the procession.

Their friends and staff members had shared hugs and sentiments with them at the cemetery chapel before the graveside service. There was nothing left to do now but go home. Shawna's heel caught on a broken piece of concrete. She lurched into Hunter, who caught her and kept her upright.

The rapid click of cameras came from the crowd of reporters and gawkers that had gathered behind temporary barriers near the cars. Questions tumbled from the reporters, one on top of another.

Shawna had not asked for this constant scrutiny, and she especially hated it today. Even during her national collegiate tennis tournaments, she had preferred to turn media attention to her teammates and coaches. When she chose to marry Hunter, she hadn't realized how high the price would be. The only privacy she could find anymore was behind the iron fence of the ten-acre estate she now called home.

At this minute, that's where she wanted to be—in the second-floor private quarters of the Georgian mansion. Where she could get out of the black linen dress and crawl into the king-size bed. Maybe she would never wake up.

She put her hand on Hunter's arm as they hurried for the first vehicle in line. Then she heard the shouted question, the one that burned to be answered.

"Governor, will this tragedy affect your reelection campaign?"

Tennessee Governor Hunter Wilson stopped and turned in the direction of the reporters. He held up a hand. "Please, give us privacy today. We've just buried our daughter."

Of course, he would drop out of the race. Shawna needed him home with her and the boys, not off traveling the state campaigning. She wouldn't mind moving into a modest home when his current term ended. He could always go back to teaching.

Their driver, a state trooper wearing a black suit with a lapel pin, opened the rear door of the black Crown Victoria.

Out of the corner of her eye, Shawna saw a tall, slim woman with long black hair stride toward the barriers. Johnnie Allen, Hunter's long-time campaign manager, who seemed to consume all of his time these days.

"The governor will resume his schedule in the next few days," Shawna heard before she slid into the back seat. She sank onto the cool leather, grateful that Mimi and the boys would ride separately in the Ford Escalade behind them.

Hunter put one arm around her shoulders. With his other hand, he brushed a wisp of hair away from her cheek. With his lazy eyelid nearly obscuring the left one, his green eyes studied her as he had at their first meeting nearly a year ago. "You okay?"

She leaned her head against the hard bone of his forearm. "Not really."

He picked up a bottled water from the cup holder, unscrewed the top, and handed it to her. She drank. The lukewarm, tasteless water flowed down her throat without refreshing her.

The cars moved along the drive, past the grave sites of the likes of George Jones, Porter Wagoner, and Tammy Wynette. Strange that Shawna's daughter would be buried among so many country music stars, including Hunter's first wife. How had Shawna's life taken such a strange twist?

Network satellite trucks, and one small white car bearing the words "The Tennessean," lined both sides of Memorial Gardens Drive. Cameramen filmed the funeral procession leaving the cemetery, then scrambled into their vehicles and followed them.

As they turned onto I-65, Shawna closed her eyes, shutting out the Nashville traffic. But the voices in her head continued to whimper. Could she ever have a life that wasn't marred by the death of people she loved?

A decision about his campaign eluded Hunter on Monday as the black Escalade with tinted windows followed him and his running companion along the quiet streets away from the Executive Residence.

Dressed in blue nylon pants and a fitted white athletic

shirt, Hunter could have passed for an ordinary businessman out for an early morning run—except for the car creeping along behind him, its headlights illuminating the way. No one would realize that his black running partner wearing an earbud was actually a state trooper.

When the trees no longer provided cover, a brisk wind pushed against him, showing him what his two-week break had cost him. His heart thundered and he struggled for breath. He had needed to be there with Shawna and baby Hannah, as crushing as those days at the hospital had been. Hearing the doctor tell them their daughter's lungs had been contaminated during delivery. Holding the tiny pink bundle too briefly as she struggled to breathe. Reaching into the incubator to stroke her smooth head. Pleading with God not to punish her for the sins of her parents.

A bird circled to the west, a black spot in the brightening sky. A vulture? Perhaps, drawn to some remnant of roadkill over on Franklin Pike? Following the usual route, the two runners turned east toward Lipscomb Academy where Hunter Lynn and Cooper went to school.

The boys had been so excited about having a sister. They didn't know her death was their father's punishment. He hoped they would never know, that his actions would stay firmly buried in the past.

Time to focus on the future.

"A lot on my mind this morning, Curtis. Not very good company." They had nearly reached the turnaround point, and they hadn't exchanged more than five words. Hunter's breathlessness betrayed how out-of-shape he really was.

The trooper, taller than Hunter's even six-feet, managed to match Hunter's pace, no matter if he sprinted or strolled. And he could talk as he ran, without gasping for breath like Hunter.

"Ah don't mind, Governor. Gives me a chance to think about the paper Ah have to write." Curtis Woods' southern drawl was more pronounced than Hunter's, a reflection of his coming-up years in South Carolina.

In sync, the two men navigated the drive in front of the school, then cut across the grass back to the street. The trail car would rejoin them at the street corner.

Hunter nodded. "What's the paper about?" Curtis, who pastored a small inner-city church in his spare time, was taking seminary courses online. He often talked about his coursework during their runs together.

"This course on First and Second Samuel is the toughest yet. I'm supposed to write about the allure of power, comparing another prominent figure to Saul."

"Shouldn't be hard to find examples." Hunter had seen the hunger for power ruin men that he had respected, in academia as well as in politics.

Curtis grunted his agreement. "My problem is deciding which one to use. I'm fascinated by some of the British kings, but there are many modern-day examples, too. Not just grasping for power, but abusing it. Entertainers, sports figures, even preachers." He glanced sideways at Hunter. "And politicians."

12

Hunter stepped on a rock he hadn't noticed and missed a step. "Yeah, I guess every occupation has a few bad seeds."

They turned through the wide gate in the iron fence surrounding the Executive Residence and ran up the curving drive to the three-story brick-and-stone house. While the trail car parked, Curtis followed Hunter around to the side and in through the family entrance. Hunter still had not decided about his reelection bid, but before he took his shower, he called Johnnie and asked her to come over to discuss the campaign.

As the vibrating spray massaged his back, he considered his accomplishments as governor: the new Japanese auto assembly plant with its five thousand jobs. Increased funding for roads and bridges without even a penny in higher taxes. More innovation in state government.

But several important measures still needed to be accomplished, such as funding technology for schools, so all children had the same opportunities. And attracting a research facility that would find cures for cancer and add more jobs.

So much more to do to help the citizens of his state. He wanted—no, he *needed*—to get back to work, both at the capitol and on the campaign trail. With another four years as governor, he could make an even greater difference.

Twenty minutes later, he rubbed his short hair dry with

a thick towel as he came out of the bathroom. Shawna lay on the king-size bed, curled into a ball just as she had been when he left for his run. Her eyes were closed, but he knew she was awake. Her long brown hair spread like a pheasant's fan across the pale green pillowcase. He sat down next to her and ran his finger along her hairline where it framed her face. The tan she'd had when they married had faded over the winter, stolen by limited outdoor activity during the last months of her pregnancy.

"Honey?" He bent down and kissed her cheek, breathing in the aura of sadness that enveloped her. "Want breakfast?"

"I'm not hungry." Her words were muffled, her lips barely moving.

He moved his hand to her back, trying to rub strength into her. "You need to eat something. I think the chef's letting Mimi make pancakes and sausage with the boys."

She pulled in a deep breath. "I couldn't eat anything."

He sensed her shivering, though she couldn't possibly be cold under the layers of blankets. She had been behaving this way since Hannah died last Tuesday, getting out of bed only to plan and attend the funeral. "Will you at least sit with me while I eat? Johnnie's coming over to talk about the campaign, and I'd like to know your thoughts."

She opened her eyes. Cold, hollow ovals scowled at him. "The campaign? You're going to drop out, right?"

Her question-that-wasn't-a-question irritated Hunter. He stood and strode to the closet. "I don't see why I should."

Shawna pushed back the blankets and sat up, scooting to the edge of the bed. She reached for her bathrobe. "After all we've been through these last couple of weeks, I thought..."

She wanted him to pull out of the race, to hide from the public like she was doing. Had been doing for two weeks. Not a chance. "I've got a job to do. I've got things I want to accomplish for this state, important things that won't get done if I don't get reelected."

"Really?" She shrugged into her robe and shuffled to the bathroom. "And I thought your family was important." She shut the door, cutting off any rebuttal.

Hunter shook his head. People reacted to grief differently, but he wished Shawna would cry and scream, rather than carrying on in such a passive-aggressive manner. Maybe she needed to talk to their pastor. He finished dressing and left the bedroom, closing the door quietly behind him.

As he neared the bottom of the family's private stairwell, he heard Mimi and the boys in the commercial kitchen, Mimi giving instructions on how to mix the batter. Having been married to an army general for twenty-two years, she ran a household with military precision, which he had appreciated when he was a single father. She even looked the part, keeping her silvery hair cropped short and tidy. But hidden beneath the disciplined exterior was a soft heart, especially for her grandchildren. If only she would show Shawna the same level of respect she demanded from the boys.

When Hunter entered the kitchen, Cooper was pouring flour into a bowl, and Hunter Lynn stood on the other side of Mimi, watching the link sausages sizzling in an iron skillet.

"Somebody knows how to start a Monday morning off right." He crossed the sun-filled room and put his arms around Cooper and Mimi. Wouldn't be long before Cooper would be as tall as his five-foot-two grandmother. He had obviously inherited Hunter's stature, not his mother's. "You're being a good helper, aren't you, Coop?"

"Yeah, Dad." Grinning, Cooper moved a long-handled wooden spoon in a random pattern through the bowl, splattering batter onto the counter. "I'm gonna make Teddy-bear pancakes."

"Teddy-bear pancakes huh?" Hunter ruffled his son's hair. White-blond like his mother's. "Can't wait."

He turned to Hunter Lynn. "Looks like you've got the piggies well under control, son."

Hunter Lynn used a spatula to push the sausage links around. He shrugged. "They're not alive, Dad."

Hunter laughed. "Good thing. I don't eat raw pork. Mimi, Johnnie's coming over to talk about the campaign. Is there enough for her?"

"Hunter Wilson, you ought to know you don't even have to ask. I'll set another place." She opened the cabinet and took out a plate. "What about Shawna? Will she be

16

eating?"

He couldn't answer that question, and the jangle of the bell gave him an excuse. "That should be Johnnie." He left the kitchen and went to greet his campaign manager.

Shawna joined them as they were sitting down to eat. She appeared to have showered, and she had wrapped her wet hair into a tight bun. Her lips turned up in a smile that didn't reach her eyes. "Hey, Johnnie. You here to take my husband on the road again?"

Shawna sniggered as if she were joking, but Hunter cringed. If she were going to argue with Johnnie, he didn't want the boys to hear. "Why don't we eat, then we can talk afterward?"

As soon as the boys finished, Hunter told them they could go to the room they shared and play the Xbox. He wasn't sorry they would have one more day off school due to a teacher workday. Even if they didn't show it, the boys needed time to grieve over their half-sister as much as he and Shawna did.

"Yeah!" Hunter Lynn gave Cooper a high five.

After they left the room, Hunter turned to Johnnie. "When can we get back out there? How much has this time off hurt us?"

"We had to cancel several events the last couple of weeks." She rose to retrieve her briefcase. Taking out a manila folder, she returned to her seat. "We have had to pass on a number of good opportunities, but we've got six months before the buzzer. And voters are rooting for you, even if they weren't your fans before." A former basketball star and coach for the University of Tennessee, she often used sports terminology in conversations.

Shawna set her cup on her saucer with a clunk. She had eaten nothing, but was working on her fourth or fifth cup of coffee. "Seriously? Are you saying that losing our daughter will help Hunter's campaign because it gets sympathy?"

"Shawna, please—"

"It's okay, Governor." Johnnie used both hands to gather her long, straight hair into a bunch at her neck, then released it and looked directly at Shawna. "That's not what I meant, Mrs. Wilson. I'm sorry if I sound insensitive. Just stating the facts as I see them."

Hunter reached over and placed his hand over Shawna's where it lay on the table. "Let's stay focused, honey. Johnnie's here to help."

Shawna turned her hand over and clasped his. "I don't want Hannah's death used as a campaign tactic."

"It won't be, I assure you. Right, Johnnie?"

"Agreed. It's out-of-bounds." Johnnie opened the folder and looked at Hunter. "There is an event scheduled for Wednesday that I haven't canceled yet. You could start a full-court press to gain grassroots support for Teaching Through Tech."

The General Assembly had adjourned in mid-April, again without including funding in the appropriations bill for computers in classrooms. "What's the group?"

She pushed a sheet of paper across the table. "It's a Parent Teacher Organization meeting in Black Rock. That's in Randall County, eastern part of the state."

He picked up the letter from the group's president inviting him to speak at their annual meeting. "Will they support our proposal?"

Johnnie drained the last of her coffee. "To be honest, I don't know. It's a mining town. The computer bill has been a hard sell in that part of the state. I think it's an opportunity for them to hear straight from you about why this initiative is important."

Mimi stood. "Sounds like a nice, quiet event to get you back into the campaign. I'll get you more coffee." She took Johnnie's cup and went into the kitchen.

"But Wednesday?" Shawna leaned her arms on the table. "That's day after tomorrow. Does he really need to go back out so soon?"

Hunter appreciated his wife's need for him, but he couldn't sit around all day holding her hand. "I'm the governor, Shawna. The people are depending on me, and this is an important issue. I've been working on this for three years."

"It's a campaign speech, Hunter." She pushed away from the table but stayed in her chair. "The bill won't come up again until next spring. It's not like you won't have other opportunities."

Mimi entered, carrying Johnnie's coffee. She glanced at Shawna, then looked at Hunter. She set the cup in front of Johnnie. "I think it's a good idea. These are ordinary folks, not high-dollar donors. Show them you want to hear what they think." She picked up Johnnie's empty breakfast plate, then her own. "Seems like the ideal way to give your campaign a reboot."

"But we haven't even decided if you're going to continue your campaign."

"Why wouldn't he continue?" Mimi set the plates down and put her hands on her hips, reminding Hunter of a Doberman facing an attacker. "If he quits now, he'll throw away his political career and any chance of being president."

He loved that Mimi still believed in him, even after he failed her daughter. But he didn't need her to defend him to his new wife. "I told you this morning, Shawna." He spoke like he would to a child. "I don't see any reason to drop out of the campaign. There's still a lot I want to do for Tennessee, and winning reelection is my best chance to see it through."

Shawna stood and glared at him. The hurt in her eyes pierced his soul, but she didn't speak.

Johnnie had been looking at her phone. She cleared her throat. "The meeting is at five their time, Governor. You could leave after lunch and be home by about seven. Seven-thirty at the latest."

The dual time zones worked in his favor this time. He stood and faced Shawna, reached out and rubbed her arms. "You see? I'll be home before the kids go to bed."

"Fine. I guess the people of Tennessee are more important than I am." She moved away from him and left the room. His heart pounding in his ears almost drowned out the sound of her feet running up the stairs.

Johnnie sat waiting with one thin eyebrow arched more than usual. Her narrow eyes studied him. "Game on?"

Hunter nodded. Shawna had married a sitting governor; after seven months, she should be used to his traveling. "Let's go for it."

Marie Wells Coutu

Chapter 2

Maybe Hunter could go on as if nothing had changed, but Shawna could not. Her whole world had turned upside down in the past nine months. Losing Hannah had been the final stone.

She remained in the bedroom the rest of the day and most of Tuesday, coming out only when Mimi ordered her to come downstairs to eat. "The boys need life to get back to normal. Besides, I'm too old to be bringing your meals upstairs to you." At 67, Mimi was nearly as fit as any drill sergeant. Still, Shawna got the point.

After breakfast Wednesday morning, wearing gray sweatpants and a royal blue Murray State sweatshirt, she went into the home office she shared with Hunter. So far, she used the room more than he did. He was much more likely to go to the capitol than to work from home.

She found a stack of sympathy cards on the desk.

Sighing, she sat down and picked up one that had a white dove on the front. Immediately, she felt the dark cloud settle on her, the one that had been her constant companion since she realized that Hannah Lea would not live. She read the sentiment from the Senate Majority Leader and her husband. Her eyes brimming with tears, she read another card, then another, dabbing at the teardrops so she wouldn't smear the signatures.

When the phone rang, she almost didn't answer, but on the fifth ring, she picked up the receiver. Avoiding Crystal accomplished nothing. Her assistant wanted to know what to do about the First Lady's appearances scheduled for the next two weeks.

Shawna's mouth dried up at the image of a bunch of old ladies who would give her sympathetic shoulder pats and cluck their tongues. "I'm still not ready to come back, Crystal."

She leaned her head against the high back of the maroon leather chair and crooked her neck to hold the phone to her ear. The room had the same high ceilings and traditional furnishings as the rest of the governor's living quarters. Here, though, the dark woods and leather even smelled masculine.

Shawna liked that, when he was elected governor, Hunter had been the one to choose these colors and accessories. The office suited her current mood more than the living room's bright flower-patterned walls, no doubt selected by Mimi. "Just cancel all my appearances for a couple more weeks."

Crystal coughed—her signal of disagreement. "Look, Shawna, I understand. But some of these people planned their events months ago. I know it's only been a week since Hannah died, but don't you think it would be good for you to get out?"

A week yesterday. Hannah Lea would have been three weeks old. She looked at the stack of sympathy cards on the desk, and visualized the scene of some charity event. "And face all those people saying how sorry they are? They don't even know what it's like." A personal response to each of the cards would be appropriate, but she had no heart for that task. "In fact, I'm going to send all these cards over to you to handle the response. I can't read any more of them, much less answer them."

"Sure, we can take care of that. I'll get someone to pick them up today." Crystal's flat tone acknowledged that she was losing the argument. "But what do I tell the event planners?"

Shawna pressed the button to put the call on speaker and stood. Why did this have to be so hard? She crossed to the bookshelf and pulled out a suede-covered scrapbook. She raised her voice to be heard across the room. "Look, Crystal, I want you to cancel them all until further notice. First Lady is an honorary position. It's not like I'm being paid to show up."

She took the large volume back to the desk, stroking the soft brown cover. Her staff did a nice job of putting together these scrapbooks for her. Maybe the clippings and photos from her courtship with Hunter would cheer her up.

Crystal's voice crackled over the speaker again. "This Saturday is the Fitness Expo, the kick-off for your Fit Kids campaign. It's been planned for months."

"The other sponsors will be there, won't they? We've got lots of support for this thing."

"Yes, but you're the face of the whole campaign. This is your primary initiative. The task force will be perturbed if you don't even show up."

Saturday was still four days away. Perhaps she could pull herself together by then, if she must. "Fine. Saturday. But nothing before then."

"Great. Mimi's representing you at the Heart Association auction today. Everything else I can cancel."

She had nearly forgotten about this afternoon. With Hunter in eastern Tennessee, and Mimi substituting for her, Shawna would be responsible for the boys after school and all evening. They were good kids but she had no experience with little boys. She'd had sisters growing up, not brothers. Mimi had taken care of Hunter Lynn and Cooper since their mother died. Shawna had been grateful, when she married Hunter, to have their grandmother to look after them.

"Shawna? You still there?"

She stared at the phone on the desk, then picked up the receiver and took it off speaker mode. "Yes, Crystal. Sorry, I was just thinking."

"Okay. Is there anything else you need? Anything I

can do for you?" Crystal sounded almost desperate, as though Shawna couldn't take care of herself.

"No, thanks. I'm going to lay low until Saturday."

After she hung up, she opened the memory album. The pages chronicled, through newspaper clippings and printouts of Facebook posts, her whirlwind romance with Hunter. Of course, it didn't start at the true beginning. The media and the public did not know the truth about their first encounter. And, if Hunter wanted to remain in politics, they never would.

Shawna stayed in the office all morning, reading the articles in the scrapbooks. Nothing like having every moment of your courtship chronicled in newspaper articles, YouTube videos, and blogs.

It hadn't been easy for him to spend time with her, given his busy schedule running the state and kicking off his reelection campaign. If they went to dinner or a show, the fact got tweeted in minutes. But he invited her to fundraising dinners all over the state and a couple of visits to the Opry. When he introduced her to the Bluebird Cafe—which became her favorite place—they had to enter through the kitchen to avoid standing in line waiting for admission. Even then, someone would manage to snap their picture with a phone and post it on Instagram. And the next day, some newspaper columnist would write about the governor's "girlfriend."

So different than when she'd been Miss Kentucky. Her sponsors had worked overtime to get her that kind of publicity. Even then, she'd have preferred to stay out of the spotlight. But she'd cooperated. It was part of what she signed on for when she entered the scholarship contest.

Likewise, Hunter had known what to expect when he entered politics. The farther up the ladder he climbed, the less privacy he had. But she had—quite literally—fallen into the spotlight with him. Her desire had been for the person, not for the position or the publicity.

One of the albums lay open to a photo taken Labor Day weekend, when she and Hunter hiked in the Smokies. She touched the newspaper clipping, thinking how she had actually wondered if ending the pregnancy would be best— for her, the baby, and the governor.

However, on that weekend trip to Gatlinburg she realized the depth of her love for Hunter, even as she carried grief over Daniel's death. And there, by Rainbow Falls, Hunter convinced her to marry him. The wedding had taken place two weeks later.

The sound of "We Are Family" blasted from her cell phone, signaling a call from one of her sisters. She picked up the device and glanced at the screen. Elissa. She groaned. There was no sense ignoring it. Her oldest sister would keep calling until Shawna talked to her.

"Hey, Ellie. I'm fine, thanks." She had always avoided

lectures from her big sister by answering questions before they were asked.

"Good morning to you, too. Glad to know you're fine, so I don't worry about you."

With the phone caught between her cheek and her shoulder, Shawna turned another page in the scrapbook and smoothed out the pages. "You don't have to worry. I'm a big girl."

She felt, rather than heard, the sigh on the other end. "Really," Elissa said. "Anyway, that's not why I called. I'll be in town tomorrow. We need to find a birthday present for Bri."

The sisters always joined forces to buy each other birthday presents, but Brianna's birthday was more than a month away. "I'm sure you'll find something perfect. Let me know how much, and I'll send you money for my share."

"Oh, no, you don't. You know the best places to look, and you have great ideas about what she'll like. I'll pick you up at ten."

Five years older than Shawna, Elissa always managed to get her way. In this case, to get Shawna out of the house. There was no other reason to shop for the present so early. She swallowed the sour flavor of caving in to her big sis. So much for laying low until Saturday. "Fine. But a trooper will have to take us in a state car."

After making the arrangements, Shawna clicked off. She placed her arms on the desk and put her head down.

She'd been Miss Kentucky, a soldier's wife, sales manager for Lake Barkley Resort, and now Tennessee's First Lady. Yet Elissa still managed to make her feel like a child.

Later that afternoon, Shawna sat on the floor by the bookshelf, scrapbooks scattered around her. She had found Cooper's baby book, from before Hunter became governor and before Lynn had died. Shawna touched a photo of the happy family, excitement over the new baby radiating from their faces. The hollow spot in her heart grew larger.

Mimi, dressed in a two-piece navy and white dress, came in. Her orange blossom cologne floated across the room. Shawna looked up at her. "Did you put this one together? A lot of love went into it."

"No, Lynn was the scrap booker. Right up until she got too weak." Mimi's terse voice suggested that she didn't want to share the memories. At least not with Shawna.

She closed the book quickly. "I'm sorry. I didn't mean to be nosy."

"It's all right." Mimi crossed her arms. "Lynn was a special person. Too bad you didn't know her."

Right. If Shawna had known Lynn, she could never have married Hunter. She got off the floor and placed that album back where she had found it. "Thank you for going to this auction today. I could not stand to see all those faces of people thinking *poor Shawna.*"

Mimi moved to the shelf and straightened the scrapbook, then adjusted the other books near it, lining them up in formation. "You'll have to before long, you know. You can't stay out of the public eye forever."

"I know. I'm going shopping with Elissa tomorrow." She picked up another volume from the floor and put it away. "And I told Crystal I'd go to the Fitness Expo on Saturday. That will be mostly kids, so it'll be easier. Maybe I'll bring Cooper and H. L."

"That would be good for them." Mimi turned toward the door. "They just got home from school. They're in their room doing homework. I told them no Xbox until after supper."

"Thanks, Mimi. We'll be fine while you're gone." She wouldn't let this woman know how inadequate she felt around Hunter's sons. As long as they stayed in their room, she had nothing to worry about.

After Mimi left, Shawna put away the rest of the scrapbooks then wandered down the hall. Stopping quietly outside the boys' room, she listened but heard nothing. They must still be studying. She moved on to the next room—the one she had set up as a nursery. Fluffy white lambs with pink bows around their necks frolicked across the green walls. She flipped the light switch, which also controlled a ceiling fan, and that set in motion a mobile above the crib. The sheep and cows and pigs chased each other in an endless circle.

She closed the door and crept to the rocking chair by the window, the chair she brought from her childhood home, the chair in which she had imagined rocking her baby to sleep each night—the baby who had never come home to this place prepared especially for her. Shawna lifted the crocheted afghan and sat in the chair. Holding the fuzzy blanket to her face, she pushed back, rocking slowly. She hummed "Rock-a-bye Baby."

The door flew open and Cooper ran in. In his hand was a neon green plastic machine gun that shot foam darts. He looked around the room but pulled up short, eyes wide, when he saw Shawna.

Hunter Lynn poked a similar toy through the open door, then peeked around the corner and fired, the foam dart hitting Cooper in the back. "Gotcha!" The older boy laughed and ran into the room, but he also stopped when he saw Shawna.

Shawna jumped out of the rocking chair. This was her private space. Hers and Hannah's. "What are you two doing? You know better than to play with those guns in here! I don't want you in this room—ever."

What was wrong with her? First the tears, and now yelling. The once-confident, self-controlled winner seemed to be falling apart.

Cooper screwed his face into a frown and threw the toy gun to the floor. "I wish Daddy had never married you!" Then he turned and ran from the room.

She looked at his older brother, whose face had taken on a surly look. He bent over to pick up Cooper's discarded weapon. "Sorry." His tone sounded more sassy than sincere.

From down the hall came the sound of footsteps

pounding down the main staircase. Shawna started. "Where's he going?" The boys rarely went into the public rooms of the house.

Hunter Lynn looked at her and shrugged, then shuffled out of the room, leaving Shawna to flounder in her failures.

After Hunter was introduced to the Parent Teacher Organization, the life-hardened men and women in the audience applauded politely, if not enthusiastically. But when he began to discuss his Teaching Through Tech legislation, he noticed scowls and raised eyebrows.

The cramped gymnasium at Black Rock Elementary School reeked of sweat, left behind by the energetic kids who had been gone for hours. Now their parents packed the bleachers, eager to hear what their governor had to say. Dust drifted in the air, caught in the slivers of light eking through dirty windows.

Hunter couldn't tell if the faces in front of him were unfriendly or only skeptical.

"The world is changing, and our schools need to change with it." He could tell he was losing the audience. "Access to technology should be just as available for your children as it is for the children in Knoxville or Nashville."

A man in the front row who was wearing a blue custodial uniform started to raise his hand, but he lowered it when Hunter continued speaking.

"Technology can keep your children from falling behind, but only if we make it available to every child. Rural school districts can't afford to keep up with the latest devices."

A chubby woman three rows up shook her head and crossed her arms.

Hunter gestured to the audience. "That's why we need state funding for Teaching Through Tech, and I intend to keep fighting for it when I am reelected governor."

A man at the end of the top row stood and descended the bleachers, each step shaking the entire metal-and-wood contraption and echoing around the room. A local reporter on the bottom row scribbled furiously in her notebook. Apparently, Johnnie had been wrong about this town being full of his supporters. He had to do something to win them over, and quickly.

He took the last page of his prepared talk and held it up. "You know, I believe in this project. But I can tell many of you have doubts." He crumpled the paper with both hands, and the sharp edges bit into his palms. "Instead of finishing my speech, I think I should listen to your concerns and answer your questions." He saw a few heads nod. The man leaving stopped at the exit and turned around.

"Could we start with the man who was about to leave? Sir, could you tell me why you are no longer willing to listen to my proposal?"

The man's face registered surprise, then red showed

briefly through his scruffy beard. He glanced around, then nodded and started walking across the basketball court painted on the floor. Hunter sensed his two bodyguards prepare for action.

The man stopped at the faded red circle and rubbed his hands on his worn jeans. "Well, Mister Governor, most of us grew up without all this technology you keep talking about, and we don't know why our kids need it." Murmurs of agreement echoed through the crowd. "Our daddies were miners, and we're miners, and our children will be miners. Some of us have smart phones and some of us have dumb phones. What good is some fancy computer tablet gonna do our kids?"

Hunter couldn't believe his ears. He thought the days of families rooted in the mining culture had ended decades ago. "That's a good question, sir. It's my understanding that companies are developing technology to make the mines safer and more efficient. Your children could be part of that innovation."

He looked around. He saw miners, a few men who could be mechanics, women who might be supporting their families as cooks or waitresses, and several teachers. "Maybe some of your children aspire to do something different. They might become engineers or musicians—or politicians." That brought a few chuckles. "Putting technology in their hands at a young age can open up the world to them, allow them to see there is more to life than living in Black Rock, Tennessee."

The comment echoed in his head. He hadn't actually said that, had he? The laughter and smiles faded to frowns. "Of course, Black Rock is a great little town. But your options are limited, right? Either you work in the mine, or the local convenience store, or wait tables at the cafe. I want your children to see that they don't have to be limited by where they live or what their parents did." He looked around. They were listening, but he still wasn't making any points.

"Any other concerns?"

The bulky woman in the third row uncrossed her arms and unfolded herself to stand, reaching out to her neighbor to steady herself. "You say this technology opens up the world to our kids. That's what I'm worried about. From what I hear, there's a lotta stuff on that inner-net my kids don't need to be seeing. Pornography, sex tapes, child molesters. Why would we want ta expose them to all that garbage?"

This one he could handle. "I understand your concern. As you know, I have two young sons, and I care what they look at, whether on TV or the Internet. The filtering programs available today are very good at blocking inappropriate content, and every device funded under this program will be equipped with the latest filters."

A man in the middle of the crowd stood up. His white shirt contrasted with the clothes of the rest of the men. "I am one of those with a smart phone. I need it to stay in touch. But my children already bug me to let them play games on my phone all the time. I don't want them to spend even more time on electronic devices."

"That's right, Pastor."

"Amen."

Hunter waited until the murmurs of approval died down, then he leaned over the podium. "Like with anything else, children need to have limits. You as parents can set time limits when they're home, and the teachers will give them limits, as well. Part of the state funding will go to train teachers not only how to use technology most effectively, but also how to keep it from being misused."

From the end of the front row, Johnnie gave him the "wrap it up" signal. "Thank you for your attention, ladies and gentlemen, and for the opportunity to share with you my vision. And thank you for your honesty. I hope you'll consider supporting this legislation that will provide new opportunities for your children."

"One more question, Governor Wilson." The reporter, a short young woman who looked like she might have recently graduated from college, stood up. "You're talking about children, but we're very aware of the recent loss of your daughter. Can you tell us how the First Lady is doing?"

Hunter gritted his teeth. He had promised Shawna not to use Hannah's death as part of the campaign. But not answering could raise more questions. "She's doing as well as can be expected. The grief is overwhelming, for both of us at times, but Mrs. Wilson plans to resume her public appearances soon."

But the reporter wasn't done. Based on her accent, she didn't grow up in eastern Tennessee. "Do you and the First Lady plan to get pregnant again, now that you're married?" Her abrasive tone told him she wasn't planning to stay here in Black Rock long. She wanted a scoop that would get attention from a larger media outlet.

Amid rumbling from the audience, Johnnie jumped up and rushed toward Hunter, whose pulse had begun to race. He couldn't believe how close this small-town reporter had come to the truth. "Excuse me?"

Johnnie grabbed his arm and pushed him aside, taking over the microphone. "Thank you, everyone. The governor needs to get back to Nashville tonight, so that's all the time we have for questions."

She pulled him away to the middle of the gym. Scattered applause and rumbled conversation followed them toward an exit. The bodyguards took their positions on each side of Hunter and escorted him through a door that opened directly to the outside. Even the sun, still high in the sky, thanks to daylight saving time, seemed to be covered in mining dust. He got into the rented SUV, and Johnnie climbed in beside him. "Let's get out of here."

Once they started moving, Johnnie's shoulders sagged. "Sorry, Governor. That question was totally insensitive."

Hunter chuckled, hoping to convince them both there was no problem. "Not your fault. She's just a kid trying to make a name for herself at a Podunk newspaper. We shouldn't be surprised that people want to make a scandal out of my relationship with Shawna."

A scandal they had avoided, so far.

Marie Wells Coutu

Chapter 3

"Cooper! The game's over. You can come out now."

Shawna marched down the grand staircase for the umpteenth time, determined to scour every public room once more.

Cooper had been gone for two hours. She had waited an hour, thinking he would return on his own. When he didn't, she looked for him everywhere, even checking under beds and in closets of the main living quarters in case he sneaked back upstairs and hid.

She had driven him away, and Hunter would be furious. They had lost their daughter, and now she had lost his son.

She hadn't meant to yell at the boys. But Hannah wouldn't be coming back to them, and her memory should be respected. Shawna stopped at the entrance to the Tennessee Room, scanned the pristine furnishings for any sign of the boy. If he had been here, he would have left evidence—a chair out of place, a dropped toy.

Perhaps he'd gone outside. But the grounds were huge. She squared her shoulders and headed to the control room in the basement. Time to confess to the security team and get their help. They had to find him before Hunter returned. Or Mimi.

She tapped lightly on the door, which opened at once. "Mrs. Wilson, is something wrong?" Lieutenant Palmer stepped aside for her to enter the room full of camera monitors, then closed the door behind her. Hoping for sympathy and discretion, she looked from him to the other trooper seated in front of the rack of electronic screens. A black man with his face turned away from her. Maybe Curtis, who ran with Hunter in the mornings. Him she could trust, but the man kept his eyes focused on the flickering screens.

"I can't seem to find Cooper. I wondered if you'd seen him, maybe going outside?"

The lieutenant grabbed a chair from the corner and rolled it over to her. "Why don't you sit down? Tell us when you last saw him."

"He got upset and ran off about two hours ago." She bounced the heel of her foot up and down. "I heard him run down the main staircase, but I thought he'd come back in a few minutes. I've looked all over on the first floor, and upstairs, too."

She nodded to the monitors, which showed the view

from cameras placed everywhere around the property except in the private quarters. This one time, cameras in the private quarters might have been a good thing. "I thought if he went outside, maybe you saw him."

The seated trooper turned to face her. Her racing pulse slowed when she saw that it was Curtis. "Yes, ma'am, we would have, but we had a group of 4-H kids here for a tour. He could have slipped by in the crowd. Would you like us to review the tapes?"

"Please. Maybe we can see where he went." She rolled her chair closer to the monitor as Curtis cued up the recording. Despite his muscular frame, his calm demeanor seemed to radiate comfort like a warm fire.

"You saw him about two hours ago?" He paused the video and ran it forward in slow motion. "There he is." The picture showed Cooper running down the main staircase. Another camera picked him up entering the main kitchen, where Jean-Claude, the executive chef, was talking to a group of about twenty children.

Curtis leaned back. "That's why we didn't notice him. He blended in with the other kids." He gave her a sheepish look. "Sorry, ma'am."

"You didn't see him come downstairs?" She struggled to keep the frustration out of her voice. This was all her fault, not theirs.

"The boys sometimes wander downstairs. We don't think anything of it. They're free to play anywhere they want." He turned back to the controls. "Let's see if he stayed with the group."

Reviewing footage from other cameras, he soon found the tour group in the greenhouse. A volunteer had shown them the vegetables being grown there. Most of the children were taller than Cooper, and the way they crowded into the greenhouse made it difficult to spot him.

"Wait!" Shawna pointed to the screen. Curtis paused the recording and backed it up. "Look, he slipped out that side door. What was he up to?"

The two troopers searched the other camera angles but did not find him again. Shawna sagged in the chair. Cooper seemed to simply disappear into the expansive lawn. He didn't show up in any of the footage from the cameras around the perimeter. The three of them carefully examined the video of the tour group boarding the school bus.

"He's definitely not there." Shawna sighed. "Surely the leaders would have noticed an extra child, in any case. But where is he?"

"Don't worry, ma'am." Lieutenant Palmer lifted his arm. "We'll find him. He's still on the grounds somewhere." He spoke into the microphone hidden by his shirt cuff, alerting the other on-site members of the Executive Protection Unit. He directed them to start an organized search of the ten-acre property.

He turned back to her. "Why don't you go back upstairs and wait for him? We'll keep you informed."

She nodded, aware they would consider her a nuisance

if she tried to help. "I should go check on HL, make sure he doesn't get into trouble, too." Both boys were her responsibility, and she wanted Hunter to know he could trust her with them. "The governor is going to be upset. Please find Cooper before he gets back."

"Yes, ma'am. We'll do our best."

Shawna kept vigil in the sitting room, pacing figure-eights from the sofa to the hallway to the window, where she caught an occasional glimpse of the searchers scouring the grounds. Hunter Lynn begged to play Xbox instead of waiting until after dinner, and she finally relented, if only to silence him. As he ran to the bedroom, he seemed unconcerned about his brother.

She turned on the television and found "Wheel of Fortune," hoping it would take her mind off the missing child, but it didn't help. When she heard footsteps coming up the private stairs, her heart beat faster. Surely the troopers had found Cooper. She hurried to the hallway.

It was Hunter. Shawna hesitated in the doorway, her insides strangled by a boa constrictor.

"Hey." He set down his briefcase. "I'm shot. Those folks aren't too thrilled with—" He strode to her and put his hands on her arms. "What's wrong?"

She stepped into his embrace, her heart thumping. "I'm so sorry. I yelled at him. I didn't mean…"

He wrapped his arms around her. "What happened? You yelled at who?"

She took a deep breath. "Cooper. The boys were just

playing, but they were noisy and … I got upset. I told them to stay out of Hannah's room. Cooper freaked out."

Hunter rubbed her back. "He's sensitive like that. It'll be okay."

"No. He ran off, and we can't find him."

Hunter felt a chill freeze his body. His youngest son, the one who looked so much like Lynn, was missing. The boy who greeted life at one hundred miles per hour, but pulled into his shell at the slightest harsh word.

He pulled away from Shawna and scrutinized her. "What do you mean, you can't find him?"

She explained what had happened. "The detail is out there looking for him now. But he seems to have disappeared."

Hunter's heart pounded like an echo in an empty chamber. Nothing could fill the void if harm came to his son. "What did you say to him to make him run away?"

Her face became a mask. "I told them both to stay out of Hannah's room. I might have yelled a little."

Cooper was somewhere on the grounds; he had to be. He would be found, or he would come out from hiding on his own. Hunter drew a deep breath. "Where's H. L.?"

"In his room, playing Xbox."

Hunter called down the hall. "Hunter Lynn, come out

here."

The boy came out and made a running leap at his dad, who caught him but didn't swing him around as usual. "Hey, son. What happened with Cooper?"

Hunter Lynn drew back. "I dunno, Dad. We were playing storm troopers with our dart guns, and she yelled at us." He frowned, nodding at Shawna. "He just ran off. You know how he gets."

Hunter squatted beside him. "Think, H. L. If he's outside, where would he go? Does he have a hiding place?"

"He could be anywhere." He shrugged, and Hunter wanted to shake him. "It's not the first time he's run off. He'll come back when he's ready. Can I go back to my game now?"

Clinching his fists, Hunter nodded. The boy ran down the hall, closing the bedroom door with a thud.

Shawna sank into a wingback chair and put her elbows on her knees. She looked lost herself. "That's the same thing he told me. I didn't know Cooper had a habit of running off."

Hunter ought to hold her, tell her it would be all right. But he couldn't until he located his son. He turned and headed for the elevator to the basement. "I'll go see what security has found out."

She jumped up. "I'm coming with you."

He glanced down the hall toward the boys' room, then shrugged. "I guess H. L.'s absorbed in his game. Come on, then."

When they knocked, the security room door opened at once. Lieutenant Palmer was alone in the room. "Governor. You want a briefing."

"I do."

The officer motioned to a large paper diagram spread out on the table. It showed the residence, Conservation Hall, several outbuildings, and the layout of the grounds. Red and black ink divided the property into sections. "So far, there's no sign of the boy. We've covered the outside perimeter and we're working our way in." His eyes met Hunter's stare. "We'll find him, sir."

"After you do, John, I want a full report of how this happened." Hunter's jaw hardened. He couldn't tolerate laxity in security. "And what will be done to make sure it never happens again."

"Absolutely." The lieutenant spoke into his sleeve. "Roger, Team Two." He marked off another area on the diagram.

For a moment, the small equipment-filled room seemed to close in on Hunter. A metallic flavor in the air constricted his throat. The electronic screens flickered, and he saw only wavering lines monitoring bodily functions. He blinked away the hated memories.

"Are you positive he didn't run out the gate when the tour group left? Maybe I should call Mark and have him alert the media. They could put out one of those Amber Alerts."

Palmer shook his head. "I've scrutinized the video.

The boy did not exit the property through the gate, and there's been no other breaches of the fence, sir. He is still within the perimeter. Alerting the media will bring camera crews and reporters here, making our job more difficult."

Hunter rubbed the back of his neck. "You're right, of course. But it's getting dark. And it'll be chilly tonight. He'll be cold and frightened. We have to find him soon."

Hunter's pulsating jaw told Shawna he was straining to control his emotions. Not that she blamed him. She felt out of control herself, and Cooper was his son, not hers. At least, not biologically.

Tension filled the control room, raising the temperature by degrees. Shawna wished Curtis was still here, with his reassuring voice and calm spirit. But she supposed Lieutenant Palmer had sent him outside to assist with the search.

A buzzer sounded, and Palmer turned to watch a monitor as the main gate opened. "Mrs. Maddux is returning."

All the moisture in Shawna's mouth evaporated. Mimi would never understand how she had let this happen. As if the boy's grandmother needed another reason to dislike her.

Hunter left to intercept his former mother-in-law. A

few minutes later, they both returned.

Mimi looked like a general going into battle, not worried but ready to attack. "Shawna, tell me how you managed to lose track of Cooper."

She related the story, providing every detail she could think of, even admitting that she had yelled at the boys.

"Mm hmm." Mimi pursed her lips. "It's been months since he's done this. Before you moved in."

Shawna's face reddened. How could Mimi blame her if Cooper had run away before?

Hunter narrowed his eyes. "You never mentioned it. How could you not tell me?"

Mimi patted his arm. "He was never gone this long, of course. I didn't see any need to bother you, with all of your responsibilities. I always found him myself, or he came back on his own." She turned to the lieutenant, her jaw set. "I know where he might be."

"Yes, ma'am?"

"Let's go find him."

The lieutenant gestured for Mimi to lead the way. Hunter and Shawna followed them outside. Mimi marched down the path toward the greenhouse. The western sky glowed orange with the sun's setting, casting long shadows from the trees. Shawna edged close to Hunter for shelter from the cool breeze.

The dark shape of the greenhouse hovered ahead of them. The troopers had already searched the building, where they had last seen Cooper on the video feed. What did Mimi know that they didn't?

Lieutenant Palmer shone a flashlight on the gravel path, which crunched under their feet. Mimi led them past the greenhouse and through the vegetable gardens. Hunter fell in behind Shawna as the group plodded across the uneven ground, freshly turned earth releasing a dank scent in the evening air. Clumps of dirt splattered into the tops of Shawna's sneakers, scratching her feet and irritating her toes. Lightning bugs among the bushes flashed their warning signals, and crickets raised an alarm at the intruders.

Finally, Mimi stopped at a small garden shed. "Cooper likes to help the gardener, and he knows where he hides the padlock key." She pointed to the hasp, which was loose from its hook. The padlock hung open through the loop, but the door had been carefully pulled shut to avoid notice.

"Cooper?" Mimi called softly as Lieutenant Palmer pulled the door open. "Cooper, sweetheart, are you in here?"

Shawna stifled a sneeze caused by the pungent odor of fertilizer. Lieutenant Palmer waved the flashlight around the dark interior, revealing jugs of weed killer on shelves along one wall. Bags of grass seed were stacked on the wooden floor, and there, stretched across two of the bags, lay Cooper.

Marie Wells Coutu

Chapter 4

Nate Matthews ran his stubby finger along the shelf of used history books. Always on the lookout for one about the Civil War, he decided to visit BookManBookWoman. It seemed as good a place as any to spend a solitary evening.

The store's owner arranged the books by general topics, but a volume about Nathan Bedford Forrest could be jammed in between one about Eisenhower and another about ancient Greece. He crouched so he could scan the titles in a tipsy stack on the floor.

"Ah thought you might be heah." Surprise at hearing the familiar soft drawl nearly knocked him out of his precarious position. He placed a hand on the pile of books to steady himself and nearly pushed the entire stack over. Grabbing the shelf with the other hand, he pulled himself upright, face to face with Deborah Hummel.

"I wish you wouldn't startle me like that, Deb. You know I don't like it."

She waved a perfectly manicured hand. "Poor Nate. I don't mean to upset you. But it's so easy to do." She leaned forward and brushed her cheek against his. "And you haven't gotten rid of that scruffy beard, I see. It scratches." She rubbed her face, smooth and creamy as it had been thirty-five years earlier, when they had served together on their high school student council.

"Hides my ugly mug. You were looking for me?"

Deb motioned to another customer down the aisle. "Can we get out of here? I'll buy you a cup of coffee."

A private conversation. He nodded, and she turned to lead the way out of the store. He followed her, ignoring the complaint from the steel rod in his right thigh. In the chilly evening, streetlights had begun to flicker on, accompanied by their characteristic hum. From the end of the block floated the notes of a guitar being tuned by a street musician. As Deb and Nate came to a small café a few doors down from the bookstore, a college-age couple vacated a tiny sidewalk table.

Nate pulled out one of the two black iron chairs and held it for Deb.

She remained standing. "You wait here and save the table. I told you I was buying. What do you want?"

She could afford it. As a stay-at-home mom, she had started an online bank, turning it into a Fortune 500 company. "Large coffee, three sugars, no cream."

He waited until she had entered the shop, then he settled himself on the chair, positioning his injured limb so it could stretch out. The jeep accident in Iraq only caused minimal discomfort now, but he was always aware of his narrow escape from permanent disability.

Deb returned with two large paper cups encased in brown sleeves. "Black coffee with extra sugar for you, soy latte for me."

Nate scowled. "Latte? You might as well drink milk."

"*Au contraire*, dear Nate. The milk makes it drinkable, but it has enough caffeine to keep me going. Unlike you, I never acquired a taste for the high-test stuff."

Nate held his cup in a mock toast. "What did you want to talk about?"

She laughed. "Trying to escape the small talk, are you? Get right to business and avoid the personal questions, right?"

He shrugged. "Nothing new."

She twirled her cup in both hands, studying him. While they'd never been more than friends, she had always been able to see behind the gruff facade he tried to maintain. "Fine. I need help with my campaign. I'm behind by nearly twenty percent. Tell me something about Governor Wilson."

Any other year, Deb might have a chance to win the election. But running on the state's minority ticket with no political experience, and against a popular incumbent presented a challenge higher than the Smoky Mountains of eastern Tennessee.

Nate breathed in the aroma of his coffee, then sipped the hot brew. "I'm not sure how I can help. The polls tell you what people think about him. He's been good for the state. And sympathy over his loss of a baby is a huge advantage."

She leaned toward him and lowered her voice. "There must be something I don't know. Something nobody knows."

A woman at the table behind Nate pushed her chair back, bumping into his. He scooted his chair, trying to move out of the way. The woman stood and turned to him. "I'm so sorry! Are you all right?"

"No. But that's not your fault." He waited until the woman and her friend left. "He's squeaky clean. It's a tough year for you to run for governor."

"C'mon. You've been in Nashville for seven years." She spread her hands wide. "Since his wife died, he's been the most eligible bachelor in the South. Are you telling me he doesn't have any skeletons in his closet? No jilted girlfriends, kids by another woman, anything?"

He scrutinized her, curious as to what happened to the teen-age girl who always stayed on the moral high ground. "Where is this coming from? Dirty politics isn't your style."

She removed the lid from her coffee cup and took a big gulp. "I don't want to sling mud, but the voters need to know the truth, don't they?"

Not sure he could see the distinction, Nate considered her question. "Most eligible bachelor or not, Wilson never even looked at another woman after his wife died. At least, as far as any of the media could tell. Until he met Shawna Moore."

"And then?" Deb's large hazel eyes pinned him in place, vaguely reminding him of the woman who was now Tennessee's First Lady. "That was a pretty short courtship, don't you think?"

Nate himself wondered, not for the first time, how the sudden marriage had come about. He toyed with the broken plastic tab from his coffee cup lid, rubbing the sharp edge with his thumb. "As far as I know, they first met at the Governor's Conference at Lake Barkley Resort. You know he was chairman of the conference, right?"

Deb nodded.

"Shawna—er, Mrs. Wilson, now—was the resort sales manager, and she was in charge of all the logistics. I noticed them together a lot that week. But, so what? It wasn't like he was married at the time. A man's entitled to enjoy the company of a beautiful woman, if he can find one who'll spend time with him." Nate shifted his weight in the chair, trying for a more comfortable position for his aching leg.

Deb turned her chair. "Maybe he wasn't married, but she was. Didn't that bother you?"

He rubbed his hand over his thigh, massaging the knots in the muscle. Did Deb have the same suspicions he had formed earlier? "I had lost touch with her after college. None of us in the media knew if she was divorced or what, only that no man was around. It wasn't until the governor attended her husband's funeral that we found out her husband had been serving overseas."

"She got over her grief pretty quick, don't you think?" Deb reached across the table and touched his arm. "I would think you, of all people, would want to know the truth about that relationship."

"Why me, of all people?" He wouldn't admit how accurate she was.

"Nathaniel." The way she said his name reminded him of his mother. "I know how much MaryAnn hurt you. You don't fool me with your false bravado."

"It's better this way. MaryAnn didn't need to be saddled with me, and I'm free to go where my job takes me." After he came back from Iraq injured, his wife had asked for a divorce and remarried within a month.

When the governor attended the military funeral for Shawna's husband, Nate had speculated about the relationship. But the possibility that Shawna Moore had acted like his own wife seventeen years earlier wasn't something he wanted to think about. Some dogs were better left sleeping.

Deb held up her cup. "Want a refill?"

He shook his head. "I'm good. I need to go."

"Listen, you and I both suspect Mrs. Wilson got pregnant while her husband was serving his country overseas."

When he pushed back from the table, Deb grabbed his hand. "Then he died in combat, and the governor married her to cover it up. Don't you think that was a betrayal to other soldiers? You owe it to all military spouses to find out the truth." She flashed her award-winning smile. "And you sort of owe me."

After he used the GI Bill to finish his journalism degree, Deb's connections had helped him get a job with *The Tennessean.* But it was his persistence and work that had earned him the spot as the newspaper's lead investigative reporter. He didn't want to ruin his chances of promotion to management by fishing around in the sewer, especially since he considered Shawna Wilson a friend. He gave Deb an apologetic smile and rose to his feet.

Deb stood and stepped in front of him, blocking his way. "You know I'd make a good governor. So, let me know if you find anything I can use against him, okay?" She picked up her pocketbook and slung it over her shoulder. "Be seeing you, Nate."

Nate picked up both empty cups from the table and headed for the trash can. "Not if I see you first."

Chapter 5

Peering into the shadowy space, Shawna sagged against Hunter. They had found Cooper.

When she saw the boy's still form, her stomach twisted. In the thin ray from the flashlight, he looked so vulnerable. He had curled into a protective ball, perched precariously on the pile of seed sacks. His red t-shirt and blue jeans were wrinkled, and his bare arm provided his only pillow. A dried trail of tears streaked his face.

She pushed past Mimi into the shed and knelt on the plywood floor. "Cooper?" She stroked his hair, touched his shoulder. She held her breath, waiting for movement. "Cooper, wake up." Please, God. Let him be all right. Hunter squatted next to her and placed his hand on Cooper's chest.

She felt Cooper shudder and saw his eyelids blink. She sucked in a deep breath. "Are you okay?"

He squinted at her. "Shawna? Dad? What's wrong?"

"Son, you scared everybody. We were about to send the Mounties to look for you." The teasing in Hunter's voice hid the concern Shawna knew he'd felt. And took the sting out of his words. He rose and held out his hand.

Cooper took it, rolled off the stack of bags, and stood. He clasped Hunter around the legs. "Sorry, Dad. I didn't mean to." His thin voice trembled. "I-I guess I fell asleep."

Hunter crouched down and pulled him to his chest. "We're glad we found you before we put out an APB. But Shawna's the one you should apologize to. Do you want to tell her why you ran away?"

Cooper shook his head. He whispered, but Shawna heard the words. "She scared me when she yelled. Not like a real mom."

He didn't say it to hurt her, but the innocent honesty in his voice pricked her heart. Tension from the last few hours oozed out of her muscles and she collapsed on the floor. "I'm sorry I yelled at you, little man." She reached out and stroked his back. "You and H. L. were only playing, but I was feeling sorry for myself. I had no right to get so upset."

Hunter pulled away from Cooper's embrace and put his hands on the boy's shoulders. "Now, what do you have to say to her?"

Cooper dropped his head. "Sorry I ran off, and you couldn't find me." He glanced up at his father, as if to see if the apology met his approval.

"Alrighty, then." Mimi stepped into the crowded shed

and held out her hand to Cooper. Shawna had almost forgotten that she and the trooper were still there. "I think it's time we got this boy cleaned up and ready for supper. He's probably hungry as a bear, after such a long nap." She chuckled as she led Cooper toward the house.

Hunter turned to Shawna and motioned toward the door. "That's that. Let's get out of here."

Ignoring his command, she moved next to him, brushed her cheek against the end-of-the-day bristles on his chin. "I won't let him out of my sight again."

He chuckled, a half-laugh without meaning. "Don't overreact and become a wicked stepmother who keeps the children imprisoned."

"No, I—" Her protest was interrupted when he tipped her face up with his index finger and planted a quick kiss on her mouth.

"It's over now," he whispered. "You won't let it happen again."

Hadn't she just said that? She opened her mouth to respond, but Hunter had already stepped out of the shed.

After supper, she and Hunter waited in the living room while Mimi put the two boys to bed. Hunter picked up the sports section from that morning's newspaper and claimed one end of the sofa. Too wound up to even consider reading, Shawna sat at the other end, clasping a throw pillow to her chest.

Once the boys had settled down, Mimi came out and perched on the club chair nearby. The smile she wore for the bedtime ritual faded into a frown.

Hunter closed the newspaper, folded it, and let it rest on his lap. "How did you know where to find Coop?"

"I pay attention. He loves gardening, and he likes to hang around with Mr. Jennings. I figured that's where he'd go, even if Jennings wasn't working today." She picked up a cloth tote from beside the chair and pulled out her current knitting project, a mass of green and yellow. "I'm just glad it wasn't fertilizer he had chosen to sleep on. We'd have never gotten that smell off him."

Shawna fingered the top edge of the brocade pillow. "I'm grateful for your help, Mimi. Sometimes I don't know what to do with those boys."

"I know you don't." Mimi arranged the bulky yarn object on her lap, studied it, and began to yank it apart. "There's no reason you shouldn't go back to work. Be the First Lady. At least you can do that reasonably well."

The room cooled twenty degrees but Hunter seemed not to notice. He slid an arm along the sofa and touched Shawna's shoulder. "That's a great idea. Maybe you could join me for a few campaign events. I'll mention it to Johnnie."

The campaign again. Why did that seem more important to him than family?

Chapter 6

"Bri would love this."

Elissa sniffed at the painted silk scarf Shawna held out.
"I was thinking something a little less ... ostentatious."

A mother of three, Elissa's tastes leaned toward the
simple and conservative, in contrast to their single sister's
flamboyant style. Not gaudy, but definitely showy. Brianna
liked to make a "statement," and the vibrant flowers on the
sheer green scarf fit. But Shawna acquiesced to her older
sister's opinion, again. She'd go along with anything to get
this expedition over with so she could retreat behind the
privacy of the iron fence.

She scanned the spacious store, with its high ceiling
and polished wood floor. Designer purses, handmade
jewelry, and one-of-a-kind gift items graced the antique
shelves and tables, but Elissa dismissed them all. They had
already tried half a dozen unique shops in the East

Nashville district. But so far, Elissa had turned down all of Shawna's suggestions. She was beginning to think Elissa just wanted to keep her from hiding at home.

Though Shawna's obvious security had drawn a few quizzical looks, thankfully no one had recognized her. At least, they hadn't tried to talk to her. Maybe Trent's imposing presence deterred them, even though he waited by the entrance door of each store.

"Oh, look at this, Shawna." Elissa swept over to an enormous wall hanging. "This would look perfect over her fireplace, don't you think?"

Shawna hadn't been to Brianna's Memphis townhouse for several months. "Are you sure she hasn't found something for that spot?"

"I'm sure she hasn't. She would have told us if she had." Elissa studied the painting of a fish on an old piece of metal. Shawna was surprised Ellie liked something with rust on it, but she had to admit it would be compatible with Bri's shabby-chic decor.

Her stomach grumbled and she realized it was past lunchtime. "Why don't we find something to eat and think about it?"

A sudden rain shower had turned the gloomy day into a soggy mess. They didn't wait for Trent to open the umbrella but jogged through the sprinkles. Knowing Ellie's recent decision to eat gluten free, Shawna pointed out a natural-foods restaurant a couple blocks away. They burst into the busy place, laughing and shaking off drops of water. Frowning, Trent followed them in, and Shawna regretted having seemed to dismiss him.

After they placed their orders, Ellie took both menus and handed them to the waitress. She leaned across the wooden table and squinted. "So, what aren't you telling me, sis?"

Shawna never could hide much from her older sister. But maybe, from her motherly experience, she would have advice to help her with raising the boys. Shawna held out her hands in surrender.

"One of the boys ran away and hid yesterday, because I yelled at him. We didn't find him for hours."

In the middle of taking a drink, Ellie sputtered and nearly choked on the water. After a brief coughing spell, she finally cleared her throat. "Sorry. But that reminded me of one time when you ran away."

"I didn't."

"Yes, you did. You said you were going to Grandmother's house." Ellie paused to sip more water. "Only you didn't know that she lived in Missouri. Let's see, you must have been about five. I think you got to the end of the block and got tired. Daddy found you sitting on the curb when he came home."

Shawna didn't recall the episode. "Well, this wasn't funny. Cooper didn't threaten to go anywhere. But he said he wished his daddy had never married me."

"Ouch."

"Then he ran off. I didn't realize he had left the house

until an hour later." She stopped talking while the waitress put their salads in front of them.

Ellie picked up her fork. "That must have been scary for you."

Shawna shivered. "I was terrified. I couldn't imagine how Hunter would feel. It was almost dark when Mimi found Coop asleep in the garden shed."

"So, he was all right?" Ellie picked at her salad.

Nodding, Shawna stabbed a cherry tomato. Juice squirted onto her hand. "He was fine. He did say he was sorry."

"That's progress," Ellie said. "I guess it's not easy being a stepmother."

"You've got that right. Getting to understand their personalities is hard. Cooper is so sensitive, but fearless. He approaches life at fifty miles an hour with his hair on fire. And Hunter Lynn can be surly. He's angry at the world. I'm not sure I'll ever win him over."

As she slowly chewed and swallowed, Ellie seemed to be thinking. "Maybe you could find something Hunter Lynn likes to do that you could help him with. Has he ever played tennis?"

Shawna hadn't lived with them long enough to find out. "I doubt it."

"Don't you think it would be worth trying? Playing tennis got you through some tough times in high school, didn't it?"

True. After their mother had been killed by a drunk

driver, Shawna had been angry. Her tennis coach had encouraged her to take her frustrations to the court. That focus had helped her not only to work through her grief but also to become a top competitor and win a college scholarship. If Hunter Lynn showed some ability, perhaps he could learn to compete with the best.

Ellie stiffened and stared at something over Shawna's shoulder. "That's Garth Brooks!"

Shawna moved to turn around, but Ellie grabbed her arm. "No, don't look. It's too obvious."

"Okay." She shrugged. "It's Nashville. Musicians can show up anywhere."

Ellie hadn't taken her eyes off the spot. "I know. But he's my all-time favorite singer. Do you know him?"

"I've met him a couple of times. He's been to some of Hunter's fundraisers. Would you like me to introduce you?"

Ellie looked at her plate, toying with her fork. "No, I'd feel like a groupie."

Shawna had never seen her sister so rattled. She had no idea Ellie would get starry-eyed over a country singer. She wanted to do this for her, show her that her younger sister had clout. "Really, it'll be no big deal."

"Could you?" Ellie's eyes glittered. "That would be super."

Shawna pushed back from the table. "Sure. Let's head for the restroom. I'll catch sight of him and naturally, I would go over to speak to him." She stood and turned, scanning the room. Ellie stepped to her side.

A tall man sat alone in the corner, shoveling rice into his mouth. A black cowboy hat sat on the other side of the table. He had dark hair, a tidy beard and mustache. But it was not Garth Brooks.

She saw no one else who remotely resembled the star. She looked at Ellie. "Where did you see him?"

"Over there. In the corner."

"Nope," Shawna said. "That's not him."

They returned to their chairs. "I'm sorry, sis. Guess I wanted to meet Garth so badly that I really thought it was him."

Shawna smiled, trying not to smirk at Ellie's embarrassment. For once, she felt like the more mature sister. "It's okay. Maybe someday I can introduce you."

Ellie changed the subject abruptly. "How's Hunter's campaign going?"

Better than the marriage. But Shawna wouldn't confess that. "Johnnie's keeping him out on the road to make sure he doesn't lose his strong lead in the polls."

"Why don't you go with him?" Ellie's gaze bore into her, searching for a crack in the veneer.

Her face grew warm under the examination. "I will. Soon enough."

"Sis. It's time you got back into life."

Back to the big-sister bossiness. Shawna sighed and put down her water glass. At least she had a rebuttal. "I've got a Fitness Expo for kids Saturday. To kick off our Fit

Kids project."

"Exercise is good for the soul as well as the body." Ellie scraped the last of the lettuce and dressing from her plate.

"I know that. Why do you think I pushed for this as my primary initiative?"

"What about tennis? Are you playing again?"

"I will, as soon as the weather allows." Shawna wiped her mouth with the paper napkin. She didn't need her sister, any more than Mimi, telling her what to do.

Ellie leaned across the table, her eyes pinning Shawna in place. "It's not only exercise you need. You know Hannah is with Jesus now."

Laughter erupted from a nearby table, drowning out the pounding in Shawna's ears. "That's what you've said. I wish I could decide whether I believe it."

"Of course, you believe it." Ellie tossed her napkin onto her plate. "You're just going through a phase. Have you talked to your pastor?"

"No. I'll be fine. Like you said, it's only a phase." Hunter had suggested the same thing, but talking to their pastor could mean exposing her true self, her doubts—and her secret. The choice she and Hunter had worked so hard to keep hidden. Shawna was unwilling to submit to that kind of heart surgery.

Ellie's expression softened. "Listen, you've been through a lot in the past year. First, Daniel's death, your whirlwind romance with Hunter—whatever that was about—and gaining two bonus kids, the pregnancy, and now losing the baby so soon. It would be good for you to talk to a professional."

Shawna didn't need a professional. She needed to rewind time. "Look, Ellie, let's decide on a present for Bri. I need to be home when the boys get out of school." Mimi would be there, but she would use any excuse to cut this conversation short.

Ellie sighed and grabbed her purse. "Fine. Let's go back for that wall hanging of the fish."

Hunter scanned the draft of a news release Mark Newton had handed him.

He picked up his pen and scratched through a couple of words, wrote in a revision. Rain and wind rattling the large windows could not dampen his confidence. He handed the page back to his public information director. "Okay, make these changes and let's have it ready for the delegation to review."

He had no doubt the people from New Chemo, Incorporated, would choose Nashville for their cancer research facility. The consultant had all but guaranteed it when they had lunch two weeks ago.

He hoped the agreement could be finalized during the meeting today. Hunter could use the boost for his campaign.

A quick knock sounded on his office door. "Come," he said.

His secretary cracked open the door and stuck her head in. "Governor, they're here."

Hunter nodded. "Bring them in."

She opened the door wide and gestured for the three to enter. The woman, petite with dark hair, wore a skirt suit in a non-traditional bright red that matched her lipstick. She smiled warmly and held out her hand. "Governor Wilson, I'm Mandy Haywood."

Immediately behind her, Philip Woods said, "Mandy is executive assistant to the CEO of New Chemo."

Hunter took her hand and held it. Her eyes were an amazing sky blue. He caught himself staring at her and released his grip. He turned and greeted the state's economic development consultant, shaking his hand and grasping his elbow with the other hand. "Good to see you again, Phil."

Phil turned to the third person. "Governor, this is Justin Fowler, Vice President of Facilities."

Fowler was a bulky man with a shaved head. He shook Hunter's hand but did not make eye contact.

Hunter motioned them to the sitting area, and he introduced Newton, Johnnie, and a policy analyst, Jared Rodgers.

His secretary returned with a tray loaded with cups, a coffeepot and a selection of bottled water and soft drinks.

She placed the tray on a table and proceeded to distribute the drinks. When everyone had what they wanted, she quietly left the room and closed the door.

Hunter inhaled the toasty aroma of his favorite coffee. "Welcome to Nashville. I trust you've had a good visit. Have you had the opportunity for any sightseeing?"

Haywood shook her head. "We went to the Grand Ole Opry last night, but otherwise, no. Phil showed us the proposed location for the research center, but that's all we've had time for."

"How'd you like the Opry?"

Fowler shook his head. "Country music's not my thing.

But Haywood beamed. "I loved it. It's so … homespun. There was this incredible family of musicians. The oldest was about twenty-one and the youngest, maybe five. Every one of them could play at least one instrument. Extremely talented."

Hunter knew the group she referred to, though he couldn't think of the family's name. He nodded. "I've seen them perform. They're incredible, aren't they?"

After a few more minutes of small talk, Johnnie interrupted. "I'm sorry to cut off this discussion, but the governor has other appointments, and I'm sure you are busy as well, so we really should get down to business."

She looked at Rodgers, who opened a folder and removed several thick documents. "Based on our previous discussions, I took the liberty of having an agreement drafted," he said.

He passed copies to each of the three visitors and handed a copy to Hunter, keeping one for himself. Rodgers pushed his square-rimmed glasses up on his nose. "If this meets your approval, we are hoping to announce your decision within a couple of days."

Haywood took the document and scanned it. Fowler let his copy rest on his lap, and Phil took the stapled document and flipped through the pages without really looking at them.

Hunter sipped his coffee, confident the document was only a formality.

Finally, Haywood looked up. "Governor, this appears to include all the points you and Phil discussed. However, …" She leaned back in her chair and crossed her legs. "We are currently leaning toward a different location. In Philadelphia."

The coffee in Hunter's mouth turned bitter. Landing the research center would help his campaign—and his legacy. Besides, Tennessee needed the investment and the jobs. He hadn't lobbied for the facility to help Lynn, but to help cancer patients like her. Shawna's image flashed in his mind, but he swatted it away. This project had nothing to do with him and Shawna.

He swallowed his alarm and leaned forward. "I'm sorry to hear that. Can I ask what changed your mind?"

Phil spoke up. "The city has offered a comparable package, Governor, with a location close to the company headquarters. I'm sorry." He held out his hands in conciliation.

Johnnie tapped her foot nervously. "We were under the impression proximity to headquarters wasn't a factor."

"It wasn't," Fowler said. He brushed his hand over his bare head. "But all else being equal, the benefits in reduced travel, shared facility staff, and infrastructure can't be ignored."

Hunter seized on his words. "All else being equal. Does that mean you would still consider Nashville if we made additional concessions?"

"What sort of additional concessions?" Haywood leaned forward and met his gaze.

Hunter glanced at Rodgers. "I'm not sure. Maybe additional tax waivers, state funding to help with infrastructure. We can find something, can't we, Jared?"

Rodgers nodded. "I'm sure we can, but we'll need a little time."

Hunter looked at Haywood, then at Phil. "Could we have a month to see what we can come up with? We'll have to get the General Assembly leadership on board with a new package."

Haywood glanced at Fowler, then nodded. "Certainly, we're willing to see what you can do. We like Nashville and the opportunity to work closely with Vanderbilt University. But I'll be honest with you. The president is intrigued with the idea of keeping operations in Philly. It will take a lot to change his mind. And we are anxious to get the facility built, so no more than a month. We'll have to move forward one way or another by the beginning of November."

Hunter's heart calmed. They still had a chance.

After the visitors left, Johnnie fidgeted with her pen. "This is not good, Governor. We were counting on making the announcement this week. Hummel's been gaining points on you, and several reporters are aware of the meeting today."

Hunter sat at his desk with his head in his hands, elbows propped on the desk. "Do we need to tell them anything?"

She shook her head. "New Chemo's decision is not final, and they did give us a month to come up with something else. For now, we'll simply say that discussions are continuing."

"Good enough." Hunter turned to Rodgers. "Start talking to the General Assembly leadership, see what you can come up with. Get them on board. We may need a special session, so we don't have any time to waste."

Chapter 7

"Have you made any plans for Hunter's birthday?"

Mimi's abrupt entrance to her home office startled Shawna. She put down the plans she had been reviewing for tomorrow's event and glanced at the desk calendar. Saturday was also her husband's birthday.

She had jotted that note to herself weeks ago, but so much had happened since. She had completely forgotten. Hard to believe she had yet to celebrate his birthday with him, but then, they had known each other less than a year.

"No, but I'll think of something. Maybe I could ask the chef to prepare a steak dinner for the two of us?"

Mimi settled into the wingback chair opposite the desk, sitting primly in her navy-blue dress. "You could, I suppose."

Shawna knew that tone. Mimi didn't approve. "What's wrong with that?"

"Oh, I don't want to tell you what to do." She crossed her legs, then uncrossed them. "But I wonder if the boys would like to be part of it. I'm sure Hunter would prefer that they were. He doesn't really like birthdays all that much."

Mimi knew more about Hunter's likes and dislikes than Shawna did. If he didn't like birthdays, why did Mimi think it necessary to ask what she had planned? Talk about being between a rock and a hard place. And the hard place had to be her husband's former mother-in-law.

"All right." Shawna leaned back in her chair. "We'll have a nice birthday dinner with all five of us." She couldn't very well expect Mimi to eat upstairs alone while the rest of them dined in style in the main dining room. This was the twenty-first century, not the dark ages of Downton Abbey, and Mimi was not a servant, but the boys' grandmother.

She should enlist the boys to help. After Cooper's escapade the day before yesterday, she needed to find ways to blend this family. "I know. I'll get the boys to help me bake a cake." She stood. "I'll go ask them right now." Working together for a common purpose always made it easier to relate to someone.

"Of course." Mimi rose and followed her out of the office. "They're in their room. I'll be in my room sewing, if you need me."

The last thing she intended to do was ask Mimi for help baking a cake. She recalled the times she had helped her mother in the kitchen, before she died. Shawna wanted to recreate that kind of pleasant memory for Hunter's sons.

She knocked on the bedroom door, then opened it. "Boys, tomorrow's your dad's birthday."

Both boys sat cross-legged on the floor, game controllers in hand. Sounds of guns blazing and characters yelling spilled from the TV. Hunter Lynn kept his focus on the game until Cooper put it on hold. Hunter Lynn squawked and threw himself backwards onto the rug.

Cooper gave her a small smile. "Hey, Shawna. Mr. Jennings helped me start some tomato plants to give him. They're in the greenhouse. Do you think he'll like them?"

She squatted beside him. "I'm sure he will, Cooper. And he'll enjoy them all summer when they produce tomatoes for his salad."

"He'll eat them on hamburgers, not salad." Hunter Lynn tossed the controller on the carpet and jumped to his feet. He hopped over Cooper and went to the small desk by the window. "I'm giving him this model airplane I made. I just have to finish putting the stickers on it. Curtis got me a state seal, so it'll look like the plane he uses."

Shawna clapped her hands together. "Very nice, H. L. You've worked hard on that, haven't you? I'm sure your father will love it."

"Do you think maybe he'll put it on his desk?" This boy, the oldest son, acted so aloof, yet all he really wanted was his father's approval.

"It wouldn't surprise me at all." She turned back

toward Cooper. "Would you boys like to help me bake a birthday cake for him?"

Cooper jumped up. "Chocolate? That's his favorite."

"Of course, chocolate. It's my favorite, too."

Cooper grinned. "Mine, too."

Shawna looked at Hunter Lynn, who was still examining the model plane. She shouldn't expect him to share his younger brother's enthusiasm. "You coming?"

He shrugged his shoulders. "I guess so."

An hour later, with the cake in the oven and the aroma of chocolate swirling throughout the kitchen, Shawna began the task of making the frosting.

"Now the tricky part. H. L., will you get out these ingredients?" She handed him the recipe card, hoping he would do something besides stand around watching.

She took out a heavy saucepan and placed it on the commercial stove, then rinsed off the beaters for the electric mixer.

Mimi wandered in. "Sure smells good. How's it coming?"

Cooper pointed to the white kitchen timer clicking on the counter. "Thirty more minutes, Mimi! Then we gotta frost it. And we can't have any until tomorrow night, after Dad blows out all the candles."

Shawna and Mimi's eyes met above the boy's head, in a rare shared moment of laughter.

"But we get to lick the beaters, right, Shawna?" Hunter Lynn turned from the pantry cabinet, a box of baking chocolate and the sugar canister clutched in his arms. He set them on the counter by the stove.

Mimi glanced at the items, then at the saucepan. She raised her eyebrows. "You're making a cooked frosting?"

Her question echoed Shawna's own doubts, but she refused to admit it. "Yes, I'm using my mother's recipe. It's worth the extra effort." She took a metal measuring cup from the cabinet. "Here, Cooper. Measure the sugar, please. H. L., you can measure the milk."

"I have a perfectly good, practically foolproof recipe for chocolate frosting. Hunter and the boys are used to it." Mimi opened the drawer where she kept cookbooks and recipes.

"No, thanks. My mother's recipe is special." Shawna turned the heat on under the pan. "Everyone loves it."

Mimi's face reddened. "Well. Good luck. Cooked frosting doesn't always turn out the way you want it to." She slammed the drawer closed and left the room.

When they heard her clumping up the stairs, Hunter Lynn actually laughed. "She's mad you didn't want to use her recipe."

"I guess she is." Shawna relaxed her shoulders for the first time since Mimi had shown up. "Come on, let's get this show on the road."

The boys took turns adding ingredients. When the mixture started to boil, Shawna removed the heavy pan from the heat and stuck it under the large mixer. But she soon realized she had a problem. The frosting was supposed to get thicker as she beat and stirred it, but it remained liquid. How long had it been since she had made this recipe? She looked at the spattered white card again. She must have left out an ingredient.

One boy stood on each side of her, watching eagerly for the brown liquid to turn into frosting. After several minutes, she turned off the mixer and stuck a spatula into the watery substance. Her voice caught in her throat. "This doesn't look good, boys. It's supposed to thicken up, but it's not." She ran her finger over the thin sauce on the side of the pan. When she licked her finger, the bitterness puckered her mouth. "It's no use. We'll have to throw it out and start over."

"Mimi will know what to do." Hunter Lynn started for the doorway. "I'll go ask her."

That was the last thing Shawna needed. She didn't believe in letting her emotions show, but tears escaped her eyes. She plopped on the high red stool by the window.

Cooper came to her and patted her shoulder. "It'll be all right, Shawna. Mimi will fix it."

She wrapped her arms around him. "I know, Coop." She sucked in a breath through her teeth. "But I wanted to make it myself. With you and H. L."

She felt foolish crying like a baby while being hugged by a confused seven-year-old, but she couldn't stop the flow of hot tears streaming down her cheeks. She cried for her mother taken from her too soon. For her baby who didn't live long enough. For this boy who couldn't remember his mother.

She cried from fear that she would never be the supportive wife that Hunter wanted, or the mother that his boys needed. She cried, and Cooper patted her back.

Going through an MRI machine would be easier, but Hunter couldn't avoid visiting the cancer unit at Vanderbilt University. This event could help in ways beyond his re-election campaign.

"Governor, this way." Johnnie motioned toward the door on their right as the group of state officials and staff moved past the nurses' station. "We have permission to videotape this patient."

Hunter froze in the doorway. Years had passed, but the look and smell of the sterile room took him back to the weeks before Lynn died. Monitors beeped rhythmically. The acrid odor of antiseptic cleansers burned his nostrils. Although the window blinds were pulled all the way up, sunlight streaming into the room couldn't dispel the impending doom.

The patient, swallowed up by tubes and blankets and pillows, could have been anywhere from twenty to sixty years old. With the metal bed raised to a forty-five-degree angle, she gave them a shaky wave and a wide grin.

"Hello, Governor." Her weak voice barely reached

him. "Come on in. I've been looking forward to your visit."

Hunter closed the door on his memories and stepped into the room. Most of the entourage, including Russell Caldwell, speaker of the Senate for seven years running, waited in the hall. Serving in the dual role of lieutenant governor made Caldwell the second most-powerful man in state government. Hunter was counting on his help to pass the legislation needed to secure New Chemo's research facility.

Johnnie motioned to the staff videographer to start recording. Then she took Hunter's elbow and maneuvered him into a chair at the woman's bedside. Now that he was closer, he could see that the patient was probably in her late twenties. Her smooth bare head showed wisps of light blond hair, and her round eyes studied him with an intense blue fire straight from heaven.

"Governor, this is Julie Fisher," Johnnie murmured. "She has stage four melanoma."

He had met a number of cancer patients during Lynn's brief illness, but few had this woman's cheerful demeanor. Julie held her left hand up, and Hunter awkwardly tried to shake it. Her grip was surprisingly strong, and she didn't let go. "I'm glad to meet you, Governor Wilson. I'm a big fan."

He leaned closer to her bed so he could hear her better. "Miss Fisher, how are you doing?"

"I'm doing great, sir." Her crooked smile warmed his heart. "They treat me like a queen, but I won't be here much longer. 'For to me to live is Christ and to die is gain.'"

Hunter recognized the Bible verse, one that Lynn had cherished. He squeezed the patient's hand, not giving but drawing strength from her. He could not think of a suitable response.

Julie turned her head to the window. "You see that tree out there?"

He followed her gaze. They were on the second floor, eye level with the branches of a magnolia tree covered in white flowers. A few of the large blooms had already withered but most remained full.

"Before all the blossoms fall from that tree, I expect to see Jesus. I'm looking forward to that." She turned her face back to him and winked. "Even more than meeting you."

Something inside him broke loose. He couldn't stifle a chuckle, and it felt good. "I don't blame you, Julie. I'd rather see Jesus than me, too."

"Yes, sir. But you've got too much to do here, first." She paused, her chest rising and falling as she took deep breaths. "Could you hand me my water, please?" Her voice had become raspy.

He reached for the plastic bottle with a bent straw sticking out. He held the bottle while she drank. "When ... when were you diagnosed?"

Her voice was stronger now. "A year ago. I've been through two rounds of chemo and radiation, but there's nothing more they can do. They've given me less than a month. And it's okay. I'm ready to go, to be done with all this pain, the limitations ..."

She closed her eyes, and he thought she had fallen asleep. But she continued to talk. "I read about your first wife, how she went so quickly. That was probably a blessing. And it's good that you finally married again. I'm so sorry about your baby."

"Thank you. Losing Hannah has been difficult, especially for Shawna."

Julie opened her eyes and pierced him with her gaze. "Tell her ... I'm going to hold the baby for her ... until she gets there."

An unwanted tear leaked out of his eye and he brushed it away. "I'll tell her."

"Governor, we need to move on. The news conference is supposed to start in five minutes." Johnnie's voice echoed as if from far away, though she was standing at his side.

Julie squeezed his hand. "I'm glad you're working on getting a research center, Governor. It's too late for me, but maybe it can save others. Don't give up, okay?"

The pressure in his chest crushed his heart, and he gave her hand one last squeeze. "I won't, Miss Fisher. I promise." He hated to leave this dying woman who was so filled with faith and joy. If only he could absorb a fragment of her peace. He stood and followed Johnnie out of the room.

He stopped in the hallway and leaned against the wall,

closing his eyes. He was barely aware that the videographer continued to film him.

Johnnie hovered. "Governor? Are you okay? I'm sorry, I should have realized how painful that would be for you. She's a winner, though, isn't she?"

He pushed away from the wall and straightened. "It's okay. I'm glad I got to meet her. Keep me posted on ... her progress." He straightened his jacket and adjusted his tie. "Let's go meet the press."

When they reached the lecture hall, a dozen reporters and half a dozen photographers waited. Hunter went right to the podium and welcomed them.

"I've just come from the room of a twenty-something woman who has been given less than a month to live. She urged me not to give up on getting a cancer research facility to locate in Tennessee. And I don't intend to. We have lost too many young people, many just reaching the peak years of their lives, to this deadly enemy."

Several reporters scribbled rapidly in notebooks while others held miniature recorders toward him. Did they understand how important this was, or was it simply another sound bite to them?

"That's why we plan to push for legislation providing special incentives for a pharmaceutical firm to come to our great state. We need to find a cure, and there's no reason it can't be done right here in Tennessee. There's a proposal on the table for a multi-million-dollar facility to be built here in Davidson County, but we are not the only state being considered. We have the academic resources and the medical expertise to support such a facility which would not only work to find a cure for cancer but would also bring in hundreds of jobs. Now we need a financial incentive to convince them to select this location."

Reporters raised their hands, and Johnnie pointed to *The Tennessean* political reporter in the front row.

"Governor, do you think research could have saved your baby?"

"We need to think about the future, not the past, and work to save as many people as we can. This facility would be a step in the right direction."

Johnnie leaned over to the microphone. "Any questions about the proposed legislation?" She pointed to a female reporter.

"I'm wondering what the senator from eastern Tennessee has to say about funding a facility in the Nashville area, instead of somewhere else in the state."

"Let's find out." Hunter stepped back from the podium, confident in the man's answer.

Caldwell hesitated, his thick eyebrows knitted together in an upside-down V. An ex-NFL player, he straightened his broad shoulders, then moved forward and bent down to the mic. "No doubt a cancer research facility would benefit the entire state, both medically and economically, but we need to see the proposed legislation and study it before I can commit to supporting it."

Hunter felt another kick in his gut. A few days ago,

Caldwell had agreed to back the incentive program. Now he was waffling. Hunter had to find a way to win his support for the project.

A breakthrough might come too late for Julie and Lynn, but there were many people like them. People who counted on him, Hunter Wilson, to succeed.

Chapter 8

A fresh wind blew across Titans Stadium Saturday morning, creating a challenging atmosphere for the Kids Fitness Expo. Shawna was glad she had pulled her long hair into a ponytail as the breeze swirled around her and the group of organizers.

"Mrs. Wilson, we'll have a brief welcome, and then you can talk about the Fit Kids initiative. But we'll want to start the activities before the children grow too restless." In other words, Leslie Simpson was saying, keep it short.

Shawna had no problem with that. She intended to introduce the program and build enthusiasm for it, but she had no desire to make a lengthy speech.

Hunter Lynn and Cooper had run off to check out the activities. More than a thousand kids wandered around the football field, scoping out the various activities they could take part in later. The largest crowds gathered around the four Titans players, of course, who had volunteered their time and were already signing autographs. The kids' excitement and the sunshine warmed Shawna, filling her with energy for the first time in days.

Around the field, stations had been set up for running, hurdles, climbing, and an obstacle course. The NFL players and several high school and college coaches would hold clinics throughout the day for football, baseball, soccer, and track and field. A portable basketball goal had been brought in for a basketball clinic, and the local Scout council had set up their mobile ropes course.

"It's almost ten o'clock," Leslie said. "Shall we see if we can get everyone's attention and get started?"

Along with Leslie and Shawna, three other members of the First Lady's Task Force on Children's Fitness climbed the steps to the portable stage. The fact that three local television stations had shown up to cover the event bode well for the fitness campaign.

Following the program, which lasted only fifteen minutes, Shawna and Leslie met with reporters.

"Mrs. Wilson, will you be joining in any of the sports?" Nate Matthews had covered sports for the Murray State newspaper when Shawna was on the tennis team. But now he was an investigative reporter for *The Tennessean*. What could he be investigating today?

"I might do that, Nate. I'm out of shape since my pregnancy, but I want to set a good example for the kids. How about you?"

He squinted his eyes, and Shawna saw the challenge coming. "As you can see, I haven't been working out much lately, either. But I might try beating you on the obstacle course. For the kids, of course."

He had gained twenty pounds, Shawna guessed, since college. Plus, he'd gone to college after serving in the army, so he probably had twenty years on her. And didn't he have a wounded leg? She could beat him easily. "What's the prize?"

He thought a moment. "If you win, I'll write a series of articles on your Fit Kids project for our website. If I win, you'll play in the Bluegrass Classic this fall.

The newspaper had already asked her to participate in the annual tennis tournament to raise money for community charities. She hadn't given them an answer. The event would take place right before the election, and she wasn't sure how much time she would have to practice. But getting more media coverage for Fit Kids would be worth the risk of embarrassing herself.

Shawna stuck out her hand. "You're on. What time shall we do this?"

Nate grabbed her hand and shook it, then nodded to his cameraman. "We need to get some video and talk to a few of the kids for the webcast. How about an hour from now? That'll still give me enough time to put a story together by deadline."

Grateful she had worn actual workout clothes under her nylon warmup suit, Shawna set off in search of Hunter

Lynn and Cooper.

The boys were working their way through the ropes course. She chewed her lip as Hunter Lynn edged along the fifteen-foot high platform. He didn't like heights, and she saw that he had chosen to avoid the rope bridge. Fearless Cooper, meanwhile, practically skipped across the bridge and prepared to shimmy down the final rope. When he reached the ground, he removed his harness and sprinted back to get in line for another round.

"Cooper," she called. "Come here a minute."

He looked around and saw her, and his smile faded. No doubt he thought she would make him quit. But he ran over to her. "Can I go one more time? Please?"

She laughed and leaned over to squeeze his shoulder. "In a minute, okay? Let's watch H. L., then I have something to tell you both."

They watched as Hunter Lynn reached the edge of the platform and hesitated. The teen-age boy supervising the activity hooked Hunter Lynn's harness onto the cable that would lower him to the ground, but still Hunter Lynn held back. He looked down at the ground, then at the rope slightly beyond his grasp, and he stepped back from the edge. The older boy spoke to him and put his hand on Hunter Lynn's back. Other kids were waiting. The boy showed him how to grab the rope. Hunter Lynn shook his head. Finally, with the Scout's encouragement, he sat on the edge of the platform. Shawna held her breath, hoping he would make the jump on his own. When he didn't, the older boy gave him a gentle push. Hunter Lynn's eyes grew huge, but the cable lowered him slowly to the ground. He unbuckled the harness like it was on fire.

"Good job, H. L.," Shawna called out. Hunter Lynn looked around until he found her, then he ambled over to her and Cooper.

She squatted down to his level. "You did it! Your dad will be proud of you. Wasn't that fun?"

The boy shrugged. "It was okay, I guess."

"You can go again in a few minutes, if you want to. But first I need to tell you both." She stood up and pointed to the obstacle course. "At 11:30, I'm going to do the obstacle course, racing a reporter. I'm hoping you'll both come and cheer for me."

Cooper jumped up and down. "Yeah! Go, Shawna!"

Hunter Lynn shrugged. "I guess we could."

"Great. I'll see you over there, then. Now go get back in line if you want to do this course again."

Cooper ran off at once but Hunter Lynn stayed where he was. He looked around the field at the other activity stations. "I think I'll check out the tunnel crawl over there. Bye."

He headed in that direction and Shawna watched one of the troopers follow a few paces behind. For the boys, having security trail them whenever they weren't at home or in school had become an accepted fact. Personally, she wasn't sure she'd ever get used to the lack of privacy.

And now she was going to be filmed in an obstacle

course race—a sport she had never tried. Why had she agreed to this? A simple footrace would have sufficed. She could do that, even as out-of-shape as she was. She only hoped she didn't embarrass herself too badly.

Maybe she could go through the course once before the race. She hurried over to the obstacle course, only to find a line of fifty-some kids, mostly teenagers, waiting. Had anyone told the starters about the challenge? She headed to the front of the line and found a volunteer wearing a red "Fit Kids" t-shirt. He looked about thirty and had to be a body-builder, from the way his arms bulged out of his t-shirt sleeves. His cropped haircut and tattooed arms screamed ex-military.

"Excuse me. I'm Shawna Wilson. Did anyone—"

"Hey, Miz Wilson. Craig Futrell." He stuck out his hand, which Shawna shook. "It's a pleasure to meet you. This is a great event and—"

"Thank you, Craig. But I need to know if anyone alerted you about the race in, let's see …" She checked her phone for the time. "About thirty minutes."

"What race?"

She grimaced. "I was afraid of that. It's an impromptu thing. One of the reporters challenged me to a race on the obstacle course, and—"

Craig wouldn't let her finish a sentence. "Cool. They're gonna tape it and show it on the news?"

Kids were waiting for Craig's signal to proceed. He waved the next pair onto the course.

"They'll videotape it for the Internet, and I suppose one of the TV stations could show it. The thing is, Craig, I've never done an obstacle course, and I really need to practice. But I don't have much time."

"Oh. You want to go next? I'll explain to the kids. Do you want help?"

She hoped not. "No, I'll try it on my own, thanks. But when Nate and his crew come, we'll need to stop the kids until the race is over, okay?"

"No problem, Ms. Wilson. We can do that. Good luck to you."

Fifteen minutes later, Shawna crawled over the final wall and collapsed on the mat at the finish line. She had made an awful mistake in agreeing to this race. She'd make a fool of herself.

"Well, well. If it isn't the First Lady." Nate Matthews stood over her. "Trying to get an advantage, or wearing yourself out before the race starts, Shawna?"

She rolled over, and he held out a hand to help her up. "Actually, I was wondering how I got myself into this." She grinned at him. "Have you done anything like this before?"

He studied the course. "Not exactly. I watched my brothers run a Rugged Maniac a couple years ago. At least with this one, there's no mud."

Shawna laughed. "That would be a pretty sight, wouldn't it?"

Nate eyed her with an odd look on his face. "That it

would. But it would make for a good YouTube video. Probably get thousands of views."

Just what she needed, the state of Tennessee laughing at her covered in mud. As if this wouldn't be bad enough. "This isn't your usual sort of story. No corruption, no scandal. What are you working on that brings you here?"

Running his hand over his bristly hair, he scowled. "We're short-handed. I'm having to do human interest stuff as well as the real stories."

"I see. Well, let's get this over with, shall we?"

Back at the start, Nate stretched while Craig held off the waiting teens. He and a couple of other volunteers moved the spectators several yards away from the course. Two TV crews were also preparing to film the impromptu race. Shawna spotted Hunter Lynn and Cooper, and waved to them. They waved back and clapped their hands, and Cooper jumped up and down.

Then Craig counted down to start the race. "Three. Two. One. Go!"

The crowd yelled as Shawna sprinted for the first obstacle, a cargo net stretching up to a platform. She found her footing in the ropes and grabbed hold above her head, climbing and pulling herself up. She reached the platform and rolled across it, where she had to crawl over another net. When she reached the other side, she looked back. Nate had reached the edge of the net.

"Yea, Shawna!" She heard Cooper's voice among the screams and cheers. Her muscles already burned and she had five more obstacles to go.

By the time she reached the next to last hurdle, she had gained even more ground on Nate. But her arms were feeling the pain. The adrenaline she felt from the competition was all that kept her going. She had to jump across a five-foot portable pool to the final platform, crawl over the last wall, and sprint to the finish. She could taste victory, and it tasted as sweet as she remembered.

But she misjudged the distance and started her jump too soon. She tumbled into the water and wound up sitting in the two-foot deep pool, with water splashing over her head. She looked up in time to see Nate above her.

"You okay?"

She nodded and stood up, shaking the water off. He grinned, leapt across the opening easily, and kept going.

Heat rose to her face. Not only had she fallen, but now she had lost the race.

"Come on, Shawna! Go! Catch him!" Cooper didn't understand giving up. She saw the faces of kids in the crowd, some laughing, some cheering.

If she couldn't win, she would laugh with them, not let herself be the object of derision. She made a show of plodding through the water and climbing onto the three-foot-high platform. Nate had already finished and was bent over, rubbing his right thigh. She smiled and waved to the crowd with both hands. Then she climbed the last wall and ran for the finish, her arms raised high in an imitation of victory.

Marie Wells Coutu

Chapter 9

Please, not a surprise party. Suspicious noises flowed from the dining room as Hunter entered the living quarters that evening.

He slipped upstairs without being noticed, loosening his tie on the way. The idea of talking politics tonight sucked the moisture from his mouth. At least he could relax until Shawna discovered him. Then, if he had to, he would deal with whatever the family had cooked up.

In the bedroom, he grabbed the remote control and switched on the TV, expecting his visit to the cancer unit to make the news. Heading for the walk-in closet, he threw the remote on the bed. He hung up his tie, then removed his shoes and placed them on the rack.

The door opened and Shawna entered. "You're home! I didn't hear you come in."

Glancing at her, he narrowed his eyes. "We're not having guests, are we?"

"No. Just family."

He shrugged off his shirt and tossed it into the hamper. "Good. I hate birthdays, and I don't want a party." He pulled on a polo shirt and stretched out on top of the bed cover.

"Mimi told me. But the boys are excited to surprise you." She lay down next to him and touched his hand, her flowery perfume teasing for his attention. "Rough day?"

He put his arm around her so she could rest her head on his chest. "You could say that. Caldwell practically—"

Hunter heard the words "First Lady Wilson" from the television announcer. He sat upright and grabbed the remote to turn up the volume. "Sounds like you made the news."

What had been on Shawna's schedule today? One of those festivals for kids. Her pet project.

She scooted forward on the bed, facing the television screen. "We had a good turnout. The boys had fun. And I think the committee was pleased."

He glanced at her to see if she was gloating. She claimed that she didn't like publicity, but she seemed eager to watch. After a cat food commercial, another teaser came on. He pressed the button to record. A video played of Shawna clambering across a sort of obstacle course, as the announcer said, "First Lady Shawna Wilson came out of seclusion today to test her skill on an obstacle course that proved challenging. Coming up on the six o'clock news."

That sounded like the lead story. And no mention of his news conference. The proposed research facility should be more important than Shawna running some race.

The camera showed two smiling news anchors behind a desk. The woman said, "First Lady Shawna Wilson kicked off her Fit Kids initiative with a Fitness Expo at Titans Stadium today. But the first lady of Tennessee wound up setting an example of what not to do."

The picture cut to a video of Shawna attempting to jump across an obstacle and splashing into the water. The video had been edited to show the movement backward and then forward again, twice. Finally, Shawna got up and climbed out of the water to finish the course.

Next to him, Shawna covered her face with her hands.

"The governor's wife took the fall in stride," the announcer said, "admitting to being out of shape, and urging kids not to follow her example."

The screen changed to Shawna, speaking into a microphone. "It's okay to fall, kids, as long as you get back up and keep trying. But even better is to stay in shape so you don't fall in the first place. That's why we're initiating the Fit Kids project."

Hunter had to admit that Shawna handled the situation like an experienced politician. She had seized the moment of defeat and turned it into a victory. In fact, she'd done so well that she had upstaged his pitch for cancer research, at the very time when he needed more support.

Keeping his eyes focused on the TV, he muttered, "Nice recovery."

Hunter's frosty comment made Shawna's heart thud.

One moment, she felt warm and cozy in his embrace; the next, he had withdrawn his arm and his affection. What had changed?

"Hunter?"

He didn't answer. His gaze was riveted to the television screen, in that way he had of avoiding conversation.

"Finally," he muttered under his breath.

She looked at the TV, where her husband could be seen entering Vanderbilt University Hospital. Of course. He had visited the cancer unit today, trying to drum up support for a research facility. That probably dredged up memories of Lynn's dying days. Even after six years, those memories had to be painful.

"I'm sure going there was difficult." She touched his shoulder. "Want to talk about it?"

"Shhh."

"…announced a proposal to increase incentives for a multi-million-dollar cancer research facility in the state. Lieutenant Governor Caldwell accompanied the governor, but when asked if he supported the latest proposal,

Caldwell would only say he needed to study it. In other news—"

Hunter clicked the remote to switch the channel. Commercial for a new car dealership. He tried a third channel. "...more on the First Lady's race on Ten at Ten."

Her normally reserved husband pressed the power button to shut off the TV, then tossed the remote on the bed. He stood and glared at her. "Congratulations. Your little escapade seems to have overshadowed my efforts to help cancer patients. Not to mention my campaign."

So, that's what was eating at his craw. "I doubt my fall will have any effect on your campaign." Though she wouldn't mind if it did do some harm. He hadn't listened when she asked him to drop out. She slid off the bed and stood up. "Anyway, they covered your visit to the hospital."

He grunted. "Gave it half the time of yours. And Channel Ten is teasing more about you for the late news. Probably won't even mention my proposal."

"Can I help it if they love me?" As soon as the words escaped, she willed them back.

His eyes blazed. But a knock on the door shut down the reply forming on his lips.

"Dad, Shawna? The chef says dinner's ready. And it's your favorite, Dad."

Hunter instantly switched his demeanor. He went to the door and opened it for Cooper. "Really? We're having rattlesnake and kumquats?"

Cooper leaped into his arms. "That is not your favorite. It's spaghetti and Italian sausage, right?"

Shawna was glad for the interruption, and for the return of Hunter's throaty laugh. She loved that laugh, which showed up more when he was with the boys. She waited until he had wrestled Cooper to the floor and tickled him into breathless giggles. "We'd better go eat before Jean-Claude gets upset. You know he hates serving his food cold."

"Yes, Jean-Claude must be respected above all." Hunter stood, held out his hand to Cooper, and lifted him to his feet. He wrapped an arm around Cooper's waist and picked him up like a football, restarting his giggles.

Shawna followed the pair, staying back to avoid Cooper's thrashing feet as Hunter carried him horizontally through the hallway. When the three of them reached the stairs, Hunter set Cooper on his feet and waited for him and Shawna to lead the way.

Cooper scurried down the broad steps and burst into the dining room well ahead of her. She smiled at his little-boy attempt at a whisper. "Here he comes!"

She entered the family dining room and turned to join Mimi, Jean-Claude, and the two boys as they shouted, "Surprise! Happy birthday!"

Hunter's face revealed genuine surprise. The room was festooned with blue streamers and a colorful hand-lettered banner proclaiming, "Happy Birthday, Daddy." Hunter Lynn and Cooper had worked on the banner after the Fitness Expo, drawing it out on butcher paper provided by Jean-Claude, then decorating it with magic-marker curlicues and "Star Wars" stickers.

"You boys have been busy." Hunter grabbed a boy in each arm and hugged them both. He didn't mention Shawna—or Mimi, who had overseen the decorating. The family sat in their usual places, with Hunter at the head of the table and Shawna on his left. The two boys sat side-by-side across from Shawna, and Mimi took the other end opposite Hunter.

A minute later, Jean-Claude returned with two large bowls. He handed one to Hunter and set the other on the table at his right. "Happy birthday, Governor. I'll be going now."

Except when important visitors came for dinner, Jean-Claude made the initial preparations for the evening meal, but Mimi or Shawna would finish and serve it. Shawna liked the arrangement. She enjoyed the freedom from planning and cooking entire meals, especially since she had never learned to cook for more than two.

Hunter nodded. "Of course. Thank you for staying."

As Shawna spooned marinara sauce over the spaghetti on her plate, Mimi spoke up. "Carole called today. She invited all of us to come hear her sing next week. Of course, we can't go."

Carole was Mimi's other daughter, the sister of Hunter's late wife. She was also a country singer, but had not yet broken out. Ten years younger, she was still in high school when Lynn died.

Hunter took the bowl from Shawna. "I'm pretty busy next week, but why don't you take the boys?"

"Yeah," Hunter Lynn chimed in. "We haven't seen Aunt Carole in a long time."

"I wouldn't set foot in that honky-tonk." Mimi's tone of voice left no room for argument. "She's playing at Tootsie's, of all places."

"Tootsie's? But Mimi, that place is famous. Lots of stars have been discovered there." Even Shawna, who knew little about the Nashville music scene, recognized the significance of an appearance at Tootsie's.

Hunter speared a piece of Italian sausage with his fork and moved it to his plate. "I'm afraid Shawna's right, Mimi. This could be Carole's big break. Lynn played there lots of times, even after she got her contract. You should go."

Perhaps Shawna imagined it, but Hunter's voice seemed to crack when he mentioned Lynn's name. After so much time, apparently, the torch still flickered.

"That is no decent place for decent people. I didn't like it when Lynn played there, either. Loud music and free-flowing liquor, that's what it is. I certainly won't take my grandsons to a place like that. They can see Carole play in a couple of weeks at the benefit concert."

Time to change the subject. "Is everyone ready for cake?" Shawna stood and headed for the kitchen. In the middle of the counter sat the chocolate layer cake, covered with her mother's frosting, thanks to Mimi's help. Four dozen birthday candles filled its top, and a blue grill-lighter lay next to it.

"Can I light the candles?" Hunter Lynn pushed through the swinging door and grabbed the lighter. "Please?"

Cooper joined his brother. "I want to help, too."

"Hmm. Let's see." Shawna stroked her chin. "How old are you?"

Hunter Lynn waved the lighter. "I'll be ten in three months."

"Shaw-na." Cooper dragged the word out. "You know I turned seven in February."

"That's right, you did. But unfortunately, the rule is you have to be nine-and-a-half to use one of those lighters. So, H. L., you can light ten of the candles. Then you'd better let me finish. Cooper, I'm afraid you'll have to wait a couple more years."

"Awww."

With flames from the burning candles warming her face, Shawna carried the cake into the dining room and set it in front of Hunter. Mimi led them in singing "Happy Birthday," and Hunter blew out the flames with one breath.

As everyone applauded, Hunter Lynn grinned. "What'd you wish for, Dad?"

"It's bad luck to tell you." He cut the cake and served it onto small plates they passed around the table.

Hunter Lynn took a big bite of cake. "You should have

seen Shawna today, Dad." He forgot to swallow before he spoke, and Mimi tapped on the table—her signal to the boys about manners. Hunter Lynn glanced at her and swallowed his food quickly. "Sorry. But Shawna was awesome. Until she fell."

Shawna forked a bite into her mouth, closing her eyes to savor the taste. Finally, Hunter Lynn had something positive to say about her. And Shawna thought he'd been bored watching the race.

Cooper jumped up and down in his chair. "She was still awesome, even if that guy did beat her. He didn't even stop to help."

"Actually, he did ask if I was okay."

"Yeah, but you were way ahead of him till then. You would've beaten him big time." Cooper sounded as excited as if he had been in the race himself.

Hunter put his fork down. "I saw her on television."

Shawna closed her eyes. Clearly her moment of fame threatened him, but surely, he wouldn't reveal his displeasure to the boys.

Hunter Lynn looked at his brother and said, "Television? Awe. Some!" He exchanged a high five with Cooper.

But Hunter kept quiet, still.

"Your dad recorded the news story," Shawna said. "If you want to, you can watch it before you go to bed."

Maybe if she bungled enough times, her husband might lose the election and they could have a normal life away from politics. In the meantime, she would keep doing whatever she could to promote the Fit Kids project, whether Hunter liked it or not.

Because, for the first time since Hannah died, today she had felt alive again.

Chapter 10

Nate turned onto the curvy two-lane road leading to Lake Barkley Lodge, eager to stretch his legs and watch boaters on the water on this early summer day.

"Almost there, boy." He reached across to Pax, his golden retriever, and patted him on the head. Pax whined. He needed a break as much as Nate did.

The hour and a half drive north from Nashville was close to the maximum he could take before his leg froze up from lack of exercise. At least traffic hadn't been too bad. For the most part, the truckers on I-24 had stayed out of his way.

Suddenly, a sharp noise echoed through the trees. Sounded like an IED exploding. Nate's startled reaction caused him to swerve into the other lane, and he braced for a collision. More explosions. He yelled, and Pax began barking frantically.

Nate shook his head. He was in his own Jeep, the sole vehicle on a Kentucky back road, not in a Humvee in Iraq, and Pax was barking. He jerked the steering wheel to the right and glanced in his mirror. No cars in sight, so he stomped his foot on the brake and rolled to a stop. He took several deep breaths, slowing his galloping heart rate to a trot. One of these days, these flashbacks would get him in real trouble.

Beyond the woods hugging the empty road, he could still hear the thuds that had pushed the play button on his memories and nearly caused him to crash. Trap shooters. He should have remembered the shooting range, since several of the governors had used it last year during the conference at the resort.

He shook his head. Nate rubbed Pax behind the ears, the silky dog hair soothing his nerves. "Sorry if I scared you, fella. Thanks for bringing me out of it."

Sunlight glinted in front of him as a brown car came around the bend. The driver slowed. Probably a park ranger, checking to see if something was wrong. The car pulled to a stop alongside Nate's vehicle, and he could read the lettering on the side. "Yep, it's a ranger," he told Pax.

Not only a ranger, but a young woman, maybe 25. Attractive, even with a wide-brimmed "Smoky" hat perched on her head. Nate pressed the button to lower his window.

"Sir, do you know that you are parked in the middle of the road?"

Nate resisted the urge to make a wisecrack about thinking this was a parking lot because of all the cars. "Yes'm. I-uh-had to stop for a deer that ran across the road. It kind of shook me up, so I was trying to calm down before I proceeded." At least the last part was true. He couldn't admit to the real reason he had stopped.

The ranger looked across into the thick woods. "A deer, huh?" She rested her arm on the door of her car. "Are you okay to drive now?"

"I'm fine. I'll be moving along."

She nodded. "Uh-huh. Just take care, and watch out for those deer." She seemed to be trying to hide a smirk. Her window whirred shut, and she pulled away.

"I don't think she believed us, Pax." He inhaled the crisp scent floating through the open window and decided to leave it down. He reached over and shut off the air conditioner. The day was not too hot and not too cold, exactly right for a short research trip.

Ignoring the sound of periodic gunshots, he shifted into "drive." The conference center should be around the next bend, and he needed to focus on his task. His best bet would be to find one of the maids who would be cleaning rooms about now. One of them might remember something interesting from the governors' conference last year.

He pulled into a parking spot on the far side of the lot. Pax woofed and stood up on the passenger seat, his tail wagging. Maybe he should have left the dog at home, but he'd wanted company during the drive. Besides, sometimes friendly Pax could break the ice better than Nate could.

After attaching the leash to Pax's collar, Nate let him out of the car and allowed himself to be pulled to the grassy area under the trees. His right leg tingled and he shook it to get the blood flowing again. If anyone noticed, they would probably think he was imitating his dog. But what did they know of his pain?

While he waited for Pax to take care of business, Nate studied his options. Down the hill, he spotted a laundry cart on the walk in front of one of the cabins. "That looks like a good place to start, don't you think, boy? Away from the curious eyes of management at the lodge."

When Pax had finished watering one of the trees, Nate led him across the parking lot to the walk.

As they neared the first cabin, a plump woman came through the door. Her black hair and wrinkled, brown skin contrasted with the bundle of white linens she carried. She stuffed them into the hamper on her cart, then pulled a clean set from the neat stack on the lower shelf.

Guessing she came from Latin America, Nate hoped she could speak English. "Good morning. Can you help me?"

"Maybe. What is it?" She did have an accent, but not so strong that Nate couldn't understand her. She kept the cart between them, and creased her forehead until her thick eyebrows almost joined.

"How long have you worked here?" He jerked on the

leash to stop Pax from sniffing the laundry cart.

She eyed Pax. "Pretty dog." Then she looked at Nate. "Four year."

Did she mean "four years" or "for a year"? Nate couldn't tell, but it didn't matter. "Did you know Shawna Moore when she worked here?"

The woman smiled and nodded. "*Si.* Very nice lady. So sad when her husband die. But she is famous now, wife of Tennessee governor."

"That's right." Nate stepped closer to loosen Pax's leash, letting him nuzzle the woman's legs. As he hoped, she bent over and stroked the dog's head. He waited a beat while the two bonded. "His name is Pax. He likes you."

"My *chiquita*—my little girl—would like a dog. But our place is too small." She shook her head, then straightened and put both hands on her laundry cart. "I have work. Why you ask about Missus Moore? You her friend?"

Good, she showed curiosity but not suspicion. Nate shifted his feet. "I knew her in college. Do you recall last year when all the governors came here?"

She nodded, her brow furrowed. "Big deal. Missus Moore was really nervous, and busy."

Careful now. Mustn't scare her off. "I know she was very busy. I was here, too. She did a great job with all the arrangements. She got to know Governor Wilson that week, didn't she?"

The cleaning woman shrugged. He had to get to the point before she lost patience.

"I want to thank you for all your hard work." He put his hand in his pocket and palmed the twenty-dollar bill he'd placed there. Then he took her hand, slipping the money into her palm while squeezing her hand. "This is not an easy job, I know. And sometimes, you probably see things, like Governor Wilson going into or coming out of Mrs. Moore's cabin, perhaps?"

The woman squinted her dark eyes. "Mister, whoever you are, I don't think you Missus Moore's friend. She is good woman." She pulled her hand away and let the twenty flutter to the ground. Pax sniffed at it. "I do my work. That's all." She grabbed a stack of clean towels from the cart shelf, shuffled into the cabin, and closed the door.

Nate had no better luck with two other maids he found cleaning cabins. One had only started three months earlier, and the other refused to talk to him at all, simply smiled and shook her head. He spotted a man spraying weeds along the path but he worked part-time, starting at ten in the morning and leaving at four. He did not remember the governors' conference. To him, one week was the same as another.

Nate took Pax back to the car and fastened his leash to the rear bumper. "I guess it's time to try inside the lodge, boy. You'll have to wait here for me." From the back, he removed the water dish and poured water from the gallon jug he'd brought along. He rubbed the dog's head. "I'm going to grab a sandwich and talk to a few people. I'll be back in a little bit."

Pax drank from the bowl, then laid down in the shade of the Jeep.

Before heading to the restaurant, Nate made his way down the long hallway lined with closed doors. He spotted a maid he remembered as she disappeared into one of the hotel rooms. The young woman's white hair and nearly six-foot height would stand out in any setting. He had talked with her several times during the week of the conference. He riffled through his memory bank for her name.

"Serena." Nate stopped in the doorway of the room she was cleaning. Her back was to him, and she turned quickly, holding a pillow to her chest. "Remember me? I was here last spring for the governors' conference."

Her eyes narrowed as she scanned him from head to foot, then her face relaxed. "Yeah, I remember you. You're a reporter, right?"

"Right. Nate Matthews, with *The Tennessean*. How've you been?" He leaned against the doorframe, casual, non-threatening.

She walked to the other side of the bed and began pulling sheets off, keeping her eyes on him. "You staying here again?"

"Nah. I'm just here for the day, looking around, talking to people."

She didn't respond but continued to gather the sheets.

"I was wondering if you remember anything special about that conference."

She tilted her head and gave him a flirtatious smile.

"Like what?"

He shrugged. "You know, the sort of thing that happens at conferences. Did you notice any, um, suspicious activity—maybe a woman going or coming from a man's single room?"

She dropped the bundle of sheets on the floor and went into the bathroom. A minute later, she added several towels to the pile. "They don't tell me how many people are staying in a room."

"Right. But you can tell, can't you?"

"Sometimes. But I don't know who's who, ya know?" She picked up a clean sheet from a stack on the dresser. "I might have seen something, but why do you care now?"

"Curious. It's my nature." He straightened and put a hand in his pocket. "You may remember I'm a pretty good tipper, so if you saw anything helpful ..."

She held still for a beat, then tugged at the sheet, making a hospital corner. "Helpful as pertains to what?"

Enough tiptoeing around the elephant. Nate stepped into the room and spoke in a conspiratorial voice. "Do you have any reason to think Shawna Moore may have been in Governor Wilson's room, or that he may have gone to her cabin?"

"You shouldn't be in here." Serena threw the coverlet over the bed and bent over to straighten it. "I liked Shawna. She could be a little ... direct. But not in a mean way. I don't want to cause her any trouble." She glanced up at him. "I could use a little extra cash, though."

He took out his money clip and pulled off a twenty-dollar bill—the same one the first maid had refused. He dropped it on the bed, but held the money clip so she could see there was more.

Serena grabbed the bill and stuffed it in her pocket. "I know Shawna missed her husband. And she did spend the night in someone's room. Twice. She never did anything like that before—or after. At least I don't think so."

Nate's chest thudded, a familiar sensation when he got close to uncovering the truth in one of his investigations. He pulled another Jackson from his clip and held it across the bed. "Whose room?"

She reached out and snatched the bill, quick as a lizard's tongue snagging an insect. "We don't know the guests' names. But I saw them together downstairs several times. And then, on TV. When she married him."

Marie Wells Coutu

Chapter 11

From backstage at the Ryman Auditorium, Hunter glimpsed his family seated in the Gold Circle on the main floor.

His annual evening of agony took on a new twist this year. He supported holding this benefit concert in Lynn's memory, but the yearly event reopened the wounds just as they began to heal. And now with his marriage to Shawna, doubt added to the pain.

Had he betrayed Lynn by marrying Shawna? Was he betraying Shawna by continuing to host the concert? The questions had roiled in his stomach all day, leaving him irritable and nervous.

Every year, he wondered if Lynn Wilson would have been forgotten by the country music community. But as before, the sold-out crowd said otherwise. Whether people wanted to honor her memory or contribute to cancer research funding, he didn't know. Or care. All that mattered was that they paid the steep price for the tickets, raising half a million dollars for research.

"Governor, it's time." The stage manager gave the signal to lower the house lights, and a spotlight came up on center stage.

Hunter made his way to the microphone. He looked down to the area where he knew the boys were and winked. Mimi sat in the front row with one boy on each side of her. Shawna sat next to Cooper, and an empty chair at the end of the row waited for Hunter to join them after he welcomed the audience.

He raised his eyes to take in the whole auditorium as the applause swelled. The rows of wooden pews were packed, even in the balcony. The Ryman's reputation as the "mother church of country music" stabbed at his heart. He hadn't been to church since ... when? His wedding to Shawna? But now wasn't the time to think about that.

"Thank you for coming tonight to show your support for cancer research. It's crucial that we find a cure for the deadly disease that took the life of my wife—my first wife, Lynn Wilson—" He hoped Shawna hadn't been offended by his slip of the tongue. After all, he and Shawna had been married less than a year. It was a natural mistake. "Six years ago, when Lynn was diagnosed with stage four pancreatic cancer, the average patient died within six months. Lynn lived five months and two weeks after her diagnosis. Now, with two new chemotherapy regimens, life expectancy is about eleven months after starting treatment. That is a tremendous breakthrough, but still leaves a lot of room for improvement."

He waited for the spattering of applause to end. "As you know, the money raised tonight will help fund continuing research—research that is desperately needed by patients and their families to give them hope for a longer and less painful life after this devastating diagnosis. I want to thank all the musicians and production staff for donating their time tonight, and I thank each one of you for coming. Enjoy the show."

The spotlight dimmed and a video of Lynn's life began playing on the immense screen behind him. Hunter waited for his eyes to adjust, then he trotted down the steps to his seat. Shawna surprised him by sliding into the vacant chair, so that he could sit next to his son. He dropped into it and draped an arm around Cooper, then focused on the video.

Lynn in a home movie, playing air guitar and singing at the age of twelve. Lynn in her first public appearance, a Knoxville talent show. The two of them campaigning for his first term in the General Assembly. Lynn in her debut at the Grand Ole Opry after he was elected state senator. The family, all together, after Cooper was born—only six months before her diagnosis of cancer.

Hunter squeezed Cooper's shoulders until the boy squirmed.

"Dad, you're hurting me." Cooper's whispered whine brought Hunter back to reality, and he released his grip.

"Sorry, son."

Cooper leaned over against his chest, continuing to speak in a low voice. "It's okay, Dad. You miss her, don't you?"

Hunter nodded.

"Me, too. I wish I could remember her."

"She loved you and H. L. very much. She hated leaving you, you know." He glanced to his right, detecting tears streaming down Mimi's face. On the other side of her, Hunter Lynn slouched low in his seat, arms crossed.

Sometimes Hunter worried about his oldest son. Unlike Cooper, Hunter Lynn stuffed his feelings. He had developed a surly attitude that Hunter didn't like. And it had become more noticeable since he and Shawna had married. But he wasn't sure what to do about it.

He had done all he could for Lynn, but it hadn't been enough. The cancer had progressed too far by the time she was diagnosed. If only he'd paid more attention and urged her to report her symptoms to her doctor earlier. Perhaps they could have saved her.

The video ended and the spotlight came up on the first performer, Vince Gill. "I had the privilege of playing this song with Lynn Wilson a couple of times," he said, strumming his guitar. "It was my favorite of all her fantastic songs, and I know it's one of y'all's favorites, too." He launched into an explosive performance of *No Secrets, No More,* and the crowd roared.

Recorded soon after receiving her death sentence, the

song had been on Lynn's final album. Hunter smiled wryly, picturing her in her hospital bed upon hearing the album had made platinum. "There won't be secrets between us, anymore," she had crooned, her voice cracking with pain and heartbreak. The only secret she'd ever kept from him had been the early symptoms of the cancer. That had killed her, and losing her had nearly killed him. Only Mimi's frequent reminders that he still had two sons who needed him had kept him going.

By the time the song ended, his vision was cloudy, but his family joined the rest of the audience in a standing ovation. All except Hunter Lynn, who remained slumped in his seat. Hunter whispered to Cooper, "I'm going to check on your brother, okay? You stay here with Mimi and Shawna."

Cooper nodded.

As the applause died, Hunter slipped into the empty chair next to Hunter Lynn. He leaned close to the boy's ear. "You all right, H. L.?"

Hunter Lynn shrugged. "Guess so. I just don't like that song."

"Why not?"

"'Cause people shouldn't have secrets from each other."

The boy occasionally showed too much wisdom for a nine-year-old. "You're right. But that's what the song means."

"You and Mom had secrets. That's why she wrote it,

isn't it?"

Hunter winced. He and Shawna, not Lynn, had a secret they hid from the world. "Not really. I think she saw what keeping secrets did to other people … one of her friends, especially. That's what inspired the song."

"Oh." Hunter Lynn sat up a little straighter as the emcee introduced Lynn's sister Carole. "I wish she was still here."

Hunter rubbed his son's head, smoothing his hair. "I know, son. I know. But your Aunt Carole looks a lot like her."

The audience loved Carole's performance of two of Lynn's songs. She was followed by a parade of other top Nashville artists, each one sharing how much they missed Lynn. By intermission, Hunter wanted nothing more than to be alone.

As soon as the lights came up, three state troopers surrounded the family, escorting them backstage to a special dressing room set aside for them. Although the Ryman was packed with stars tonight, many of whom were Hunter's personal friends, his security detail would take no chances.

Mimi excused herself to wash up, laughing about her tears ruining her makeup. Shawna, who seemed extremely quiet, retreated to an overstuffed chair in the corner. Hunter pulled a chair close to hers, not wanting her to know how much he missed Lynn. "Everything okay, honey?"

She studied him, her dark eyes penetrating his mask.

"Sure. But I'm realizing what big shoes I have to fill. She must have been a wonderful person, from what everyone says."

"She was." He couldn't say any more without choking up, so he sat still, not talking. Cooper and Hunter Lynn came over to them, and he held out his arms. The boys eagerly moved into his embrace. The sadness in their little faces pierced his heart. "I'm still here, boys."

"Dad," Cooper said. "We were wondering something."

"Okay. What is it?"

Hunter Lynn was the one to speak next, affecting the know-it-all tone of the big brother. "You loved Shawna's baby more than us, didn't you?"

Hunter blinked. "Why in the world would you say that?"

"Seems like you've both been really sad since she died." Hunter Lynn shrugged. "And maybe we remind you too much of Mom, and you'd rather forget her, now that you have Shawna."

What had Hunter done—or not done—to make them think this? He pulled both boys in closer. "No, son. I did not love Hannah more than you. It's different, because we didn't have her very long." He looked over their heads at Shawna. She was leaning forward, concern crinkling her forehead.

"As for wanting to forget your mother, you couldn't be more wrong. She was a special person, and I'll never forget her. I don't want you to forget her, either. H. L., do you remember how she would read a story and sing to you at bedtime?"

Hunter Lynn's brow creased. Then his eyes got big. "She used to sing *I Love You, Baby,* didn't she?"

"She wrote that song for you when you were born."

"Mimi sings it sometimes. But now I think I remember Mom's voice instead."

Hunter mussed his son's hair. "That's good. Hold onto those special memories. You boys help me to keep the best parts of her close to me." He noticed a gleam in Shawna's eyes. "And marrying Shawna doesn't take any of that away. I have enough love to go around, you know."

In spite of his words, Hunter's failures plagued him. His love for Lynn had not saved her. Based on the doubts his boys had expressed, he hadn't done a good job of loving them, either. And recently, his actions toward Shawna didn't reflect his true feelings. He was away from her far too often. But he had an obligation to the people of this state.

Chapter 12

Kids surrounded Shawna, covering the high school football field somewhere in the eastern part of the state. Cheers of delight and encouragement rang from parents who watched their children take part in the various events.

The summer air held the scent of rain, and dark clouds hovered in the western sky. She'd attended fourteen Fit Kids Festivals in the past six weeks. And she had at least two more scheduled every week from now until school started again. If the number of participating kids proved anything, the Fit Kids campaign could be considered successful. At least she had done one thing right since becoming Tennessee's First Lady.

Crystal strode up, a Nikon camera hanging around her neck. Wearing navy capris and a red top, Shawna's twenty-four-year-old petite assistant could be mistaken for one of the high school students. She had worked as a marketing intern for Shawna at Lake Barkley, and they made a good team. "I've got several great photos of kids having fun and competing. Oops, I mean *participating*." She wrinkled her nose.

Crystal shared Shawna's disdain for the decision of the Fit Kids committee that events should be non-competitive. How could you have an obstacle course, long jump, and races and expect that kids wouldn't compete? Shawna's days of competitive tennis had taught her that an athlete worked harder when challenged by others who were as good or better.

But today's politically correct values had won out over her objections. Though the program was figuratively hers, citizen involvement was crucial to its success, so she had silenced her protests. The project awarded certificates for participation and completion, rather than first, second, and third-place finishers.

She and Crystal watched ten boys run a hundred-yard dash. Four of them outpaced the rest of the field until near the end, then one boy put on a burst of speed. The other three tried to keep up, but the boy finished with a two-stride lead. His victory dance showed his satisfaction with himself, and the next three finishers congratulated him.

Shawna laughed. "See, you can't keep kids from competing, even with no prizes."

"Miz Wilson." She felt a tug on her shirt and looked down at a little black girl of about five.

Shawna squatted down to her level. "What is it,

sweetie?"

The girl looked at her with large round eyes. Two black braids stuck out from her head. "I like these games. I wish you could be my mother, so we could do this all the time."

Startled, Shawna nearly fell over. She reached out to hug the girl. "I'd love that, but I'm sure your mother would miss you. You know you can play lots of these games even when we're not here."

The girl's face lit up. "I guess we could. I'll tell my brothers." She ran off toward a small group that seemed to be waiting for her.

Shawna stood and stretched. Seeing all the children at these festivals reminded her of her own loss. God knew the pain she felt when she recalled holding tiny Hannah in her arms. She had been trying to bargain with God, asking him to give her another baby.

Of course, as little time as she and Hunter had spent together lately, getting pregnant seemed unlikely. He might think more of her if she could connect with his sons. Especially Hunter Lynn, who continued to be mostly hostile. She still had not asked him about trying tennis. The sport had been her lifeline in high school, pulling her out of depression and helping her find her balance. Maybe it would be the answer for H. L., too.

The thunderstorm held off until a ribbon had been distributed to every child. Shawna was grateful she didn't have to drive in the torrential rain. The expected four-hour trip turned into five as her driver slowed down when the worst of the downpour limited visibility.

By the time Shawna arrived home, the boys were already in bed. Hunter had left for another campaign trip that afternoon, and Shawna found Mimi alone in the living room.

Mimi put down her knitting needles and picked up the remote control. She paused the replay of *Downton Abbey*. "It's about time you got home. The boys wanted you to read to them."

Why did Mimi make her feel as if she were a teen-ager out past curfew? She wasn't Lynn, and nothing she did would ever please this woman. "I told you I was going to Johnson City today."

Mimi picked up her knitting, and the needles clicked rapidly, like an impatient toe-tapping. "Seems like you're gone more than you're home. Doesn't seem right for a mother—even if you are just their stepmother."

Shawna bristled, both at the "just a stepmother" reference and the criticism. Only a few weeks ago, Mimi had urged her to resume her duties, and now that she had done so, she was judging her for not being home. "I have responsibilities. You said so yourself. I'm attending to my 'First Lady duties,' as you called them."

"Hmph. You sure you're not just avoiding H. L. and Cooper?"

"Avoiding them? Why would you say that?"

Mimi shrugged, not looking at her. "Thinking out

loud. They already lost their mom. Somehow, I don't think a grandmother is a good long-term substitute." She continued to focus on the blue-and-white yarn object taking shape in her lap.

The fuzzy yarn looked soft and cozy to Shawna. She plopped down in the chair opposite the older woman. "What are you talking about, Mimi? You've done a great job for six years. The boys love you." She couldn't believe she was complimenting this woman who had just insulted her.

"Of course, they do. And yes, I have taken good care of them. But I won't be around forever, you know. Since Hunter chose to marry you, you really should try to act like a mother."

"As a matter of fact, I'm going to start giving them tennis lessons next week."

"Aren't they too young for tennis?"

Of course, Mimi wouldn't approve of any idea Shawna had. "There's a new approach for younger children, with smaller rackets and smaller courts. I think they'll like it."

"I see." Mimi's knitting needles clicked.

"What are you making?"

"This? Oh, nothing. I need something to occupy my hands." She stashed her knitting project, along with the yarn and needles, in a cloth tote bag. She switched off the television. "It's late. I'm going up to bed."

Shawna waited until she had headed up the stairs, then blew out a breath, turned off the lights, and went into the bedroom. Mimi was wrong. Shawna wasn't trying to avoid the two boys. She simply didn't know how to relate to them. Or to Mimi. You couldn't please some people.

Chapter 13

"Who's picking up the governor tonight?"

"Let me check, ma'am." Lieutenant Palmer put Shawna's call on hold but returned moments later. "Curtis is scheduled to meet the plane."

"Good." Shawna found it easy to be around Curtis. She lifted the phone from her shoulder where she had rested it. "I'd like to go with him."

"Of course, Mrs. Wilson. I'll let him know." His voice indicated his skepticism. "The schedule shows him leaving for the airport about ten."

"I'll be ready. And please don't mention it to the governor. I want to surprise him." Shawna clicked off and dropped the phone on the bedside table. Five more hours. Hunter had been campaigning in the eastern part of the state since Tuesday, and she longed to see him again. To hold him and be held.

She went into the closet to select an outfit—something alluring. She and Hunter had not been intimate since before Hannah's birth, and the distance between them seemed to be growing. She needed reassurance that he hadn't married her only because of the pregnancy.

Maybe the charcoal gray dress she'd been wearing when they met. The color enhanced her hazel eyes, Hunter had told her. She pulled the hanger from the rack and held up the knit sheath. Had she lost enough weight to get into it again?

Only one way to find out. She shed the two-piece suit she had worn to the office. Then she shimmied into the dress, pulling it over her head and smoothing the soft fabric over her hips. Surely Hunter would notice how well it fit her, maybe even recall the feelings he had for her last summer.

Her loneliness back then had led to a bad decision, but she did not regret marrying Hunter. And she wanted to make that clear to him. Besides, being around children all week at the Fit Kids programs had convinced her she wanted another baby.

There was a rap on the bedroom door. "Shawna, dinner's ready."

Shawna left the closet. "Thanks, Mimi. I'll be down in a minute." She slipped off the dress and laid it neatly on the bed, then put on jeans and a casual shirt. Once the boys went to bed, she'd have time to take a leisurely bath, fix her hair, and "glamour-up," as Ellie liked to call it.

She waited until dinner was over and the boys had left the table before she told Mimi about her plans. She got the expected reaction—raised eyebrows.

"You're planning to surprise him?"

"Yes." Why shouldn't she surprise her own husband? It wasn't any of Mimi's business, anyway. "He's been gone five days. I thought he might like being welcomed home."

Mimi rose and started clearing the dishes. "Hunter is a good man. He's not a playboy."

That thought had never occurred to her. "I know that. It's just that—well, he's been gone a lot lately, so I want to do something special for him." She didn't have to defend her actions to this woman, so why was she?

Mimi came to Shawna's side of the table and picked up her plate. "Go on and get ready. I'll put the boys to bed." She took the stack of plates and headed for the kitchen, but at the door, she stopped and looked back. "He does love you. I can see it, even if you can't."

Stunned, Shawna sat in silence. For once, Mimi seemed to approve of Shawna's plans.

Curtis pulled the SUV into the parking space at the state hangar a few minutes before ten. He picked up his cell phone and made a call. Then he turned and looked over the back of the seat. "They were delayed by weather en route, so they're still about twenty minutes out. Do you want to wait here or inside?"

Easy question. The butterflies in her stomach wouldn't let her sit still for long. "I'll wait inside. But, Curtis ..."

How could she explain without being too obvious?

"Yes, ma'am?"

"Would you mind, um, would it be possible for you to wait out here? I'd like to have a few private moments with the governor." She hoped the dark car kept him from seeing her flushed face.

Curtis's white teeth shone when he smiled. "Yes, ma'am. Trent's traveling with him, so I'll let him know, as well."

Shawna paced around the two rows of cheap vinyl seating in the tiny waiting room. Charter terminals sometimes had plush seating and a choice of beverages, but state government couldn't spend money on luxuries. A single coffeepot, the carafe half-full, sat on the counter at one side of the room. The coffee smelled like it had been made that morning and left on the burner all day. She chose to pass.

Even this late at night, an occasional jet passed overhead to land at the nearby commercial airport, each sudden roar causing Shawna to shudder. As she waited, her frayed nerves tormented her. Hunter didn't like birthday parties, but what if he didn't like to be surprised at all? Mimi would have warned her, wouldn't she? Unless she hoped Shawna would fail.

The door from the hangar opened, and a short man wearing mechanic's coveralls came in, whistling random notes. He stopped short when he saw Shawna and let out a long whistle. She felt like a prom queen at a mud wrestling match. On top of that, her feet were killing her. She sat in the nearest chair and slipped her feet out of the four-inch heels.

"Ma'am?" The mechanic seemed uncertain what to do about her. "Do you need some help?"

"I'm waiting for the governor's plane to come in." The man still seemed confused. She smiled. "I'm Mrs. Wilson."

"Ah. Of course." His eyes grew large. "Uh, I'm sorry about that, um, that, you know, the whistle thing. I wasn't expecting a lady all dressed up like you. I didn't mean anything by it."

The poor man was afraid of losing his job over a sexual harassment complaint. She shook her head. "Don't worry about it. I caught you by surprise."

"Yes, ma'am, you did. Thank you." He shuffled his feet. "Well, if there's anything you need …"

"No, thanks. I'm fine."

He nodded and continued on his path to the restrooms down the hall. Before he returned, Shawna heard an engine. She put her shoes back on and went to the door the man had entered from. Looking through the building to the open doors at the end of the hangar, she saw lights, then the nose of a small plane, which rolled to a stop right outside.

Shawna considered whether to walk through the hangar and greet Hunter with a big kiss as he came down the steps of the plane. She should have brought him flowers. That would have really surprised him. As she imagined the look on his face, the ends of her lips turned up.

No, she would wait here for him. Let him walk through the hangar, expecting Curtis or one of the other troopers to meet him. She let the door close and took a seat in one of the chairs that faced the door, resisting the desire to remove her shoes again.

Finally, someone pushed open the door and Trent came through. He nodded and smiled, then continued toward the exit. Hunter followed him, head bent. He raised his head slowly, as if it took all his energy, and halted in the doorway when he saw her.

"Shawna! What are you doing here?" He rushed to her, and her heart pounded. Delighted to see his excitement, she stood to greet him. But instead of hugging her, he squinted at her. His lazy eyelid drooped nearly shut, and she watched him force it open. "Has something happened to one of the boys?"

The door opened again and Johnnie trudged in, pulling a suitcase on wheels. "Hunter, I'll get with you tomorrow on that—" The door slammed behind her. "Oh. Shawna. Didn't know you were picking him up."

Shawna looked at her husband's campaign manager, who had just spent five days with him on the road. "I decided to come with Curtis and surprise him." She looked back at Hunter. "Nothing's wrong. The boys are fine. I wanted to see you, that's all."

Johnnie headed for the exit. "You kids have fun, but watch your curfew. Hunter, I'll call you tomorrow. Good night." She headed out into the dark parking lot.

When she was gone, Shawna turned to Hunter and put her arms out. "Aren't you glad to see me?"

He stepped forward and embraced her. "Of course, I am. It's good to be home."

She clung to him and whispered, "It's good to have you home. I'd like to show you how much I've missed you." She moved her face toward his and kissed his lips. He didn't turn away, but he didn't return the kiss, either.

"It's nice of you to come." He pulled away from her. "It's been a tough week and I'm bushed. Twenty-five events in five days ... must be some kind of record. Johnnie's trying to kill me. I want to go home and get some sleep." He headed for the door and held it open for her. "Let's go."

He hadn't even noticed the dress she had worn for him. Apparently, Mimi was wrong. He had married her to avoid a scandal, not because he loved her.

Marie Wells Coutu

Chapter 14

Nate hit his right thigh with his fist to stimulate circulation. He'd been sitting in this musty office for twenty minutes, waiting for the senator to return from lunch. If the senator had a good story for him, the wait would be worthwhile.

The high ceilings and old windows in the War Memorial Building kept the rooms from ever being a comfortable temperature. The door opened and Senator Phil McCracken sauntered across the oriental rug. Never in a hurry, even when he knew someone waited. "Nate. Good to see you."

Nate struggled to his feet as McCracken reached him, and they shook hands. The senator's fleshy hand reminded Nate of a lumpy pillow. "Senator. Thanks for giving me your time."

The older man shook his head and moved behind the

massive cherry desk. "Nonsense, son. I always make time for my favorite reporter." He brushed both hands down his ever-present red tie as if it had been out of place. Despite having added fifty pounds in the last four decades, the seventy-eight-year-old man remained fastidious in his tailored black suits and white shirts. He lowered himself into the oversized wood and leather desk chair.

Nate returned to his own plain chair and pulled out his cell phone. "I'm sure you say that to all the reporters, sir. But you asked to see me this time." He checked that the phone was ready to record and held it up. "Do you mind?"

McCracken brushed his hand through the air. "Go ahead. Got nothing secretive to talk about."

"What did you want to discuss?" Nate pushed the red dot to start the recording.

"Transportation. Specifically, airports for small communities."

Nate almost dropped his phone. He laid it on the desk between the two of them. "Airports? Not exactly my area of expertise."

The senator leaned back and rested his elbows on his bulging stomach, tenting his fingers together. "I realize that. But this is really a story of collusion."

"I see." Nate rubbed the bristles on his chin. "What kind of collusion?"

McCracken whirled his chair around to face the window. Gray skies hung over the city, promising another rainy day. "Businesses need convenient airports.

Communities need businesses. It's a simple equation." He turned to face Nate again. "But someone is putting out propaganda against them, claiming all sorts of fiction about how much they cost and how much money they lose. I want to know who's behind these opponents."

"And you called me because …?"

The other man slapped his desk. "Confound it, you're the bulldog. It's a good story, don't you see? Whether it's left-wing environmentalists or right-wing anti-government folks, whoever's putting up the money to oppose the airports has an agenda. And their agenda is not what they claim it is. Find out what they're up to."

Nate nodded and pulled a notepad from his pocket. He didn't want to be diverted from investigating the governor's marriage, but perhaps he and the senator could be useful to each other. "Okay, if you've got some names, I'll look into it. But I'd like your help on something else."

"Sure, sure." McCracken nodded. "I know how it works. What do you need?"

"By the way, I meant to ask about your family, sir." The senator's district had a reputation of being one of the most conservative in the entire state, and "family values" had been a cornerstone of his long tenure in the state senate.

He reached for a framed photo sitting on his desk and showed it to Nate. "They're all fine. Look how big my grandchildren are getting. Youngest one's already learning to drive." The picture showed the senator and his wife seated under a large oak tree, surrounded by three middle-aged couples and seven teens and young adults. "That was taken at our fiftieth anniversary celebration in May."

"My, just look at them." Nate leaned forward, impressed by the smiling faces and apparent closeness of the family. "Congratulations, sir. I didn't realize you had celebrated such a milestone."

McCracken turned the photo back toward himself and positioned it precisely as it had been. "No worries. We kept it under the radar. Only the family and a few close friends. But all the family came. Pretty good considering how spread out they are with jobs and college and all."

"I'm sure that was really special for you and Mrs. McCracken."

"Sure was." He chuckled. "She was in hog heaven. Now, how can I help you?"

Nate relaxed against the back of his chair and stretched his legs out in front of him. "I know you and the governor have been close since he got into politics. I believe you were his mentor, weren't you?"

The senator smiled. "I don't know about that, but I tried to share what I knew with him. He learned pretty well, I think."

"He's been a popular governor, for sure." Nate chose his next words carefully. "But what would the people in your district think about him having an affair with Mrs. Wilson? While her first husband was still alive, that is."

Senator McCracken's smile faded like a rain cloud covering the sun. "What are you saying, son?"

Nate toyed with his ballpoint pen. "I thought you'd have heard the rumors. Seems they may have been … intimate … during that governors' conference last summer. You know, the one where they met? That was before her first husband was killed in Afghanistan."

McCracken brushed the idea aside with a wave of his hand. "Everybody knows that's when they became friends. Nothing more than that."

"Maybe not. Respectfully, though, if you do the math, it's a strong possibility that Mrs. Wilson—or Mrs. Moore she was then—became pregnant at that time, not later. Which explains the short courtship after her husband was buried."

"Look, Hunter's my friend, and he's devoted to his family. If you expect me to help you sully his reputation, you are chasing the wrong dog's tail. Sounds like you've been listening to his competition." He leaned forward and clasped his hands on the desk. "Now, do you want the names of those groups opposing the airport in my district, or not?"

Nate had pushed as far as he could today. He decided not to mention his talk with Serena, the resort maid. "Sure. But if you learn anything specific about the governor and his wife, would you let me know? I wouldn't mind proving the rumors wrong."

Even if the rumors were being propagated by Deborah, they left a sour taste in Nate's mouth. If they were true … well, he wasn't sure he wanted to know the truth. And that didn't bode well for his career as a reporter.

Shawna shepherded Hunter Lynn and Cooper onto the concrete patio, facing a long, windowless wall of the pool house. "We'll start here while you learn to hit the ball."

After three rainy days, the sun had returned. The sweet smell of freshly mowed grass filled her nostrils. She dumped out two cans of balls, and the boys ran after them, laughing as the yellow balls bounced off the concrete and rolled down a small hill. When they had gathered them all, they ran back to her and dropped them at her feet.

She handed them each a racket—blue handle for Hunter Lynn, red for Cooper—then she held out her own racket. "Okay, boys, we're going to start by learning how to hold the racket. Grab it like you're shaking hands with it."

Hunter Lynn shook his racket up and down. "Nice to meet you, Mr. Racket."

Cooper imitated him. "Yeah, nice to meet you."

"Stop copying me."

Cooper edged away. "You can't make me."

"Boys, stop it." Shawna took Hunter Lynn's hand and positioned it on the racket correctly. "Now, you hold it like this, and you swing it like so." She moved his arm slowly to demonstrate the forehand stroke. "Practice that swing while I show Cooper."

As she stepped away, Hunter Lynn swung the racket as she had showed him, but nearly hit her. Shawna jumped out of the way barely in time.

"H. L., you have to watch what you're doing. Make sure nobody's around before you swing, okay?"

"O-kaay." His tone told her he didn't like her correcting him. Teaching him to play might be harder than she'd expected.

She showed the same movement to Cooper. After they had taken several practice swings, she picked up a tennis ball and bounced it. "Watch the ball." When it reached the top of its bounce, she hit it toward the blank wall. The ball caromed off the siding, and she had to run to hit it again. When it flew back at her, she reached up and caught it with her hand. "See how easy that is? I want you to practice hitting it against the wall, and see how long you can keep it going. H. L., you go first."

Hunter Lynn bounced a ball and hit it on the first try, but missed the return. It buzzed by him and landed on the patio and kept bouncing. "That's all right. Try again." She picked up two balls and handed him one.

This time, he managed to hit it twice before missing. He ran after the ball but it rolled off the concrete and stopped in the grass.

While Hunter Lynn retrieved the first two balls, Shawna stood in front of Cooper and handed him one. "Your turn, Coop. Let's see what you can do." Cooper dropped the ball and it dribbled off to the side of the pavement.

She handed him another. "Bounce it a little harder."

Cooper did so, then gave the racket a full swing from twelve to six o'clock, but he whacked only air. "Awww, shoot."

Shawna picked up the two remaining balls. Learning the timing hadn't been easy for her, either. "Don't worry, you'll get it. Keep your eye on the ball and time your swing."

This time, Cooper managed to connect with the ball, but he angled the racket so that the ball bounced off the patio instead of hitting the wall. Still, he jumped up and down. "I hit it, Shawna. I hit it!"

"Yes, you did! But keep your racket straight. Try it again." She handed him the last ball.

Just as he bounced the ball, Hunter Lynn came up the hill, clutching his racket and four balls. "I'm not gonna go after all your balls, Coop. You can chase your own next time."

The sudden comment startled Cooper mid-swing, and he missed again. "You made me miss on purpose!" He turned, aiming the racket at Hunter Lynn.

A metallic taste rose in Shawna's mouth. Cooper was the quiet, sensitive one, not the angry one. He wouldn't really hit his brother, would he? She stepped forward and grabbed Cooper's racket. "It's okay, Cooper. You'll have another chance. But we don't hit anything with the racket except tennis balls, and definitely not your brother."

Hunter Lynn put the balls on the ground and positioned them so they wouldn't roll away. "When do we get to play a game, Shawna? I can't wait to beat Cooper."

"You have to learn to volley first. When you can hit the ball consistently, then we'll start playing some fun games." She instructed both boys to work on hitting the balls against the wall, while she retrieved the stray balls. After about twenty minutes, Hunter Lynn could keep the volley going four or five times, and Cooper could hit it two or three times.

Shawna heard Hunter's SUV approach and pull into the parking area. "Okay, boys, you're both doing great. Let's call that a day. Tomorrow we'll get on the court and try something a little more fun."

The boys dropped their rackets and ran to meet their dad.

"Boys, you can't leave your rackets here. And we need to pick up the balls." Shawna shook her head and walked over to where she had left the cans for the balls. After gathering all six balls and putting lids on the cans, she picked up the boys' rackets, the handles wet from their sweaty hands. She felt more exhausted than if she had played three tie-break sets.

The next afternoon, Shawna took the boys to the tennis court next to the pool. She positioned them, one on the right and one on the left side of the court while she lobbed balls to them from the other side of the net. Both boys chased

' more balls than they hit.

Finally, Hunter Lynn plopped down on the hard surface. "You said this would be fun, Shawna."

Cooper agreed, dropping onto the court beside him. "Yeah. When do we get to play a game?"

She had worked with younger players before, coaching and mentoring them. But, she realized, she'd never taught complete beginners. All she had to go on was her own experience learning the game. Boredom had brought her to it, and it had taken several buckets full of persistence before her talent had shown up.

"Boys, I understand your frustration. But you can't really play a game until you can return the ball over the net. There's no magic formula. Watch the ball and figure out where it's going to go. That's where you aim. Come on, let's try again."

This time she hit a soft shot, landing the ball right in front of Hunter Lynn, who hit it back to her. It landed short of the net, but they celebrated. "That's it, H. L.! But hit it a little harder next time. Your turn, now, Coop."

She used the same shot, but Cooper tried to hit it in the air, using a two-handed underhand stroke. He caught the ball with his racket, but it went high overhead before landing two feet behind him.

Hunter Lynn laughed. "The net's in the other direction, dork."

"No name calling, H. L. Cooper, hold the racket the way I showed you yesterday."

"My arm's tired. Can I rest?"

Maybe it would be better if she worked with one boy while the other took a break. "Okay, you watch while H. L. and I practice."

But at the end of an hour, all three of them were ready to quit. They collapsed on the lawn beside the court. Blades of grass tickled Shawna's legs, but she was too tired to move. She couldn't see continuing this day after day.

"Watching an imaginary game, are we?" Hunter called from across the yard. Shawna hadn't even noticed when his car pulled in. He strode over to where they sat. The boys jumped up and he embraced them both at once. Then he held out a hand to Shawna and pulled her up. "How's it going?"

She moved to kiss him, but he turned his head for a cheek-kiss instead. She pretended not to notice. "They'll get it, I think. But I could use your help."

"My help? I don't play tennis, remember?"

"You can hit the ball over the net, can't you? I need someone to hit the balls to us so I can stand next to the boys and help with their strokes."

Hunter squinted. Both boys latched onto his legs.

"Yeah, Dad, will you?" Hunter Lynn said.

Cooper looked up at him. "Please, Dad?"

Hunter squatted so he was at eye level with them. "Listen, boys, I would like to do this, and as soon as the election's over, I will. I promise. But right now, with this campaign, I don't see how I'll have time. You boys understand, don't you?"

"Yeah, I understand." Hunter Lynn, his face appearing to be set in stone, picked up his racket and headed for the house. Shawna looked after him and wondered what it would take to soften his attitude. But Hunter's frequent absences didn't help.

Cooper pursed his lips, but nodded. "Sure, Dad. You gotta keep your job, right?"

Hunter ruffled the boy's hair. "That's right, son. I'd sure like to keep being governor." He looked at Shawna. "Maybe you could find somebody else to give them lessons. Isn't there a club or something?"

She shrugged. "I know there's one at Centennial. I'll call tomorrow."

He pecked her on the cheek. "That's the spirit. It'll be easier on you, won't it?"

Teaching the boys certainly had been harder than she expected, but passing the responsibility off to someone else wouldn't help her get any closer to Hunter Lynn.

Hunter checked his watch. "I have a meeting tonight, and I'll have to leave in an hour. Do you suppose dinner's ready?"

Once again, he had managed to avoid spending time with her. Only in this case, he would also miss out on helping his sons. Guess she needed to find a substitute for their dad.

Chapter 15

"We should talk about our game strategy, Governor."

Hunter couldn't resist replying to Johnnie's athletic lingo with more of the same.

"All right, Johnnie, who's going to control the ball?"

Hunter and his staff had gathered for their daily briefing in the sitting area of his spacious state capitol office. Their agenda today focused on the education funding bill, and the meeting in an hour with the chairman of the Senate Education Committee.

From her chair across from him, Johnnie threw him her famous "look." Her dark black hair and smooth skin made her appear closer to thirty than her actual age of forty-four.

"You have to manage the court, sir." She took advantage of her youthful looks, and her almost six-foot height, by wearing short skirts and cropped jackets. Most women her age would look slutty or desperate in those clothes, but the wardrobe worked for Johnnie—perhaps because she kept her focus on her job, not on the men around her. Leaning forward with characteristic intensity, she pumped her fist. "Funding technology for schools could clinch the election for you, based on our polls. But Senator McCracken is not onboard yet. We need to win him over."

Hunter put his fingertips together, making an A-shape, and looked around at his aides. "What will he want?"

"Roads in his district are in bad shape, and one county has proposed a new airport." Brandon Wells, a twenty-something kid two years out of Vandy, pushed his glasses up on his nose. He had made infrastructure his area of expertise.

"Do they need the airport? Will the benefits outweigh the costs?"

Brandon flipped through his notes. "Need is relative, of course. The community wants it to attract industry. Most of the landowners are opposed, but the county officials insist it would be a moneymaker."

Hunter reached for his coffee cup and inhaled the smooth aroma. "Sounds like we need to steer clear of that one. Let the locals sort it out first. Anything else on McCracken's agenda?"

Teresa Lacey cleared her throat. Hunter's liaison to the Education Department reminded him of his fifth-grade teacher. Big-boned and sagging in all the wrong places, she had a mind sharper than almost everyone Hunter knew. "Unions are strong in his district. And we don't have support on Teaching Through Tech from the teachers' union yet."

"What's the hold-up? This technology could make their jobs easier."

"For the younger ones, yes, those who grew up with computers. But there are enough old fogeys like me—" She laughed, and so did everyone in the room. Teresa, a technology whiz, was the first to embrace any gadget that came along. "A lot of older teachers have trouble catching up, so there's concern they'll be forced out of their jobs if they have to teach with computers."

Hunter nodded. "Okay. Let's look for ways to win over the union. Phasing in the program, special training for experienced teachers, maybe?"

"We could suggest that you and McCracken visit a school that's a model for using technology," Johnnie said. "There's a district about an hour away that has really embraced technology with amazing results."

"Great idea, Johnnie." Brandon's sarcasm lowered the room's temperature by ten degrees. "Schools are out for the summer."

Johnnie cast a heated look at him. "I know that. But there might be summer school programs. If not, we schedule the trip for early September. That's still enough time before the Education Committee meets in late October, right before the election."

Hunter couldn't let the meeting deteriorate into bickering. "Okay, then. Johnnie, figure out the best time for that trip. I'll mention it to the senator, with a date to be determined. He'll be here …" He consulted his watch. "… in fifteen minutes, so let's adjourn for today."

As the staff gathered up their materials, Hunter's receptionist came in and handed him a folded piece of yellow paper. Hunter opened it and read. "Julie Fisher died this morning, at 9:30, Vanderbilt Hospital."

He dropped his chin to his chest. Though he'd spent only a short time with her, the loss scraped loose the scab on his own heart. After a moment, he looked up. "Thank you. Please find out about the service, and see if I can work it into my schedule. And send a nice flower arrangement."

When Hunter met with McCracken, the senator expressed concern about the teachers' union, as Teresa predicted. "You know I can't support this bill without the union on board, Hunter."

The two had remained friends even after Hunter no longer needed the senior man's guidance in navigating the legislative byways. McCracken's thin hair had now turned white, reinforcing his reputation as a statesman, in spite of his expanded waistline.

"Of course, you can't, Mac. But surely, we can win them over. How about if you and I go visit Shelbyville, this district that's using technology in all the schools? Invite the union leadership. Should be a good opportunity to show them the benefits and persuade them there's nothing to fear from implementing a program like this."

Something about McCracken's manner changed. "I don't know how to say this, Hunter, but I'm not sure I want to be seen as aligning with you."

Hunter rubbed his fingers across the smudges on his desk. The glass top squeaked in protest. "What do you mean, Mac?"

McCracken shifted uncomfortably in his chair. He coughed, then cleared his throat. "I've heard ... rumors, Hunter. Rumors that concern me, if they're true."

Hunter frowned and leaned forward. "What sort of rumors?"

He pressed his lips together. "About you and Shawna. And the baby."

The pulse in Hunter's neck throbbed. "You're listening to rumors about—about our private lives? No one—I repeat, no one—has a right to talk about our baby. Hannah Lea was a precious gift, and we are still reeling from her loss."

"I understand that." Mac's voice rolled like thunder. "But someone's trying to turn it into a scandal. Like, maybe, the two of you had a ... a liaison ... before Shawna's husband died."

Hunter couldn't bear any more of this discussion. He stood. "Mac, you and I go way back. If you're going to start listening to rumors now ..."

The senator, equal to Hunter in height, stood and placed a hand on Hunter's shoulder. "I know, Hunter. But my district is super conservative. I don't want to get caught up in something—"

"There's nothing for you to be caught up in." At least, Hunter hoped, nothing that could be proven. "This education tech bill is a win-win. The children of this state need an advantage like this. Why wouldn't you support that?"

"I'd like to, Hunter. But I won't go down with the ship. You understand."

Chapter 16

When the boys' tennis lessons ended Tuesday afternoon, Shawna met them courtside at Centennial Tennis Center. "Are you up for a little more practice time?"

Hunter Lynn shrugged. "Sure. I want to enter that tournament in October."

He had a natural ability and had grasped the technique quickly. If he kept it up and built up his stamina, he would be ready for serious competition soon.

"I'm tired, Shawna." Being younger, Cooper grew bored more quickly than H. L. "Can I go over to the monkey bars instead?"

She frowned. The busy park could make it hard to keep track of him, but she knew Cooper loved to climb. Though she and H. L. could play tennis at home, the governor's residence had no monkey bars. However, the youth-sized courts here were better for H. L.

Shawna looked at Trent, who stood within earshot. He turned toward the playground, then nodded. "I'll be able to watch him and you both from here, ma'am."

She gave Cooper permission to go, then she and H. L. went to find an empty court. As they took their places, Shawna reminded H. L. what his teacher had told him. "Keep your grip firm and extend your arm."

Between serves, she tried to encourage him. "Way to go, H. L. Put more power behind your swing." Or "Keep your eye on the ball. You're doing great!"

After losing two games to her, Hunter Lynn was tiring. But he needed to work on endurance. "Good game, H. L." Shawna met him at the net. "Another set. You can do more."

He glared at her, but took the ball and moved to his starting position. He started this game strong, but quickly slowed down. His technique slipped as he grew more tired, and he swung wildly, missing easy shots.

"Watch your grip," Shawna called to him as she prepared to serve. "Keep your feet loose. Don't take your eye off the ball."

He barely swung, and let the ball roll to the fence, giving Shawna game point. He bent over, hands on his knees.

"Come on, H. L. Go get the ball. You serve this time."

He stood up and wiped his arm across his forehead. He shook his head. "Nope, I'm done."

She headed for the middle of the court. "Don't quit

now. If you want to play competitively, you need endurance, too."

Hunter Lynn walked over to pick up the tennis ball, then threw the ball at her. Shawna grabbed it in mid-air. He glared at her. "Maybe I don't wanna play in a stupid tournament. You don't make it fun. You yell at me too much."

He turned and stomped away from her, swatting at invisible balls with his racket.

Shawna would do best to hold her tongue. If she spoke to Hunter Lynn about his outburst, she'd surely say something she would later regret.

He headed for the crowded playground, where he joined Cooper on the monkey bars. Other kids went down the slide or pumped their legs to go higher on the swings. Hanging by one arm, H. L. spoke to his brother, then dropped to the ground and ran toward the waiting car.

Shawna walked to the edge of the tennis courts and watched Cooper coming her way.

"Hey, Shawna. What's with H. L.? He snapped my head off."

Poor Cooper. She put her hand on his shoulder and steered him to the car. "Don't worry about it, sweetheart. He's just in a bad mood. Did you have fun?"

"Yeah, but I wish we could've stayed longer." He ran to the SUV that Trent had moved close to the entrance. Having a chauffeur had its advantages, even if the real purpose was security, not convenience.

Cooper chattered during most of the short drive home, but Hunter Lynn sat on the far end of the seat, sulking. Shawna responded to Cooper with an occasional "Uh-huh" and "Okay." She wanted to smile for him, but she couldn't muster one up.

At home, Hunter Lynn jumped out as soon as Trent stopped the car. By the time Cooper and Shawna got upstairs, he had locked himself in the bedroom. Cooper banged on the door. "Come on, H. L. It's my room, too. Let me in."

Shawna reached the top of the stairs in time to hear Hunter Lynn's muffled reply. Cooper responded, "I'm telling Mimi." He ran down the hall toward the living room. "Mimi, H. L.'s bein' mean."

When Shawna entered the living room, Cooper was already sitting in Mimi's lap. Mimi wrapped her arm around him. "What happened?"

"I dunno, but H. L. got really mad. Now he won't let me in the bedroom."

Mimi looked at Shawna, who sat down in the other armchair. "He and I were playing tennis. I was encouraging him and giving him advice. He was doing great, just getting a little tired. The next thing I knew, he threw the tennis ball at me and yelled that he didn't want to play." Her shoulders dropped, the energy drained out of her. "About the time I think we're getting along fine, he does something like this. I don't know what to do with him."

Mimi motioned to Cooper that she wanted to get up. "I'll be right back. Come on, Cooper."

She went down the hall with Cooper behind her. "Hunter Lynn, open your door right this minute." Moments later, Shawna heard the turn of the doorknob. "Now, H. L., you cannot lock your brother out of the room. I don't care what happened, you be nice to Cooper."

The sound of the door closing reached Shawna about the same time that Mimi returned. She put her hands on her hips. "You see, Shawna dear, you have to be firm with him. This is what happens when you let them have their way all the time. H. L. has got to learn to respect you. You're too soft on both boys. You shouldn't let him get away with talking back to you." She turned abruptly and headed for the stairs without another word.

Shawna leaned back in the chair and closed her eyes. So much for being accepted by the boys or Mimi. What kind of mood would Hunter be in when he came home tonight?

She heard Mimi's steps coming back up the stairs, followed by a knock. "H. L., Cooper, I made cookies while you were gone. Would you like some?"

Mimi didn't chide Hunter Lynn for his behavior at all. Apparently, this was a case of "Do as I say, not as I do." Shawna rose and headed down the hall. Her mouth watered from the chocolaty aroma as she passed Mimi, who handed a plate of freshly baked chocolate chip cookies to Cooper through the open bedroom doorway.

Shawna went into her office, closed the door, and sank into the desk chair. On top of the desk, a scrapbook lay open to the last completed page—photos of Hannah Lea. She couldn't think of one thing in her life that she had done right, at least since she gave in to desire with Hunter.

A tiny knock sounded on the door, so soft she might have imagined it. When it was repeated, she said, "Come in."

The door opened and Cooper appeared, holding a small plate of cookies. "I thought these might make you feel better."

As Hunter climbed the stairs, the only sound came from the mantel clock in the dining room chiming the hour. Only ten o'clock.

Even when Shawna didn't wait up for him—which was more often recently—Mimi usually watched television while she knitted awhile before she went upstairs to bed.

The living room lamps were still on, but no sign of either of the women.

Expecting to find Shawna sound asleep, he opened the bedroom door stealthily so as not to disturb her. But when his eyes adjusted to the dim light, he saw the bed empty—untouched. Where could she be?

He turned and retraced his steps, but this time as he walked down the hall, he noticed light coming from under the office door. He turned the knob and looked in. "Shawna?"

Her head lay on her arm, stretched across a type of notebook on top of the desk. A scrapbook, it looked like.

"Shawna? Are you all right?" His pulse raced. She had come out of her depression, hadn't she? Three long strides and he reached her, praying she hadn't done something stupid. He touched her shoulder. "Shawna?"

She jerked straight up, blinked her eyes, and shook her head. "What time is it?"

"Ten o'clock. You fell asleep in here?"

Shawna rubbed her eyes. "I must have." She rubbed her arm, where red pressure marks indented the skin. Then she closed the scrapbook and pushed it aside. "I was working on Hannah's book."

"I wondered. Mimi must have gone to bed early." His heart had calmed down, but he sensed something had happened today.

"Maybe so." She pushed away from the desk and stood up. "I didn't realize how tired I was. I guess tennis wore me out today."

He waited, ready to hug or kiss her if she wanted, but she turned to the other end of the desk.

"Shawna, did you and Mimi have an argument?"

Halting at the door, she gave him a quizzical look. "Me and Mimi argue? Why would you think that? We get along fine, don't you know?" She sneered. "No. Today it was Hunter Lynn. He doesn't respect me, and I don't know what to do about it." She left the room without further explanation.

Hunter collapsed into the chair and rested his elbows on the desk. Tomorrow, he would ask Mimi what had happened. Then he needed to speak with Hunter Lynn. The boy had to learn to respect Shawna.

He pulled the scrapbook closer and flipped it open to the middle. He studied a photo of Hannah Lea with H. L. and Cooper bent over the incubator, their faces pressed to the glass. They had tried to get the baby to smile at them, but she had only cried. The boys hadn't understood what was wrong with her.

There were many things Hunter didn't understand now. He had lost his ability to be a good husband. Shawna had practically shut him out of her life. It had been his fault, though. Avoiding her, working or campaigning all the time. Now it sounded as though his boys were causing trouble. Probably rebelling because he had not been around.

He closed the book and put his face in his hands. His campaign slogan, "He's a Winner," ought to be changed to "Hunter Wilson. He's a Failure." Because that's the way he felt most of the time.

Chapter 17

Nate figured he'd better start practicing if he was going to play in the charity tournament, as he had promised Shawna. He'd soon find out whether his leg would hold up to the stress.

He finally found his old tennis racket in a large box in his hall closet, where it had been since he moved into this apartment three years ago. The box hadn't even been opened since he separated from MaryAnn. It made no sense to keep all this stuff. Besides the tennis equipment, the box contained framed photographs, souvenir salt and pepper shakers from their honeymoon at Niagara Falls, a blanket they'd received as a wedding present, and who knew what else. He really should give the stuff away.

But that would wait for another day. He intended to find out if he could still play tennis. He checked the old terry cloth wristband and decided it would work well enough to catch the perspiration. He needed to stop somewhere for new tennis balls. He hoped he could find someplace to practice without a lot of people around, a challenge on a blue-sky, August day.

An hour later, Nate found a spot at Centennial Park where he could hit balls off the backboard. The courts were busy, and he realized he looked out of place in his long pants. Too bad. With his scarred leg, he wasn't about to put on shorts. That would scare people off, for sure.

At first, his muscles didn't want to cooperate, and his judgment was off, so he spent a lot of time retrieving balls. That reminded him of his first attempts at playing tennis in middle school. But after he got the kinks out of his leg, he was able to focus on hitting the ball, and his skill, such as it was, seemed to return. He could do this after all. He relished the exercise, but realized he would need to get serious about training if he expected to play an entire match by the end of October.

After succeeding at a long volley, he bent over to catch his breath. When he stood up, he saw a woman with a racket over her shoulder crossing the court. Shawna Wilson.

"You looking for someone who can hit the balls back to you, or do you prefer an opponent that doesn't talk back?" She walked closer to him and swung the racket in a wide arc. "Hey, Nate. Looks like we had the same idea."

"I hate to admit it, but I probably have a lot more work to do than you. You don't want to play against me yet."

She held a tennis ball in her hand. "Mind if I join you hitting against the board, at least?"

Nate gestured for her to go ahead. Preparing to swing, she held the ball at arm's length. "Hunter's boys are taking lessons, so I thought I'd use the time to work on my own game."

"Why aren't you teaching them yourself?" Nate prepared to hit his own ball.

Shawna dropped her ball and hit it against the board. "Tried that." She stepped to her left and used a backstroke to catch the rebound. "Didn't work."

They practiced side by side for several minutes, until Nate realized he'd had enough for the first day. He swung and missed the ball, then walked over to where it landed. "Tell you what, Shawna. Give me a couple weeks, and I'll let you beat me."

She grabbed her ball in the air and turned to him. "You're on. See you two weeks from today, same time? Weather permitting, of course."

An amusement park wasn't what Shawna had in mind when she offered to take the boys swimming. Before school started, she wanted to give them a special day away from the gated governor's compound. But to them, swimming didn't mean a typical pool.

"We can swim in our own pool anytime," Hunter Lynn had whined. "This is different."

The two ganged up on her, begging to go to the waterpark on the shores of Percy Priest Lake. When she finally gave in, their whoops of excitement convinced her she had made the right decision. She invited Ellie and her children to meet them here.

Now she and Ellie were stretched out on lounge chairs at the edge of the Lazy River, soaking up rays before summer came to an end. Ellie's oldest daughter had a summer job, but her two sons had come. They weren't much older than H. L.

After a dozen trips on the family raft slide and a few races down the Twin Cyclones, Shawna and Ellie had retreated to the lounging area. All four kids were tall enough to enjoy the water activities without an adult, and from here, she could keep an eye on Hunter Lynn as he floated on a tube, as well as on Cooper splashing in the wave pool.

All in all, it had been a good day. The step-cousins got along well and had taken turns splashing each other and their moms. Hunter Lynn hadn't even complained when Shawna and Cooper cooperated to make him fall off the raft.

She licked her lips, grimacing as her tongue picked up a bit of sunscreen from her upper lip. She released a deep sigh.

"What is it, sis?"

Shoot. She hadn't meant for Ellie to notice. "Nothing. Just wishing Hunter could have come. He'd have enjoyed playing with the boys."

"Campaign rallies take him out of town again?" Ellie turned her head and peered over her sunglasses. "If I were you, I'd start to ask myself if this campaign is a way to avoid staying home."

Had Ellie read her thoughts? "I'm sure that's not the case. But it has become a more challenging election than he expected."

Not exactly the truth. Hunter rarely talked to her lately, and he claimed she didn't need to join him for any of the recent campaign stops. "As long as the boys are out of school, why don't you simply enjoy spending time with them?" he'd said.

She lifted her head to check on H. L. again. There he was, floating next to a boy about his age. She leaned her head back, closing her eyes against the bright sun.

Drops of water splashed on her and she opened her eyes. "Look, Shawna, my tooth came out!" Cooper jumped up and down next to her lounge chair. He held out his hand, a tiny tooth grasped between two fingers.

Nearby, a couple of other women applauded. "Good for you," Ellie said.

Shawna handed him a towel, which he held to his mouth. "It finally came out on its own?" The tooth had been loose for days, but Cooper hadn't wanted help in pulling it.

He pulled the towel away and showed her the bloodstain. "Yeah. I was getting out of the pool and tasted blood, then I noticed the tooth loose in my mouth. I'm glad I didn't swallow it." The resulting gap in his mouth gave him the appearance of a grinning jack-o'-lantern.

Shawna held out her hand. "Want me to hold it for you, buddy?"

He dropped it into her palm. "I want to leave a note for the tooth fairy. Do you think she'll let me keep the tooth and still leave me money?"

Ellie leaned over. "Cooper, that tooth is worth at least five dollars. If the tooth fairy at your house doesn't give you that much and leaves the tooth, you come to my house. We have a generous tooth fairy."

"Thanks, Aunt Ellie!" He dabbed at his gum with the towel and frowned. "It's still bleeding."

"It'll stop in a few minutes." Shawna pointed to a vacant chair next to her. "Sit here and keep pressure on it with the towel."

Cooper did as she said, but after only a minute or two, he checked the towel again. "I'm going back in the wave pool." He dropped the towel on the chair and ran off.

"That was fun, but I think your driver was concerned." Ellie pointed to where Trent stood watching them. "At least he wore athletic clothes today, instead of a suit."

"I guess," Shawna said. He still looked out of place, fully clothed with dark glasses and standing by the fence alone. "With so many celebrities around, I suppose people are used to seeing security guards in all sorts of places."

Ellie leaned her head back against the chair. "It's hard to imagine you or the boys being a target of violence."

"I know." Shawna closed her eyes. "Better safe than sorry, they say. But it's not like I have a choice. A trooper's always with us."

A rumble of boys yelling came from the farthest area of the Lazy River. Shawna scanned the crowds, looking for the disturbance. There. Several kids had crowded at the edge and were yelling at someone in the water. The lifeguard, a teenager herself, blew a whistle and climbed down from her stand, heading toward the group.

Shawna couldn't see Hunter Lynn, and the crowd blocked her view of what was happening in the water. She stood up and took off her sunglasses. She put her hand above her eyes as she moved in the direction of the disturbance. She sensed Trent moving away from the fence as well.

Before she and Ellie reached the group, the lifeguard had arrived on the scene. From what Shawna could tell, two boys had been fighting in the water, and they had to be separated. The lifeguard then gestured that the boys had to leave the water. Shawna realized one of them was Hunter Lynn. Her mouth went dry.

"He started it." Hunter Lynn pointed to one of the other boys, a pudgy boy as tall as the lifeguard. "He kicked my tube. On purpose."

"Did not." The bigger boy protested. "You started it."

The lifeguard held up both hands. "I don't care. No fighting allowed. Both of you, out. Any more trouble and you'll have to leave the park."

Shawna stomped over to Hunter Lynn and grabbed his arm as he climbed onto the concrete deck. "Hunter Lynn Wilson, what were you thinking, getting into a fight?"

The other boy, who had crawled out of the water, snorted. "Hunter Wilson? Ain't that the governor's name?"

"Dork," Hunter Lynn said.

Shawna tightened her grip. "You know better than that. What will your father say?"

Hunter Lynn mumbled under his breath.

Before she could respond, Ellie stepped up beside her. "Sis, you don't want to make a scene here." Shawna's face warmed. First H. L.'s insolence, now her sister lecturing her.

But the crowd around them had grown larger instead of dispersing as it should have. Another boy pushed into Shawna, his wet swimsuit leaving cold water on her bare legs.

Trent held out his arms, moving the watchers back. "This would be a good time to get out of here." He guided them toward the concrete building that held the changing rooms.

At the wall of built-in lockers, Shawna inserted her key and stepped back so Hunter Lynn could retrieve his things. He didn't look at her or speak, just pulled out a rolled-up bundle of clothes, then stomped into the men's room.

"I'll get Cooper for you. It's time we got going, too." Ellie stopped at the chairs and collected the towels they had abandoned, then headed for the wave pool.

Shawna removed Cooper's clothes from the empty locker, then closed the door, leaving the key in place.

When Ellie returned with Cooper and her sons, Shawna asked if they had seen how the fight started.

The oldest one shook his head. "Sorry, Aunt Shawna. We were both over at the waterslide. H. L. didn't want to come with us."

She nodded. "Thanks anyway, boys." She would have to take Hunter Lynn's word for what happened.

After she and Ellie dried off and changed clothes, they found the four boys outside the front entrance gate. Trent had moved the SUV closer. H. L. and Cooper had already buckled in, and were showing their cousins the extras built into the special vehicle.

Shawna didn't want to end the day on a sour note. "How about we all go for ice cream?"

"Yeah!" Cooper bounced on the seat, straining at his seat belt to lean out the door. "Can I have a peanut butter and fudge sundae?"

Standing next to the car, Ellie wrinkled her forehead, reminding Shawna of their mother. "You're going to reward Hunter Lynn after he got into a fight?"

Shawna gritted her teeth, hating that her sister pointed out her mistake. "Why should I punish Cooper when his brother was the one who got into trouble?"

"I get that, but taking them for ice cream doesn't send the right message."

"Well, I promised. Are you coming or not?" Shawna motioned to the open door of the SUV.

Ellie shook her head. "I don't think so. Traffic's already going to be bad enough." She motioned her sons out of the vehicle. "Come on, boys. We have to go."

"Thanks for coming." Shawna threw an arm around her neck. "I'm sorry H. L. ruined the day."

"Nonsense. We had a great day. But you have a chance now to teach Hunter Lynn how to control his temper." Ellie pulled back and looked at her. "Don't blow this."

Between Ellie and Mimi, Shawna couldn't avoid the realization that she had a lot to learn about being a parent.

Chapter 18

"Really, Hunter? I thought this weekend was about taking time off from the campaign."

A long weekend away to celebrate their first anniversary had been Shawna's idea, but Hunter had managed to work in a campaign stop. His wife didn't understand how much he wanted to win another term as governor.

"It is, honey. We'll visit these schools first, then we'll go on to the park. Johnnie set this up weeks ago. Senator McCracken will be here, too."

The Friday morning visit to the high-tech school district was more or less on the way to the state park where he had made reservations. With Shawna's growing popularity, having her along to talk with the students could boost support for his Teaching Through Tech initiative.

She raised her eyebrows. "Didn't you say you and Mac

had a disagreement?"

"A minor one." As long as Mac didn't bring up the rumors again. "Remember, he's chair of the Education Committee. They'll be meeting in October to review the proposal, so I need his support."

She shook her head. "I don't see how that will help you in the election. It won't be taken up by the General Assembly until next year, will it?"

Hunter stretched one arm out across the back of the car seat, draping his hand on her shoulder. "If we have support from the teachers' union and the committee recommends it, it's as good as done."

She sighed. "Obviously, I don't have anything to say about this stop. What do you want me to do?"

"We'll be touring some classrooms and talking to students. You're good at talking with kids. That could make good video footage, Johnnie says."

"Of course. I should have known she'd be coming."

He heard the rancor in Shawna's voice every time she mentioned his campaign manager, and Johnnie hadn't even wanted Shawna to come today. What was it between those two? Johnnie seemed to believe Shawna was a detriment to his campaign. Best to keep the two apart as much as he could. Not that he could do that today.

Staring out the window as they passed white fences and green pastures of horse farms, he shrugged away the problem.

In the next half hour, the tidy, expansive pastures

changed to rough fields and barbed wire fences surrounding tiny farmsteads and houses in need of paint. Johnnie had said half the students in this district were financially disadvantaged, and the farms gave witness to that fact.

"It's the perfect example of how technology can give underprivileged students a chance," Johnnie had insisted. "It's remarkable what this district has done with very little funding. Think what they could do if the state helped."

The vehicle stopped in front of a small two-story building dating from the 1940s. Johnnie waited for them, along with three reporters she had invited.

"I see your friend Nate is here." Hunter offered Shawna a hand as she exited the SUV. "Doesn't seem like his usual kind of story."

"No, it's not." She seemed a little too pleased to see the man. "But he did say he sometimes covers for other reporters. Maybe that's the case today." She moved past Hunter and went to greet him. Knowing Matthews as a hard-nosed reporter who was always sniffing out scandals, Hunter hoped he had no reason to be looking for one today.

Johnnie stepped up beside Hunter, accompanied by a middle-aged woman with dark skin and reddish-brown hair. "Governor, everyone's here now. I'd like to introduce you to Principal Murphy."

"Welcome to Kennedy Elementary School." She shook hands with Hunter and Senator McCracken, then with Shawna as she rejoined the group.

The principal gestured toward the entry. "I thought we'd start in the computer lab, where we have two home-bound students on Skype waiting to meet you."

The old building had evidently been given a recent facelift—perhaps in preparation for his visit. The walls bore fresh coats of paint in bright, primary colors, and the worn linoleum floors shone. In the computer lab, they found two dozen desktop monitors of various ages hooked to mostly newer computers. Students about Hunter Lynn's age and older filled most of the chairs, and a young male teacher wandered among them, apparently checking their work.

After introductions, the teacher motioned to two monitors in the front row. Each one had a camera mounted on top and a student on the screen. "Please, sit here and meet our remote students."

Hunter indicated Shawna should take one of the two chairs. "I'll lean over your shoulder." Shawna's involvement would play well with the reporters who gathered in the background. He motioned to the other chair for Mac, who seemed unusually quiet today. Hunter needed him to engage with the students, to grasp the difference technology could make.

A huge boy filled the screen on McCracken's computer. The student on Shawna's monitor, a pale, thin girl, appeared to be sitting up in a hospital bed. The girl gave a small finger wave. "Hey."

"This is Ashley," the teacher said. "Ashley, this is First

Lady Wilson."

"I know." The girl smiled shyly. "I heard about the baby you lost. It made me really sad."

Shawna blinked. "That made me sad, too, Ashley."

If only Hunter could protect her from these reminders of their loss. But there was nothing he could do. His wife had to learn to cope.

"I can't go to school like most kids." Ashley moved her camera to show the bed and her room, decorated in pink and green ponies. "I have crest scleroderma. It's a rare disease. I get these buildups of calcium, and I can't sit or move around. I've had surgery like every other month."

When Shawna spoke into the microphone, her voice sounded husky. "You seem really brave, Ashley."

Ashley turned the camera toward the corner of the room. "When the pain isn't too bad, I use this electric wheelchair, and I can go to school." She returned the camera to her face. "But when the pain is real bad, like today, at least I can see and hear what's going on."

"It can't be easy to deal with so much pain."

Ashley shrugged. "I've had it all my life, so I guess I don't know any different."

Hunter leaned over and put his head next to Shawna's so they were both in the picture. "Ashley, I'm Governor Wilson. How does having a computer help you?"

"Hey, Governor. I'd be lost without my computer. Sometimes when I have to go to the hospital, I get behind on my lessons. Then when I feel better, I use online classes to get caught up. But whenever I can, I'd rather be learning along with the other students like now."

"Ashley, is there anything you need that we can help with?"

She grinned. "I'd really like a pony, but Mommy said I should quit asking for one. We couldn't feed it if I had one."

Hunter laughed. "Then I guess we'd better not send you a live pony. But I'll see if we can't find something you'd like."

Hunter turned his attention to the boy on McCracken's monitor, whose name was Albert. Because of his size, Hunter could imagine the teasing he got.

"Albert had trouble relating to his peers and teachers in the classroom," the teacher said. "He has embraced online learning and now is back on track. He's been extremely successful and even helps other students with math and science."

After a brief conversation with Albert, Senator McCracken said he was convinced.

"I'm impressed with how you're using this technology," Mac told the teacher and principal. "I can see the need for state funding to enable every school district to implement a program like this."

He turned to Hunter. "I'm ready to support your proposal, and I'll do everything I can to gain the union's support." He speared Hunter with a sharp look. "But don't let me down."

Hunter felt a surge of excitement through his veins, even as he absorbed Mac's warning. If the truth came out, he would no longer be able to count on Mac's support—for this or any other of his legislative proposals.

Outside the school, Mac slipped away when Hunter stopped to talk with the reporters. Matthews asked the first question. "Governor, Senator McCracken previously suggested that implementing technology should be left to individual school districts. He seems to have changed his mind, but what will your proposal cost the state?"

Before Hunter could answer, the older classes poured out of the school onto the playground. Seeing the television cameras, several of the kids ran to the fence to watch. Hunter tried to ignore them. "Each school district will be able to implement the technology as they see fit for their students, but many districts cannot afford adequate equipment without help from the state. For the first year, we are asking for one hundred dollars for each of the one million students in our state."

An argument was brewing at the fence. One of the boys' voices grew loud and angry. "You don't know that."

Another reporter thrust a microphone in front of Hunter's face. "You're asking for one hundred million dollars? Where will that money come from?"

Hunter tried to focus on the question, not on the arguing boys. "I believe the cost not to pass Teaching Through Tech will be ten times as much."

"Do too!" another boy yelled. "Heard my daddy say

that's why they got married."

"Nah. Gov'ners don't do that. Besides, she looks like a nice lady."

"Hey, don't push me. My daddy knows about that stuff."

Hunter's ears burned. Clearly, those boys were talking about him and Shawna, but they were too young to be discussing sex, much less the sex life of the governor. Hopeful that the reporters would ignore the exchange, he ended the interview. He grabbed Shawna's arm and headed for the vehicle.

During the two-hour trip to Fall Creek Falls, Hunter tried to forget about the argument between the two kids. Instead, he talked about what the school district had already accomplished and the benefits of his Teaching Through Tech program. Shawna nestled up to him, and he put his arm around her and kept talking. He didn't notice when she fell asleep.

Chapter 19

As Shawna snuggled close to Hunter in the back seat of the SUV, her mind drifted to tonight. She'd been looking forward to a romantic evening, just the two of them. She wanted to talk about having another baby—and to start trying.

Normally she enjoyed listening to Hunter talk about his legislative proposals, especially when they pertained to education. He felt so passionate about making sure that every child had access to a good education, one that would open up better opportunities.

But today, he sounded more like he was trying to avoid talking about anything personal. Did he not want to celebrate their anniversary? Maybe this trip only reminded him that he'd been trapped into marrying her.

She snoozed as he talked, and she didn't wake up until she heard Hunter ask Curtis to stop the car. She sat up and looked out the window. They had pulled off the pavement onto a narrow, gravel shoulder. Trees crowded the vehicle. Hunter opened the door and climbed out onto the roadway, letting the door slam shut. Curtis jumped out right behind him.

Trent turned around. "Everything is fine, Mrs. Wilson. The governor wants to take a look around, I believe."

Curious, Shawna turned and peered out the rear window. Hunter trudged through the weeds and brush to a side road they had just passed. He bent over and moved a large red object lying on the ground. A stop sign that had been knocked down. He spoke to Curtis, who pulled out a cell phone and placed a call. As he talked, Hunter returned to the car.

He slid into the back seat next to Shawna. "Don't know how long that sign's been down, but it's a hazard. I noticed it on the ground as we passed. Curtis is calling it in. We'll wait here until highway maintenance comes to fix it."

Shawna jiggled her foot as they waited. They weren't on a tight schedule, but she wanted to get to the park so she could be alone with her husband. It seemed like an hour passed, and only two cars came through the intersection. With Curtis standing in the road, both cars slowed to a stop until he waved them on. Finally, a state patrol car arrived. Shawna checked her phone and saw they had actually waited only fifteen minutes. The driver, a uniformed trooper, turned on his flashing lights and angled the car across one lane at the intersection. He got out and spoke to Curtis, then strolled over to their car.

The trooper leaned over and looked in the window. "Good afternoon, Governor. Mrs. Wilson. Sorry this caused you delay." He nodded toward Curtis. "Your driver said you were the one who noticed the sign down, Governor. Much appreciated."

Hunter nodded. "Wouldn't want an accident to happen because of it."

Curtis opened the front door and got behind the wheel. Outside the vehicle, the newly arrived trooper stood up straight. "No, sir. But I'll stay here until the maintenance truck arrives, so you can be on your way."

A few minutes later, they arrived at the state park. Their large cabin featured a deck that extended out over Fall Creek Lake. A fire blazing in the large stone fireplace added the comforting scent of burning wood to the pleasant autumn air.

After getting unpacked, Hunter and Shawna changed to casual clothes and took a walk, followed, as always, by one of the security detail. Apparently, it was Curtis's turn. On the opposite side of the lake, they found deserted tennis courts and ball fields. Shawna knew from working for Kentucky State Parks that business slowed down after Labor Day. Weekends would be busy during the leaf-peeping season, but the trees wouldn't reach their peak colors for another month or so.

A distant yell proved they were not alone in the park.

A few feet away, Curtis stiffened and turned in the direction of the sound. A second scream was followed by laughter.

Peering in the same direction, Shawna spotted a person in a red shirt zooming down a wire cable. He was experiencing the thrill of swinging through the trees. She grabbed Hunter's hand and tugged him toward the registration office. Hiking trips had helped them get to know each other when they started dating. Maybe the adventure course would bring back that togetherness, at least in a small way. "Come on, I've never been on a zip line. It should be fun."

He planted his feet, resisting her efforts to pull him forward. "Neither have I, and I'm not going to try it now."

She tilted her head and stared at him. "What? Why not?" Though Hunter preferred a routine, he'd never refused to try something new when she asked—whether it was playing bocce ball or eating sushi.

He seemed reluctant to answer.

Another scream came from the direction of the zip line course.

"Hear that?" Hunter pulled his hand away from hers and put both hands in the pockets of his nylon jacket. "If you must know, I don't like heights."

"Really?" She started to laugh but stifled it when she realized he was serious. "But—what about those hikes we took in the mountains ..."

"I guess you didn't notice that I stayed away from the

cliff edges. I'm not about to step off a platform with my feet swinging loose in the air. Trips in the helicopter are bad enough." Normally self-assured, now Hunter looked like a boy caught stealing a piece of candy.

"How did I not know this until now?"

"No one knows, except Curtis." He tipped his head toward the trooper a few feet away. "And Lynn knew, of course. But it's not something I'm eager to admit."

Shawna sashayed up to him. "So, what other secrets do you have, Governor, that I should know about?"

He shook his head. "You go ahead. I'll cheer you on."

There would be no sharing of the adventure. At first, she refused to go alone. But she needed to try something new, to prove to herself she could still meet a challenge. She decided to give the adventure course a shot. "How about you, Curtis? Will you come with me?"

"No, ma'am. I can't do that while on duty. I'll stay with the governor and watch."

She nodded, and the three of them proceeded to the office, where Shawna signed up for the next time slot available, starting in fifteen minutes. The woman at the desk directed her to the outside shed. There, a pimple-faced teen-aged boy handed her a harness. He showed her how to step into it and pull it up like a pair of shorts, then he draped straps over her shoulders and hooked all the pieces together. He tightened the entire contraption by pulling on the chest strap until she felt like a trussed turkey ready to be cooked.

Hunter pulled out his cell phone and snapped a photo of her. "Where are the TV news people when we need them?"

"Very funny." She waddled across the grass to the area the kid directed her for training. Another young man, probably a college student, showed her and three other people how to hook onto the cable, launch off a platform, and brake near the end of a line. They took turns practicing on a line four feet off the ground, then headed as a group to climb the ladder to the first platform.

From twenty feet up, Shawna looked down and waved at Hunter and Curtis. They waved back, and Hunter said something, but the distance and the required helmet she wore kept her from hearing him. She shook her head and jumped off the platform.

"Woo-hoo!" She whizzed past tree branches and over a small stream, relishing the breeze on her face and the semblance of flying. The cable sloped down to the next platform, and Shawna picked up speed as she approached the first landing. Another worker, who was supposed to help her land, motioned frantically with the "slow down" gesture. She applied the hand brake and barely avoided slamming into the employee. He caught her, but as she swung in for the landing, her right foot hit hard against the wooden platform.

She stumbled, but gained her footing as the young man helped her clip the next line onto her carabiner. "You all right?" he asked.

Her big toe throbbed. "I'm fine. That was great."

He directed her around the tree, where a rope bridge led to the next zip line. Despite the pain in her toe, she completed the course, which included crawling across a cargo net and maneuvering over a balance beam high above the ground, with no further incidents.

Her pulse continued to race as she made her way down the ladder of boards nailed to the last tree. Hunter met her at the base. "Have fun?"

"Oh, yeah. You should try it. It can't be as scary as running for governor, and it's much more fun." She proceeded to disconnect the straps on her harness.

"No, thanks. I enjoyed watching you, though."

Shawna's toe had nearly stopped hurting but felt slightly numb. She would not mention her clumsiness, though she would probably lose the toenail. Hoping that Hunter wouldn't notice, she forced herself to walk without favoring that foot.

On the way back to their cabin, they detoured onto the trail that led to Fall Creek Falls. As they followed the hard-packed dirt and stone path, Shawna's sore toe protested, reminding her of the injury.

The path wound uphill through oaks and poplars, still covered in green foliage. Gradually, the trail climbed until they were level with the treetops on the right side. Even though a wooden railing protected them from sliding down the embankment, Hunter didn't speak. He hugged the inside of the path, staying close to the rock-covered hill that sloped upward.

As they approached the creek, the roar of water splashing into a basin at the bottom echoed through the canyon. They reached the overlook, stopping well before the edge, and gazed across at the narrow waterfall. Water foamed and sprayed as it cascaded over a rock outcropping before plunging straight down a couple hundred feet.

Shawna gasped, her breath stolen by the sight. "Beautiful!"

A second, smaller cascade descended to the right, and the two streams of water joined in the pool at the bottom and rushed toward the lake. The late afternoon sun caused the spray to twinkle at them.

Hunter reached for her hand. "No rainbows, but I thought you'd like it."

"I do! It's so very high."

"Higher than Niagara Falls. Only not as wide, and not nearly as much water. We claim it's the highest waterfall east of the Mississippi." Now that they were more than two feet from any incline, Hunter had relaxed—a little. He leaned closer to her and pretended to whisper. "You didn't hear this from me, but I read on the Internet there are other waterfalls with the same claim."

She glanced at him, and the wink from his lazy eye caused her heart to lurch. "I don't believe it. This one is spectacular."

Even though Curtis hovered ten feet away, Hunter kissed her.

Sharing this hike, this view, this moment, her hopes for a romantic evening soared.

Marie Wells Coutu

Chapter 20

Hoarseness infected Deb's normally sugary voice when Nate took her call that afternoon. A hazard of an ambitious campaign schedule, he supposed. "Nate, honey. Anything new?"

As was his habit, Nate had holed up in his apartment to write his article, and had nearly finished it. Hunter's campaign stop had been impressive, with Shawna's presence adding a nice touch. But with Deb's single-minded focus, she wouldn't want to hear about the morning's event.

"No, Deb. I've got no more leads." Even the argument between the two boys at the school had not stolen focus from the governor's technology funding proposal. Nate couldn't tell if the other reporters understood the conversation, but he felt sure it had caused Governor Wilson to end the interview so abruptly.

He chose not to mention that incident to Deb, especially since her people had fueled the rumor mill. Perceived success would likely light a match he couldn't put out. "Don't you have your own platform you can promote?"

"Sure, I do." Deb paused to clear her throat though it didn't help much. "Lower taxes, more jobs."

Nate's focus drifted back to his computer screen. He had ten minutes until deadline. He had made the little girl—Ashley, he corrected himself—the focus of his story. She could be the poster girl for the legislative push to gain approval of the education technology project. In fact, she could be a poster girl for the governor's reelection campaign. Nate wished he had the resources to give her the pony she wanted. Albert's progress was touching and important, but cuteness trumped pathetic every time, at least when it came to news. Nate clicked his mouse to send the article to his editor.

"Did you hear me, Nate? I need something more. The rumors are gaining me a little ground, but facts would sure help."

Nate rose from his chair and stretched. "You really want to make this a negative campaign?"

"I don't want to, but the voters need to know the truth about their beloved governor."

He stepped out onto the balcony. Truth could be messy, and not easy to discern, regardless of what Deb believed. Traffic from the street below made it difficult to hear her next words.

"Nate, I'm going to be in Nashville Saturday for the State Fair. We need to meet. I might have that new lead you're looking for."

She persisted in wanting to expose the scandal—if there was one. He knew where the circumstantial evidence pointed, but he'd just as soon leave well enough alone. "I didn't say I was looking for a new lead."

Brief silence. Then, "Would you prefer I passed the information to someone else? One of the TV stations, perhaps?"

He would, if he didn't care about his career. But his editors knew of his friendship with both Deb and Shawna. If another media outlet broke the story first, and had solid information to back it up, he would lose his reputation. And, quite likely, his job. He chewed his lip, but made the only decision he could.

"When and where?"

Sometimes, he wished he could flip the calendar back and find another way to start his career. A way that didn't leave him indebted to a politician.

During a quiet steak dinner at Gaul's Gallery, the park's restaurant, Shawna could see Hunter relaxing. He gazed into her eyes, and the past few months became a haze. Maybe losing Hannah had been only a nightmare, and she had imagined Hunter pulling away from her.

But as she took the last bite of her pie, he cleared his throat. "Johnnie says I need to be on the road the next few weeks. Fundraising dinners, rallies, kissing babies—you know, all the usual."

Shawna felt the warm sensations drain from her body. Just when she hoped they could spend more time together, he would be traveling around the state. With Johnnie. He tried to sound as though he hated to be gone, but he failed. He loved being governor, and he loved campaigning. Shawna hadn't minded when they first married, but now, saving the world—or at least the state of Tennessee—seemed to be more important to him than saving their marriage.

She stretched her hand across the table. "That stop sign today. You had to do something about it when you saw it had been knocked down, didn't you?"

He took hold of her hand and stroked it with his thumb. "That's what I do. When I see a problem, I look for a way to fix it. Then I make sure it gets done."

She sighed. "I guess that's what makes you a good governor. And one of the reasons I fell in love with you. But I wish …"

When she didn't continue, he turned her hand over and studied her palm. "You wish what?"

"Nothing. Never mind." She pulled her hand away and grasped the cloth napkin off her lap. This was a weekend to celebrate their anniversary, not to whine.

"Seems like I can fix all kinds of problems. But I don't know how to fix you."

She studied her hands as she twisted the napkin in her lap. "I don't need 'fixing,' Hunter. I'd just like you home more."

"Once the campaign's over, I will be, I promise. But right now—"

"Hunter, could we not talk about the campaign any more tonight?"

"Of course, honey. What would you like to talk about?"

"Us. Hannah Lea. Trying for another baby. Our future."

"That's four topics. Pick one." He grinned at her, winking his lazy eye. Usually, she liked it when he teased.

But tonight, she didn't want to be teased. "Actually, it's only one. They're all related."

He pulled back his hand and plucked the napkin off his lap, tossing it on the table. "Then perhaps we'd better go somewhere we have privacy."

Shawna winked. "My thoughts, exactly. It is our anniversary, after all."

When he didn't respond, but merely stood and held his hand out to help her, her stomach knotted. Maybe they still weren't on the same page.

He took her elbow and steered her out of the restaurant, then turned left, away from their cabin. "Let's walk," he said.

"In the dark?"

"Trent will follow us. There's no need to worry."

She gritted her teeth. "I wasn't worried. But ... how much can we see at night?"

He stopped and looked at her. "It's a beautiful night with a full moon. We don't have to see anything, just walk. And talk, of course, like you wanted. Is that okay with you?"

She didn't want to argue with him. "Of course. It is a nice night for a walk." She tipped her head against his chin, and he kissed her forehead.

He took her hand and they headed away from the lake. It wasn't smooth walking, so Hunter borrowed a flashlight from Trent. He aimed the beam so it would reveal any potential hazards ahead. Twigs and rocks crunched beneath their shoes, and similar sounds behind them reminded Shawna of their shadowy guard.

She'd almost become accustomed to the constant security, but at times like this, knowing someone was always within earshot made her feel like she was being strangled. And Mimi thought Hunter might run for president someday? Certainly, security then would be quadrupled or more.

An owl hooted in the woods to their right, causing her to jump. Hunter let go of her hand and put his arm around her shoulders, drawing her close. "I'm fine," she said. "It startled me, that's all." But his nearness sent warmth flowing through her body.

The sound of water rushing over rocks grew deafening. It couldn't be the waterfall they'd visited that afternoon. They had gone in the opposite direction. Soon the path angled downhill along the banks of a creek that descended over several small rapids. They slowed their footsteps.

Hoping the noise of the water would prevent their follower from hearing her words, Shawna said, "I'd like to have another baby."

Hunter's arm around her tightened. "Of course, we'll have another baby."

"I mean sooner, rather than later."

"But it's only been a few months. What if—" He stopped walking, withdrew his arm, stuffed his hands in his pockets, and stared over the river. "I don't want you to be disappointed again."

Sounded more like he didn't want to deal with her grief again. "The doctors said meconium aspiration is rare. The chance of it happening again is less than ten percent."

"I know what they said. But they didn't anticipate any problems the first time, did they? Doctors don't know everything."

She couldn't argue with that. But she refused to let fear prevent her from living. "I don't want 'what if's' to determine our future, Hunter. If we did that, H. L. and Cooper would never leave the house, we would never have gotten involved, and—"

"I'm not letting it determine our future. But I don't think we should rush into having another child so soon."

She jerked around to look at him. "Rush into it? You've barely touched me in the five months since Hannah died. That's a whole lot different than last summer when we first met. You couldn't keep your hands off me." She clamped her mouth shut and stepped back. She'd gone too far and she knew it. In the moonlight, she could see his jaw clench. She glanced up the hill where Trent stood guard, waiting in the shadow of the trees. Of course, he showed no reaction, as required by his position. But if he had heard …

It didn't matter. The security detail who'd been with Hunter at Barkley Lake Resort had certainly known about their clandestine meetings. No secrets for a sitting governor, especially one who was also the most eligible bachelor in the state of Tennessee. But smack-dab in the middle of the Bible Belt, knowledge of what they had done—especially since she had been married to a soldier—could kill his political career.

Maybe that would not be such a bad thing. At least, for their marriage. Perhaps then they could find the passion of those early days again.

In the darkness, she barely saw Hunter shake his head. "I don't recall you protesting too much at the time. But since you hated it, you needn't worry now. I'll keep my hands to myself."

He stormed up the hill the way they'd come. As he

passed, Trent began to follow, then hesitated, looking back at her.

Shawna, speechless, understood the man's dilemma. He was responsible for both the governor and the first lady. She hurried up the hill, nodding when she reached him. Without saying a word, they followed Hunter back to their cabin.

No secrets, indeed.

Chapter 21

Mist settling over the hills blocked the sunrise from Hunter's view the next morning as he set out on his morning run with Curtis.

It had been a sleepless night, not at all what he'd had in mind for the weekend. He kept failing Shawna, but he didn't know what to do about it.

"Let's stick to the roads. Those trails would be too rough to run on." Not to mention the danger of sliding down the steep embankments.

Curtis nodded. "Good choice, sir." Since they would be running only in the state park, with limited traffic, the troopers had decided to forego the trail vehicle and leave Trent behind with Shawna.

As they ran uphill away from the lake, Hunter heard the cry of an owl. *Who, who.* Should be *why, why.* Why did he find it so difficult to treat Shawna the way she deserved?

She had done nothing but try to please him, to make a good life for them in spite of their bumpy start.

He couldn't deny his initial attraction to her had been primarily physical, but even when they first met, he had admired her intelligence and her abilities. In fact, if she weren't so grief-stricken over losing Hannah, she'd probably be as good a campaign manager as Johnnie—if she acquired the same passion to see him succeed.

He kicked into high gear and attacked the next hill, pulling a stride ahead of Curtis, though not for long. Shawna couldn't help him get reelected as long as she didn't care if he won or not. Politics defined him. It gave him a sense of purpose, and she had known that from the beginning of their relationship.

"Curtis, have you figured out women?"

Curtis let out a snort. "No, sir. I don't think that's possible." They rounded a curve in the road and faced east. The sun's rays pierced the mist and colored the cloud-streaked sky with varied shades of pink and orange. "Life is sort of like that sky, I think. There's moments of beauty and clarity mixed with fog. Some parts will never be revealed unless we shine a light on them and see them as God intended."

"Is that your sermon for the week?" Hunter winced. He had not meant to make fun of the man's part-time pastoral role.

"Sorry, Governor. I was talking to myself more than to you."

They passed the campground dump station, and the stench of yesterday's garbage assaulted Hunter's nose. "No need to apologize, Curtis. I hope you'll never be afraid to say what you think." Maybe a trooper like Curtis speaking truth would have helped him avoid the affair with Shawna, and the secret burden that he now dragged behind him every day.

When Hunter returned to the cabin, Shawna was in the shower. They had planned to spend another night, but the suitcase lay open on the bed, fully packed except for their clothes for the day.

He opened the bathroom door and stepped into the steam-filled room. "What's going on? Why is the suitcase packed?"

Shawna shut off the water and reached through the shower curtain for a towel. "We might as well go home. We've seen the falls. We had our anniversary dinner. There's nothing else to do here."

"There are two waterfalls we haven't seen, and miles of hiking trails in the park. And you can do the adventure course again, if you want."

She stepped out of the tub and wrapped the towel around her. "I don't think so. I'm not in the mood."

As he turned on the shower and checked the temperature, he glanced at her in the mirror. "Are you sure?"

"Yes. You can spend a little time with the boys before you head out to campaign." She didn't slam the bathroom door, but she closed it behind her in a way that ended the discussion.

Hunter swallowed the remark that nearly slipped out of his mouth. He wanted to make up for the disagreement they'd had last night, spend time enjoying the scenery—and each other. The weekend should have been their time to restore their rocky relationship, get it back on solid ground. But once again, he had blown his opportunity.

Chapter 22

Hunter stayed in his office until after ten o'clock, reading policy reports and studies regarding the economic benefits to states of attracting corporate facilities.

Finally, when the words began to blur together, he called his driver for the evening. "Ready, John. Let's go home."

Exhaustion overtook his body when he sank into the back seat of the SUV. He closed his eyes and felt the strength drain from his body. The sounds of the city, already muffled by the bulletproof glass, faded as if he were sinking into a hundred feet of water.

When had everything become so difficult? His earlier campaigns had seemed like running across a grassy football field compared to this one. This felt more like he was stuck in mire, with every step sucking at his feet, tugging at his shoes, pulling him further into the muck. His approval rating had fallen below sixty percent for the first time since he took office, and recent voter polls showed his lead slipping away.

The car stopped and he opened his eyes. They couldn't have traveled more than a few blocks. He could see flashing red lights off to the left. At the nearest corner, a street musician leaned against a brick building, strumming his guitar under the neon sign of a Broadway honky-tonk. "What's going on, John?"

John caught his eye in the mirror. "Sorry, sir. I should have taken a different route. Seems like a disturbance at one of the bars. Police responded, and traffic's a little backed up. We'll be out of this mess in a minute or two."

He could hear Mimi saying, "I told you so." Nashville's music clubs and police worked hard to maintain a safe atmosphere downtown, but sometimes, people drank too much and started fights. Still, the popularity of the city's nightlife continued to grow. He and Lynn had enjoyed many exciting nights during the early stages of her career. He had even introduced Shawna to several of his favorite spots, but he had no taste for such entertainment now.

A policeman waved their car through the intersection, and soon they left the congestion behind. Their arrival time didn't concern Hunter, however. Home only represented more failures.

He dreaded facing Mimi with the news that the cancer lab was now on life support. She had been so excited when he told her the laboratory might be named for her daughter.

"The Lynn Maddux Wilson Research Center? That has a nice ring to it," she had said.

But his legislative initiatives, including his education bill, had bogged down, with dams at every turn.

Then there was Shawna. Why couldn't he stir up any desire for her? She was beautiful, smart, and a model First Lady. She tried hard to be a good parent to Hunter Lynn and Cooper, even though she wasn't their birth mother. Certainly he had loved her at first; he had not married her only because of the baby.

The baby. Hannah Lea had been born so fragile, battling to live for two weeks and losing. That's when they had lost everything. For weeks, he couldn't even look at Shawna without thinking of their dead child. Even now, after nearly five months, he struggled with his feelings about the baby's death. Had it all been his fault?

He was the one who had initiated the advances. Shawna would not have been unfaithful to her husband if he hadn't pressed her, he was sure of that. And he should have known better than to make love to Shawna without protection. But it had been so long … Until Shawna, he hadn't been with a woman since Lynn died. Or really, since her cancer diagnosis.

He shook his head and focused on their surroundings again. No point in going back over history. He couldn't change any of it. He peered out the window as the car turned into the drive and passed through the large iron gates. He could see light shining through the living room windows. The rest of the second floor looked dark.

Shawna didn't usually wait up for him, but occasionally she did—if she wanted to talk. He was in no mood tonight for another long discussion. Not after the disastrous weekend. He wanted to crash.

When he went in through the family entrance, he found Mimi in the dining room. She cradled a cup in both hands, looking up when he entered. "Hunter. Goodness, you look tired."

He hated to, but he knew he should tell her about the research facility.

He took a cup from the top of the buffet and poured himself some coffee. "It's decaf, right?"

"Always, dear."

He added sweetener and took a seat across the table from her. "You're right, Mimi. I am tired. I got bad news today."

She pushed a plate of cookies across the table. "Then you need one of these. I baked them today."

He took one of her famous chocolate chip cookies. Even though the state hired a full-time chef, Mimi enjoyed baking and often invaded the kitchen to whip up something for him or the boys. They all loved her for it.

Which made it even harder to tell her the news. He sucked in a huge breath. "Mimi, remember that cancer research facility I told you about?"

"The one that corporation is going to build near the

Vandy campus?" She lifted her cup and sipped.

"That's the one." He shook his head. "It looks like we won't be getting the facility, after all."

She set her cup down and studied him. "Tell me what happened."

He recounted the conversations he'd had that day with legislative leaders. "There's still a chance, if we can get more concessions from the legislature. But I'm afraid that's a long shot. The other party isn't convinced that we should be giving incentives to corporations. They call it 'corporate welfare.'"

Mimi nodded. "I've heard that. But surely, for cancer research ..."

He pressed his lips together. "We barely had enough support for the initial package we offered them. And after today, I'm not especially hopeful." He dropped his head. "I feel like I've failed Lynn. And you. Again."

She reached her weathered hand across the table and patted his arm. "It wasn't your fault, Hunter. You know that. Lynn should have gone to the doctor sooner, when she first started hurting. But she didn't. You've got to stop blaming yourself."

He sighed. "You're right, of course." She spoke truth, but that didn't eliminate the pit in his stomach.

They heard steps on the stairs and looked toward the doorway. Shawna appeared, dressed in sweatpants and a Murray State sweatshirt. "I thought I heard you come in." She went to Hunter and leaned down to him for a kiss.

He gave her a quick peck.

The eager look on her face disappeared. "I waited up for you. How was your day?"

"Long. I was telling Mimi. We may not get the research facility."

She started to pull out a chair and sit down. "Oh, I'm so sorry. What happened?"

If she sat down, he would be stuck explaining it all again. "I'm pretty tired. I'll tell you all about it tomorrow. You go on to bed. I'll be up in a few minutes."

Her shoulders sagged, and she looked from him to Mimi. Hunter hated himself for hurting her, but Shawna didn't understand the obligation he felt to honor Lynn's memory.

Shawna pushed the chair back in. Her voice was cool and flat. "If that's what you want. Good night, Mimi."

Hunter studied the coffee remaining in his cup and waited for her to leave the room.

Shawna trudged up the stairs in her slippers.

She had stayed up, hoping to have a small celebration of their anniversary, since the weekend had been such a failure. She wanted to talk to Hunter, hear about his day, maybe even share an intimate moment. Instead, he chose to talk with Mimi, probably so he could avoid her.

Fine. If that's the way he felt, there was little point in staying around. She had lost him.

She had misjudged him. Their relationship had been purely physical, after all. At least on his part. The marriage was a sham, to avoid a scandal, keep her from telling the world about the baby. Had he thought she would accuse him of sexual assault?

She let out a bitter laugh. She had fallen for him, in spite of her love for Daniel. A woman could love two men at the same time, couldn't she? So no, she could never have called it rape or anything similar.

And she had been as eager to keep their secret as he had. There was Daniel's family, and her sisters, to consider. Better to have a whirlwind romance, even if her pastor and friends thought the grieving widow was marrying on the rebound.

Now they could congratulate themselves for being right. But at least they would never know the real reason for her haste. She reached the bedroom and retrieved a small suitcase from the closet, set it on the bed, and opened it. She would take enough clothes for a few nights. Tomorrow she would ask her staff to pack up the rest and send it to her.

Send it where? She grabbed several items of underwear and tossed them in the bottom of the open suitcase. The family home where she grew up had been sold when her father died five years ago. Both sisters had busy lives of their own. She couldn't impose on them, nor could she face any of them and admit her mistake. Either mistake—the affair or the marriage.

Maybe a friend? Tricia would understand, and would be glad to have her. But she couldn't simply show up. She added two pairs of slacks and three shirts, folding them carefully and placing them on top. She grabbed two pairs of shoes and the book she'd been reading, then she zipped up the suitcase.

She would go to a hotel tonight and call Tricia tomorrow. She couldn't stay here one more night, knowing Hunter didn't even want to talk to her. Could barely stand to look at her. Hadn't he avoided looking at her a few minutes ago?

She lifted the suitcase and thumped it on the floor with determination. She would not cry or yell. Even if this was the end of her marriage.

Chapter 23

"She's not Lynn, is she?"

Hunter looked up from his coffee cup and stared at Mimi. "What?"

"I said, Shawna's not Lynn. She doesn't fight back like Lynn would have. And she doesn't know how to handle H. L. and Cooper. She tries to use kid gloves when what they need are leashes." Mimi rose and filled her cup with more coffee. "Want more?"

He placed a hand over his cup. "No, this'll be enough for me. Why are you so hard on Shawna? She's trying her best. Being a parent is new to her. She didn't get to learn what to do as they grew."

Mimi returned to her chair. "I'm only saying that she's not Lynn. I know you miss my daughter. I miss her, too. She was special, and no one can ever replace her."

Is that what he had been doing, trying to replace Lynn?

Not when he first met Shawna, for sure. She was nothing like Lynn, yet for the first time in six years, he had found a woman attractive and interesting. He had fallen in love. It hadn't lessened or replaced the love he still felt for Lynn. But he had finally been able to envision a future with another woman.

"I'll never stop loving Lynn, you know that, Mimi. But I love Shawna, too. Only in a different way." He shook his head. "At least, I think I do. I want to be a good husband and father, but ever since we lost the baby, it's been so hard. I'm afraid she doesn't love me."

Mimi sipped her coffee, held the cup to her lips. "You know, I was upset when you first started dating her. I don't know what I thought, that you'd be a bachelor the rest of your life?" She stared beyond him, somewhere out the window into the past. "Then when you married her and she moved in, I worried I was being replaced. I had enjoyed representing you at events and presentations. But I figured she wouldn't want your ex-mother-in-law around to remind you of what you'd lost, especially once the baby was born."

She fell silent, and Hunter felt he could speak without interrupting. "You could never be replaced, Mimi. The boys need you. You've been a lifesaver since their mother died, and now you're as much a part of our family as I am."

She smiled, a sad smile. Like the one Lynn had used in the weeks before she died. Hunter's heart cried silently as he remembered.

224

"I know. Shawna has told me almost the same thing. I was foolish to think I would be out of a job." She reached for a cookie and took a bite, chewing and swallowing. "You're right about her trying to be a good parent. And she is learning. The boys are more comfortable with her, and she with them." She grinned. "I think there's hope for her."

He waited as she finished her cookie. He knew there had been friction between the two women, of course, but he hadn't known what to do about it. It wasn't like staff, where you could direct them to work things out and get along—or persuade one to resign. He was relieved to hear Mimi saying positive things about Shawna.

The mantel clock signaled the hour, and he counted the chimes. Eleven.

"It's not too late, you know."

"Not too late for what?"

"For you and Shawna." She waved away his protest. "Being a grandma doesn't mean I'm blind. I know things have been rough for you lately. It's obvious your weekend away didn't go well. You came back early, and you've both been sullen."

Hunter stared into his nearly empty coffee cup. "Didn't go well" was putting it mildly.

"Isn't today your actual anniversary?"

The realization hit him like a slap. No wonder Shawna had waited up for him. He'd blown a chance to make up for the botched weekend.

"Hunter." Mimi spoke softly, as she often did when

correcting the boys. "It's not too late to get back what you had when you first got married. You need to court her. Date her like you did before you married. Romance her. Love is an action, Hunter. You make the effort, and the feelings will follow."

Hunter drained his coffee cup, hope growing like a tiny sprout shooting through compacted soil. Perhaps Mimi was right. He needed to court Shawna again. It was too late tonight, but he would start tomorrow. He'd send her flowers and take her out to dinner.

Shawna couldn't leave without telling Hunter. After all they had been through, that would not be fair.

She sat down on the bed to wait for him, her suitcase at her feet. He said he'd be up shortly.

A few minutes later, the door opened and Hunter appeared. "Shawna, let's—" He stopped short, apparently having noticed the bag.

"Hunter." She forced his name out through her constricted throat.

He stared at her, shock in his eyes. "What's this? Are you going somewhere?"

She swallowed, curled her fingers until her nails dug into her palms. "Yes, Hunter. It's not working. You don't want me here. I'm leaving."

He covered the space between them in two long steps. "No. You can't."

He'd given her an order rather than asking her to stay. A clear distinction. "Why not? Worried about your campaign?"

He spread his hands. "No. I mean, yes, of course. It will hurt the campaign, but … I care about you, Shawna. And the boys. They're finally warming up to you."

He cared about her. She believed him. Or wanted to. "I-I don't know how to handle them. I'm no good at it. And Mimi resents me. I can't take all that and you ignoring me, too."

"I know I've made mistakes. I'd like another chance."

She looked up at him. "Another chance for what?"

He sat on the bed and took her hand. "To be honest, I don't know. But I'd like to make it up to you."

She couldn't speak. She felt like the rope in a tug-of-war, being yanked in two directions. She wanted to give in, to stay with him, but she couldn't stay in a marriage in name only.

"Please. Don't go. I'd like to take you out to dinner tomorrow night. We can talk."

She pulled her hand free of his. "All right, Hunter. But I don't see any point in my sleeping in here. I'll go to the guest room tonight."

Before he could respond, she stood and grabbed the handle on her suitcase, towing it behind her as she left Hunter sitting on the bed.

As Shawna passed through the living room, she found the television on. A late-night talk show with a self-proclaimed psychologist as host. She left the suitcase behind the sofa and plopped down, grabbing the remote. But before she could shut it off, the host said, "Can you maintain trust in your relationship when secrets get in the way?"

Shawna held her hand with the remote in mid-air. She and Hunter certainly had secrets, though not from each other.

She decided to watch the program. As the commercials ended, Mimi came in from the hallway and settled in her usual chair. She picked up her knitting bag and nodded toward the TV. "I was about to watch this. You don't mind, do you?"

Mimi had seemed to soften toward her in recent days. Shawna shrugged. "I don't care."

The guests included two couples. One of the wives had confessed to having an affair, and the husband was still struggling to forgive her. The other couple, whose faces were blurred to protect their identities, had immigrated illegally from Mexico and lived in the U.S. for twenty years.

"Your families are still in Mexico, and none of your

friends and neighbors, not even your children, know that you aren't legal citizens. That's a pretty big secret to carry," the host said.

"Si, yes." The man's voice was altered electronically. "We live in fear that someone will discover us and send us back. Since our children were born here, they are citizens, but we would not want to go back without them."

"And does that put a strain on your relationship with each other?"

The wife answered this time. "Oh, yes. It is like, what do you say, the elephant in the room? We think about it all the time, but we can never talk about it."

Shawna curled her toes. That's how she felt, only the elephant was on her back, not just in the room. Did Hunter feel the same way?

The host was closing the show. "Secrets create barriers you aren't even aware of. You begin to wonder if your partner is hiding something else from you. Sometimes the best thing you can do for your relationship is to come clean and face the consequences."

Shawna offered the remote to Mimi.

Mimi shook her head. "You can shut it off as far as I'm concerned."

Shawna did so.

Mimi tucked her knitting back into her bag but held the bag on her lap. "I kept a big secret once." Her voice sounded far away, as though she were traveling back in time. "I was fortunate it didn't destroy my marriage."

When Shawna didn't say anything, she continued. "You see, when we first married, my husband spent a lot of time training and trying to advance his career. And another man, an older man I worked with, gave me the attention I was missing from my husband. I knew it was wrong, but I convinced myself I could love two men at the same time."

Shawna looked at her now, understanding mushrooming in her chest. "What happened?"

Mimi nodded. "I had an affair. Only one time did we … after that, I broke it off. I had even quit having my quiet time with God. But I started reading my Bible again, and I asked and received God's forgiveness. I still carried the secret around with me for years, though. Afraid that if I told my husband, he'd never trust me again. Afraid that if he found out from someone else, he'd leave me."

Shawna understood the tug-of-war between honesty and fear of repercussions. She and Hunter had talked about possible outcomes before they married, when they'd decided to keep the pregnancy secret.

"Finally, after his first heart attack, I confessed to my affair thirty years earlier. And he forgave me. Our last few years together were the sweetest of all, because finally he knew everything about me, and loved me in spite of it. Almost as much as God does."

Shawna couldn't look at her, sure that her own secret would show in her eyes. She said nothing.

Mimi placed the bag on the floor next to her chair and

stood up. "Everybody has secrets. It's what you do about them that affects your future."

Shawna was beginning to see that the secret she and Hunter shared was keeping them from trusting each other. Tonight, she'd been ready to leave rather than allow Hunter to reject her. And she hadn't exactly shown Hunter that she was committed to this marriage for the long haul. But what could she do about it now?

Chapter 24

Dawn couldn't come soon enough for Hunter.

Shadows in the bedroom echoed the shadows from his past. He had lost one wife to cancer, and couldn't even succeed in getting a research facility built as a legacy for her. He'd lost his honor when he pursued Shawna, knowing that she was married. He lost his daughter, and now he might be losing Shawna.

Finally, as light began to seep through the cracks around the draperies, he threw aside the covers and reached for the phone. Curtis would be expecting him to jog this morning, but he was too tired. Curtis answered on the first ring.

"I'm not running this morning. I want to go to the office right away. Can you have a driver here in thirty minutes?"

"Yes, sir, no problem."

He clicked off and headed for the shower, where he let the hot pulsating water flood away the sluggishness from lack of sleep. He was governor, and he needed to be alert for whatever the day might bring.

As he passed the living room, he noticed Shawna curled up on the couch, still dressed. She had never made it to the guest room. He detoured into the room and stood watching her for a moment. Her mussed hair fell into her face. Furrows in her smooth forehead betrayed her troubled sleep. He hadn't treated her well last night. Instead of romancing her, he had acted like he owned her.

He bent over her and stroked her hair, brushing it with his fingers away from her face. Then he leaned forward and kissed the top of her head, hoping she wouldn't wake up. She needed the rest. He only hoped she would be here when he came home tonight.

By the mid-morning staff meeting, Hunter had scanned the morning newspapers and caught up on his email. His communications director, Mark Newton, was first to arrive for the meeting.

"We may have a problem, Governor."

Hunter looked at him as he gathered a notepad and his coffee cup from the desk and headed for the seating area. "What sort of problem?"

Newton dropped onto the sofa next to Hunter's preferred chair. "You know I told you Nate Matthews was digging into your relationship with Shawna. He's still snooping around, asking questions of anybody and everybody that will talk to him."

Hunter swore under his breath. "Why do they have to keep bringing up the baby?"

Newton shifted uncomfortably. "Governor, I need to ask you. Is there anything you haven't told me? Is there something for him to find if he keeps digging?"

Hunter sank into his chair and exhaled. "There is. Shawna was pregnant when we married."

"Is that all? We can brush that off. It's not all that uncommon these days. Lots of people guessed that, anyway."

Hunter shook his head. "There's more. When we ... when Shawna got pregnant, she was still married. That is, it happened before she got word that her husband had been killed in Iraq."

"Oh." Newton didn't speak for a few moments. "So, it was an extramarital affair. That's bad enough in the Bible Belt, but she was married to a soldier at the time. To some people, that could be unforgivable, even though he died."

Hunter nodded. "Exactly. That's why we've kept it secret. Not only for my campaign, but for her sake, too. If this gets out, she'll be hated by military families all over America. I don't want her to have to deal with that."

Johnnie entered the room then, followed by the other aides. Hunter didn't need everyone knowing what he had confessed. He greeted them and, as soon as everyone was settled, said, "Let's get started. What do you have, Johnnie?"

"I've been talking to the General Assembly leadership, trying to gauge support for the Teaching Through Tech bill. It doesn't seem to be there yet."

"Okay. It won't come to a vote until next session. We can keep working on it, right?"

"Yes, sir. I think we need to redouble our efforts to get the public behind it, keep showing how it can benefit students. Make some more school visits. It could help your campaign."

He nodded. "Set it up." This wasn't rocket science. His staff could deal with this without him. He'd rather be working out his problems with Shawna. Or figuring out how to keep nosy reporters out of their personal lives. The media would love knowing that Shawna was planning to leave, wouldn't they?

He turned to Jared Rodgers. "How about the research center?"

Rodgers opened a folder and handed him a single sheet of paper covered with text. He passed copies of the same sheet to the others. "Here's a list of ideas for additional incentives we might offer. I've talked to some of the legislative staffers, and the first ones are the most likely to get approval."

Hunter tried to focus on the list as Rodgers explained the ideas. But he soon realized his concentration was fading. "I'm sorry, folks," he interrupted. "I can't do this today. Let's resume this discussion tomorrow."

Shawna woke up when she felt Hunter hovering over her, but she kept her eyes closed. She did not want to face him yet, so she didn't move until he had left the living room. She had fallen asleep on the sofa after Mimi went to bed, and now she had a crick in her neck along with a splitting headache.

She called her assistant and told her she would not be coming into the office. "The little demolition man in my head won't stop using his jackhammer. I'm going to rest."

"Of course," Crystal said. "You don't have anything on your calendar today. Hope you feel better."

Shawna hung up and headed for the bedroom to lie down. Thankfully, the boys had not come out of their room yet. She didn't want them to know about the problems between her and their dad. At least, not yet. Mimi would get the boys off to school.

She spotted her suitcase where she left it last night and stopped short. She should move into the guest room, like she had told Hunter. Or was there still hope for her marriage? She wanted to think so. But sleeping in separate rooms didn't seem like a recipe for reconciliation.

She drew a deep breath and grasped the retractable handle. Glancing between the two doorways, she made her decision. She dragged the bag back into the master bedroom and stashed it in the closet. But she wouldn't unpack it yet.

After taking two tablets for her headache, she crawled under the covers and fell asleep. When she woke up, her growling stomach told her lunch had passed. A sandwich on a small plate sat on the bedside table. Looked like pimiento cheese. Mimi must have brought it. Her headache was gone, but Shawna did not feel refreshed. The cloud of last night's disagreement with Hunter still hung in the room. Had she overreacted? Maybe, but why be married if she still felt alone?

She stretched, kicking the blanket back, and turned to put her feet on the floor. She would eat, then find something to do until Hunter came home. They had much to talk about over dinner tonight.

She spotted her Bible on the nightstand, where it had sat untouched since Hannah died. Before that, she had lapsed into reading it sporadically instead of daily, like she used to. She'd once had a faith as strong as Mimi's, but she had let procrastination and doubt interfere. She knew better. Even Cooper made a habit of reading his children's Bible before bed every night.

What had she done with that daily reading guide Mimi had given her back in January? She opened the drawer and found the folded booklet listing suggested scriptures for each day of the year. She looked up today's date, then turned to the passage in her Bible. The fifty-first chapter of Psalms. Ironic. King David had written this Psalm after being confronted about his sin with Bathsheba. She read his plea for God's mercy.

But hers and Hunter's situation was different. Hunter had not been responsible for Daniel's death. The fact that she had been pregnant when she married Hunter was no one's business but theirs. Especially since Hannah had died.

She closed the Bible and placed it back on the table. She had started reading it again. That was enough, wasn't it?

She polished off the sandwich, then she pulled on jeans and a t-shirt and headed for the stairs. A massive arrangement of red and lavender roses was moving toward her up the staircase. Mimi's body seemed to be behind it, then her head peeked around the expanse of flowers.

"These are for you."

Shawna's breath grew shallow. She'd only seen arrangements that large at funerals and weddings. She waited at the top of the stairs and reached out for the glass vase when Mimi got close enough. Its weight surprised her, but Mimi held on until Shawna had control of the bouquet. "I've got it," she said.

Moving into the living room, she searched for a suitable location to place the flowers. The mantel, opposite the television. Inhaling the sweet fragrance, she lifted the vase and rested it at the end of the mantel while she moved a statue out of the way. When it was in position, she opened the miniature envelope and removed the card.

Shawna, We need you. Please stay. —H

She tucked the handwritten message into her jeans pocket, away from the prying eyes of Mimi and the boys.

The roses were gorgeous, but the sentiment—no mention of *love*, only *need*. Sure, it was nice to be needed, but she wanted more than that. Love, devotion, commitment, trust—those were the things she needed.

Maybe she could stay until after the election. Two more months. But after that, she couldn't say. She did know, however, that she would not throw herself at her husband like she had last weekend. She could not stand another rejection.

Chapter 25

"Don't you like your duck?"

Shawna looked at Hunter as if he had two heads. She had eaten less than half of her meal and had said very few words. He didn't know how to break down her wall.

She pushed her plate toward him. "You can have it. I'm not hungry."

The small private dining room at 5th and Taylor that Hunter had reserved provided the intimacy he'd wanted, and the restaurant consistently received rave reviews. But it had all been wasted on Shawna tonight. For that matter, even his veal T-bone had lacked flavor, but that had more to do with his discomfort than with the food.

Hunter reached out and moved her plate aside, laying his hand on the table palm up. She didn't take the hint. "Shawna, what can I say?"

She leaned back in her chair and shook her head, her

hazel eyes glistening in the candlelight. "There's nothing for you to say, Hunter. Being governor is important to you. I get that, and I'll do whatever I can to help you get reelected. The state fair's coming up, and I'll be there smiling and telling people what a great governor you are."

She took a sip of water, set the glass down, and kept her hand on it, using her thumb to wipe condensation off the outside. "And you are, Hunter. Tennessee's lucky to have you as governor. You have vision and passion, and you care about people."

He didn't want a campaign speech from her. He pulled back his hand and picked up his napkin, dabbing at his mouth. "You're one of the people I care about, Shawna." He dropped the napkin onto his plate.

"That's the problem, isn't it, Hunter? I thought a husband and wife were supposed to put each other above everyone else, not on an equal level with—" She waved her hand around the empty room. "With the rest of the citizenry."

"You're not—" He almost said she wasn't simply another voter to him, but that seemed pointless. Didn't the roses he sent mean anything to her? "I don't send two dozen roses to the rest of the citizenry."

Her mouth twisted up in a melancholy smile. "That's good to know. They are lovely …"

Their waiter entered the room and rushed to the table. "Will there be anything else, Governor?" He picked up Hunter's plate.

Hunter looked at Shawna, who shook her head. "Thank you, Martin. Bring us the check, please."

Martin reached for Shawna's plate. "Would you like a box for this?"

"No, thanks." Shawna moved her water glass closer to him. "I'm done with this, too."

The waiter left, and Shawna forced a laugh. "Maybe I should take the duck home for H. L. and Cooper."

"I don't think that's worth it. They would be appalled that you'd eaten one of those cute creatures." Hunter smiled, eager to keep up the banter, but regretting that nothing had been settled between them.

When the waiter brought the check, Hunter handed over a credit card. Muted sounds of chatter and laughter filtered through the walls, customers in the main part of the restaurant enjoying their food and companions. Shawna's gaze flicked around the room as she pretended to study the artwork, the high ceiling and open rafters, anything to avoid looking at him, it seemed. What had happened to the desire she displayed only a few days ago at Fall Creek Falls? He should not have pushed her away.

Hunter signed for their meal, then looked at Shawna, who appeared to be studying her lap. "Ready to go?"

She raised her head, and he wanted to lose himself in her expressive eyes. She licked her lips. "If we're going to get through these next couple months, Hunter, let's just be friends. Okay?"

The air left the room, and Hunter heard nothing but the

thumping of his heart. Friends. Just friends. He regained his breath and nodded, slowly. "If that's the way you want it. Just friends."

She pushed back from the table and stood up. She had nothing more to discuss, apparently.

Lieutenant Palmer met them at the door of the restaurant and spoke into his shirt cuff. A minute later, he escorted them out. The Escalade moved slowly up the block to pick them up.

"Governor! Shawna—I mean, Mrs. Wilson." The shout caused Palmer to make an abrupt turn, shielding Hunter and Shawna from whatever danger approached.

Hunter looked around Palmer and frowned. Shawna's reporter friend, Nate Matthews, hurried toward them. Hunter had no patience for reporters tonight. But he touched Palmer's arm. "It's all right. We know him."

Shawna had also turned. "Nate!" She stepped past Palmer and met Nate a few steps away, giving him a hug. "Nice to see you."

She appeared eager to see him. Hunter dug his fingernails into his palm and joined the two of them. He held out his right hand. "Matthews. I'm not answering any questions. You'll need to go through my office for that."

Nate shook hands with him. "Of course, Governor. I'm not working tonight. I hadn't expected to run into you, but I wanted to say hello."

Hunter waited, the noise from a tour bus making conversation difficult. The blue-striped bus stopped at the corner, spewing diesel fumes into the air.

Hunter put his hand on Shawna's back. "I didn't think reporters ever stopped working."

"Now, Hunter. Nate's just being friendly."

"And I'm just setting the ground rules." The SUV pulled alongside them, and Hunter glanced at Palmer. "Our driver's waiting for us, Shawna."

She nodded, then looked at Nate. "I'll see you on the court, Nate."

As the car pulled away from the curb, Hunter asked, "What did you mean you'd see Matthews on the court?"

She shifted position and adjusted her seatbelt. "Exactly what I said. Sometimes we play tennis while the boys have their lessons on Thursdays. It's good practice for the tournament next month."

Odd she hadn't mentioned practicing with Nate Matthews before now. What else did he not know about his wife's activities?

Hunter shook his head. He had no reason to be suspicious. Shawna and Nate had been friends in college.

But, according to what she said tonight, she and Hunter were only friends, as well.

Chapter 26

The rumble of applause reached Nate's ears as soon as he entered the exhibit hall on the state fairgrounds. Deborah Hummel's speech to small business owners must be a success.

He waved off the eager campaign volunteer who greeted him, and her smile disappeared like ice cream dropped on a hot sidewalk. Fine with him. He didn't need to be schmoozed or solicited for money.

When Nate let himself into the semi-dark theater, he found only about half of the two hundred seats full. He slid into one of the cushioned red chairs on the empty back row.

Deb's impeccable style, perfected by her handlers, reinforced the aura of the successful entrepreneur. Her economic development plan resonated with this audience, small as it was. "If a stay-at-home mom can build a multi-million-dollar bank, like I did, then anyone with ingenuity and determination can start a business. Small businesses are the backbone of our state, and they are our future."

When that round of applause died down, she outlined her plan to encourage start-up companies. Nate had always liked Deb's common-sense approach to problems. As she concluded her speech, he remembered why he had admired her, even back in high school.

"Most of you already have a business, and you may be thinking, *Why would I want to stimulate competition?* But I ask you to remember when you were first getting started—how much it meant to you to make that first sale, or get that first customer. Don't think of my program as giving you competition. Think of it as an opportunity for you to give back, to give someone else a hand up instead of a handout."

Nate joined the audience in the standing ovation, momentarily putting aside his journalistic objectivity. On second thought, he'd left that behind when he agreed to investigate Shawna Wilson's pregnancy. He stopped clapping and slumped back into his seat to wait for Deb. She spent the next twenty minutes greeting individuals, and he noticed she took extra time with several women.

Finally, when only a couple of people waited to greet her, Nate shuffled down the aisle to the front of the auditorium. Deb was listening to a skinny, thirtyish man, but she saw Nate and nodded. "That's a really interesting idea," she told the man. "I wish you the best of luck." She patted the man's arm and executed a graceful dismissal, turning toward Nate. "You made it. What'd you think?"

Nate accepted her brief hug. "Great speech, Deb. Sounds like a good plan, and the audience seemed to approve."

She took his arm and gestured toward the exit. "Let's go explore the fair while we talk. Do you mind walking?"

"As long as you don't mind a turtle's pace. This humidity's killing my leg." He pushed open the door. The warm breeze on his face felt more like July than mid-September.

"I would die for some of those mini-donuts." Deb angled toward the row of food vendors. "You want something?"

The sweet odor of donuts cooking in hot oil turned his stomach. "Nope. I'll wait over by that tree." He made his way to a big oak tree near the street and leaned against it. Mini-donuts had been his ex-wife's favorite fair food, too. Some reminders he couldn't escape.

Deb approached him, holding a paper bag of the bite-sized treats with one already in her mouth. "Mmm." She held the bag out to him.

Nate pushed her hand away. "I said I don't want any."

"Fine. More for me, then." She took another donut from the bag, but held it in her hand. "What have you learned?"

He glanced around. Too many people close by. "Let's get away from the crowd." Deb hadn't yet reached the status of being recognized by everyone, so they didn't attract any attention. Nate led this time, away from the food line-up toward the livestock barns. Since many fair-goers skipped those, they would be able to talk without concern of being overheard.

When they had left the crowds behind, Nate stopped and faced her. "I don't know why you want to do this, Deb."

Deb licked powdered sugar off her fingers. "I told you, Nate. Wilson is a popular governor. To beat him, I need an edge."

They started walking again. A teen-aged girl riding a chestnut horse passed them. Right in front of them, the horse dropped a smelly deposit. Absorbed with her donuts, Deb would have stepped in it if Nate hadn't grabbed her arm.

"You have good ideas, Deb. Great ideas. Your ratings are rising, and if you keep getting your message out, you could have a real shot at winning this thing. Why throw stones at Wilson?"

They reached the end of the lane and turned around to head back. "You haven't told me what you've found out. Have you got anything?"

Nate's leg throbbed, and he bent to massage it. "All I've got is a maid at the resort who says she knows Shawna spent the night with a man during the conference. Two nights, in fact. But she didn't actually see her entering or leaving the man's room."

Deb crumpled the empty donut bag. "I knew it! It had

to be Hunter, right? You said they spent a lot of time together that week."

He straightened and shrugged. "Yes, but—"

She rubbed his arm. "Nathaniel, you are so close to a big story here, you don't even see it. Tennesseans love their soldiers. They don't want a governor who would break up a marriage, especially a military family. And that's exactly what he did, if you think about it."

Nate's stomach churned. The truth wasn't that black-and-white. But his own failed marriage slapped him in the face. As much as he liked Shawna and Hunter, the bitter taste left by his ex-wife's betrayal returned.

He pointed to a bench by the sidewalk. "Can we sit?"

Deb tossed her trash into a bin at the end of the bench, then sat next to him. "Who can confirm our suspicions? There must be some way."

"I've got no more leads. Medical records would be the only real proof, and those are legally off-limits. I can't turn in a story with what I've got. My editor would skin me alive."

"There has to be a way." She pulled a cell phone out of her pocket and tapped it several times. "Look, I don't know if this is legit, but it's worth checking out." She handed him the phone.

He took it and listened to a voice mail message from a young woman. "Ms. Hummel, I admire you so much, and I want to help you get elected. I have information about Mrs. Wilson's baby that might be useful to you. Call me back if you want to talk." He looked at Deb, curiosity winning over logic.

"You know I can't contact her." Deb looked at the people strolling past. "That wouldn't look good. But you can talk to her, find out what she knows. Then decide if you can use it or not."

Nate's curiosity had been piqued. He copied the number to his phone. He would call the woman that evening. Probably would turn out to be nothing, but, after all, he was called the "bulldog." He couldn't give up on a story as long as he had a possible source with more information, even a story that turned his stomach as much as this one did.

Chapter 27

Shawna's cheeks ached from smiling as she spoke with fair-goers who stopped by Hunter's campaign booth Sunday afternoon.

"You are lucky to be married to such a wonderful man," said a plump, white-haired woman. She held onto Shawna's hand with both of hers. "I just love what he's doing for the schools. My grandbabies sure do need them computers he's gonna give them. You tell him he's got my vote. And my husband's, too."

"Yes, ma'am. Thank you." Shawna managed to pull her hand away and turn to the next person in line, a tall man holding a "Reelect Wilson" brochure. Judging from his odor, he had been working with livestock.

"Good afternoon, sir. Do you have any questions?"

The man looked her up and down and smiled. Or rather, leered. Goosebumps popped up on the back of Shawna's neck. "Nah, I just wanted to meet you. Not every day I get to talk to a beauty pageant winner."

Shawna leaned back, trying to avoid the man's breath. He had also been drinking beer, it seemed. "I hope you'll be sure to vote for the governor in November," she said, dismissing him.

Shawna found she actually meant it when asking people for their vote. Fixing things, improving life for people, gave Hunter purpose. And he'd been effective. Today she had seen how much the citizens appreciated his efforts and needed him to finish the job.

But the man with the beer breath didn't move on as she expected. "Four more years," he yelled. He raised his arms to the dozen fairgoers waiting to speak with her. "Four more years." A few people responded, then more joined him in repeating the chant, turning the quiet gathering into an impromptu rally. The man became a cheerleader and ran out into the thoroughfare, where passersby stopped to watch the spectacle.

Shawna's feet hurt and she felt the beginning of a tension headache at the base of her skull. The drunken man's behavior ruined any hopes of meaningful conversation with others. She looked around for help. The young volunteers in the back of the booth looked at her and at each other. Their handbook had no guidance for a situation like this.

If only Hunter would return. He would know how to handle this. But his duties judging the fair's talent show would keep him busy for another half-hour.

Shawna shot a pleading glance at Curtis, who waited off to one side of the booth opening. He nodded, and moved out into the noisy crowd. He put a hand on the disruptive man's shoulder, leaned over, and spoke to him quietly. The man looked at Curtis, and his face went still. He nodded, lowered his arms, and shouldered his way through the crowd, away from the booth. Without a leader, the chants of "Four more years" slowly ebbed, and people began to drift away.

Curtis returned to the booth. "He had too much to drink, ma'am. I don't think he'll bother you again."

Shawna's pulse calmed and she smiled apologetically at the couple who were next in line.

"Miz Wilson, bless your heart. I lost my baby girl to cancer three years ago, so I know what you're going through," the woman said. "We're real happy the governor's building that cancer center here. It'll be a real blessing."

Shawna thanked the woman. She might not have her facts straight, like many voters, but her enthusiasm made up for her lack of knowledge.

She spotted Mimi and the boys returning from their trip to the midway, and she took the opportunity for a break. A volunteer stepped up to hand out brochures and buttons, but the long line quickly dispersed.

Cooper carried a red and blue teddy bear and wore a huge smile. "Look what I won at the shooting gallery, Shawna!"

She bent down to take a closer look. "That's quite a prize, Cooper. You must be a really good shot."

"Well, I had to keep trying. And Mimi helped."

Shawna glanced at Mimi, who shrugged. "He was having fun. What's a grandma to do?"

"Who wants a silly old bear?" Hunter Lynn sported a farmer's straw hat, tipped back on his head. "I could've won one, too, if I'd wanted one, but I'd rather have this hat."

"And you look mighty sharp, H. L." Shawna tweaked the hat, moving it slightly forward. "Let's all get some water and cool off." She nodded to the back of the booth as H. L. adjusted his hat. Nothing she touched could be left the same.

As they entered the private area, a teen-aged boy and girl broke off a kiss. The girl blushed, and the boy studied the ground. "Sorry, Mrs. Wilson," he said. "We were about to go back to work." He grabbed the girl's hand and pulled her out the door.

Shawna shook her head and dug a bottled water out of a cooler full of ice. She sank into a chair in front of a giant fan. The boys took their water bottles and sat cross-legged on the floor by a checkerboard. "I'm black," H. L. said.

"You're always black." Cooper propped his bear beside him. "Why can't I be black?"

"'Cause I called it first." H. L. moved a checker to start the game.

Mimi claimed a chair next to Shawna's. "Boys, play

quietly or don't play." She twisted the cap on her water and took a sip, then looked at Shawna. "You doing okay?"

Shawna gulped some water. "I'm fine. A drunk man came by and got the crowd all hyped up. He had them chanting, 'Four more years! Four more years!' I thought he was going to start a riot or something."

Mimi laughed. "Sounds like he wanted to let off steam. At least he was for Hunter, not against him. You see all kinds at the state fair."

"I guess." Shawna closed her eyes and leaned her head back, rolling it from side to side. Mimi had campaigned for Hunter before and knew what to expect. Shawna found this type of campaigning much different from the staid, high-dollar fundraising dinners and the smaller, "town-hall" type meetings. The fair booth left everything to chance—no plans, no speeches. Only passing out literature, shaking hands, and answering questions. Exhausting.

The noise level outside their little cocoon rose suddenly, with a smattering of applause. Hunter's voice broke through Shawna's musings. "I'll be out in a few minutes, folks."

The flaps opened, and her husband slipped through. At least, she thought it was Hunter, but he was half-hidden by a four-legged stuffed animal.

H. L. jumped up, spilling the checkerboard. "Dad, that's a ginormous horse!"

Cooper ignored the spilled checkers and ran to his dad. "Wow. Is that for us?"

Hunter managed to make the brown toy stand by itself, then he squatted so he was face to face with the boys. "No, boys. I'm sorry. Shawna and I talked with a girl last week who's not as lucky as you two. She can't walk, and she's in pain most of the time. She has to have operations and misses a lot of school."

Shawna swallowed the lump in her throat and leaned forward. "That's right, boys. Her name is Ashley. She's very brave. She said she wanted a horse, but they couldn't afford to keep a real one. I think your dad got her one she could take care of."

Hunter Lynn swung one leg over the animal, but he had to grab hold of the toy's neck to keep it from flopping onto the floor. "Hey, that's cool. Maybe she'll be able to ride this horse."

Hunter lifted H. L.'s hat off his head. "Maybe so. Where'd you get this spiffy hat?" He perched it on top of his own head.

"I won it, Dad. Like you won this horse, didn't you?"

Hunter's laugh warmed Shawna's heart. "I tried, but after my first four balls missed, the man took pity on me and let me buy it."

Cooper found that so funny that he threw himself on the floor, giggling and kicking his feet. Hunter stepped over him to reach Shawna and give her a brief kiss on the cheek. "I'd better get out there. My fans are waiting."

She nodded, aware that his "fans" would always take precedence over family. "I got talked into participating in the FFA pie-eating contest. I have to go to the Creative Arts Building in a few minutes."

Hunter lifted an eyebrow. "Another chance to embarrass yourself?"

She shrugged. "Why not? It shows we're real people."

"Better you than me. Maybe the kids and I will come watch." He tweaked her chin, an affectionate gesture that caught her off guard.

To Shawna's surprise, she found herself competing in the "celebrity" round of the competition against a local TV personality and Deborah Hummel. She had met Hunter's opponent only once, at a debate in Clarksville. A successful entrepreneur, the woman had seemed charming and intelligent. If Hummel hadn't been running against Hunter, Shawna thought she might like her.

Today, however, Hummel appeared agitated. "Mrs. Wilson. The governor sent you to eat humble pie for him, did he?"

Shawna wouldn't let this woman irritate her. She fixed her best smile in place. "I didn't know that was on the menu. What kind are you having?"

"Currants. What else?" Hummel smirked. "My campaign could use the money."

Shawna groaned at the bad pun, and Hummel faked a laugh. "Just kidding you. Let's have fun with this, shall we?"

"Agreed." Shawna took a seat at the table facing the audience. A handful of students wearing the distinctive blue jackets of the Future Farmers of America waited in folding chairs, along with some casually dressed adults and a few families with small children.

Two FFA students produced black plastic garbage bags with openings and slipped one over each of the three contestants so that only their heads stuck out. As a young man explained the rules, Shawna's stomach knotted. No hands allowed; with her arms inside the garbage bag, she couldn't use them anyway. Whoever finished her pie first, or ate the most in five minutes, would be the winner. Of course, the pies were raspberry, her least favorite fruit. Why couldn't they have used chocolate?

The emcee counted down from three, then gave the signal to start. Shawna pressed her face into her pie. Getting the pie into her mouth without a fork was challenge enough, but to chew it quickly and swallow while taking another bite proved nearly impossible. And messy. Pie filling went up her nostrils and covered her cheeks. She could only imagine how she looked. Why had she let herself be talked into this? The roar of jeers and cheers from the audience filled her thoughts. She turned her head to one side to bite at the crust, and felt the sticky filling glob onto her hair.

Relieved when the buzzer signaled that time was up, she sat up straight and glanced at her competition. Seeing the red glaze covering their faces, Shawna couldn't help but laugh. No doubt she looked just as ridiculous. She had finished three-fourths of her pie, while Hummel had eaten away only spots. The TV anchorwoman had beaten them both, having gobbled down nearly the entire pie. Bits of piecrust in her blond hair attested to her determination to win the contest.

A female FFA student offered Shawna a wet towel for her face and helped her remove the plastic bag. Shawna stood and held out her hand to the winner. "Congratulations. And don't worry. I won't be asking for a rematch."

When she stepped off the stage, she found Nate Matthews waiting. "Good job, Shawna. I thought you might win that one."

She groaned. "I hope you're not writing a story about this."

"Nope. It's my day off. I'm here to enjoy myself."

Hummel left the stage and walked past them. "Nate, Shawna. Have a good one."

"You, too, Deb." Nate's eyes flicked from Hummel back to Shawna, an odd look that she couldn't read. He waited until Hummel was out of earshot. "That always sounds funny to me. Have a good what?"

Shawna nodded. "I know what you mean."

Nate didn't say anything, but only stood there. Did he want something? Finally, he shook his head, as if clearing his thoughts. "Well, nice to see you again, Shawna. Take care."

He turned and wandered along the row of exhibits, appearing to study the baked goods and home-canned foods on display.

Shawna couldn't remember Nate ever acting so strange, as if he had something to ask her, but had changed his mind.

"Looks like we missed more than the contest."

Shawna whirled to find Hunter standing next to her, his eyes focused on Nate. The hard edge of his jaw reflected the stiffness in his voice. But she had nothing to be ashamed of.

"Hunter! What are you talking about?"

He tipped his head in the direction Nate had gone. "Matthews. I know he's your friend, but he's also a reporter."

"He's not working today." Did Hunter still think she wanted media attention? She shrugged. "Anyway, I lost. But I did beat Deborah Hummel."

He studied her, his face an unreadable mask. "Seems like the media loves you more when you lose."

Her own words from months ago haunted her. "I'm just trying to be a good sport," she had told him. "If you can't handle that ..."

The rumble of conversations around them broke through her consciousness. This was too public a place for a disagreement.

Shawna managed a humorless chuckle. "Too bad you didn't see me with pie on my face."

Idiot.

Nate stared, without seeing the blue and red ribbons decorating the plates of cookies.

He almost asked Shawna Wilson for the truth, right then and there. He should have. But with so many high school kids around, the time seemed wrong to ask such a personal question.

Besides, did it really matter? Deb thought it did. Part of him did, too. The part that remembered how his wife had cheated on him. But another part questioned the need to ruin two more lives, not even counting Hunter's kids.

Shawna's first husband had died a hero. If her unfaithfulness were revealed, would that tarnish his memory? And bring more pain to his family?

On the other hand, Deb might be right about the lies. Voters had a right to know their governor had not been truthful. People were tired of politicians with secrets.

Why did Nate have to be caught in the middle between his two friends? Was this what journalism had become in the twenty-first century—digging up dirt on one candidate to provide an advantage to another? That wasn't what he signed up for when he returned to college after being injured in the Sandpit.

But at his age, what else could he do with his life?

Chapter 28

Shawna picked up her Bible from the bedside table.

She'd been trying to get back into the habit of reading it daily, but she'd forgotten this morning. Maybe she would have a few minutes of quiet now, while the boys were doing homework.

After settling on the loveseat in the bedroom, she opened the book to the ribbon marker. Psalm Ninety. She read a few verses, then three rapid knocks sounded on the door, full of urgency. She sighed and closed the Bible. "Come in."

Mimi opened the door and rushed in, grinning. "Shawna, sorry to interrupt, but there's something you'll want to see, I think."

Shawna's heart sped up and she started for the door but Mimi shook her head. "No, go out on the balcony. Look on the tennis court."

Turning abruptly, Shawna went to the glass French doors that opened onto the small balcony. She strode to the side facing the tennis court and leaned over the wide stone wall that enclosed the area. Peering down, she squinted to get a better view. Was that Hunter Lynn out there alone? He must not have had much homework.

Mimi joined Shawna at the railing. "I saw him out the window. He looks determined."

The boys had continued their tennis lessons, but Shawna had not practiced with them since the day H.L. had shouted at her. Better to avoid another scene like that one.

The boy swung his racket at a tennis ball that did not make it halfway to the net. His swing had improved in the past few weeks. He bent down and picked up another ball from a mesh bag and repeated the swing. That ball went further but bounced several feet before the net.

H. L. paused, adjusted his stance, then his grip, and took a couple of practice swings. He bent over and, taking a ball from the bag, served a ball that still fell short of the net. He stomped one foot but grabbed another ball, and tried again.

"Our court is standard size. He's not used to that." Shawna straightened. "I need to tell him he can move closer to the net." She turned toward the door to the bedroom.

"Do you?"

Shawna stopped and looked back at Mimi. "What?"

Mimi kept her gaze focused on the court. "Don't you think he knows it's a bigger court?"

Looking from Mimi to H. L., Shawna struggled to understand. "Then, what's he doing?" Mimi knew more about her grandson than Shawna ever would. "And where did he get so many tennis balls?"

"He asked me to get the balls for him. But he didn't explain. Maybe you should just watch him awhile."

Curious, Shawna pulled the nearest rattan chair closer to the edge of the balcony, and sank onto the striped cushion. Mimi claimed another chair. For once, Shawna felt a companionable silence between them, with only the distant *whack* of H. L.'s racket on the ball for background noise.

Shawna studied H. L., watched him shake his head as another ball fell short of the net. A chattering squirrel jumped from a nearby oak tree and ran along the railing, then disappeared below the ledge they sat on. Hunter Lynn picked up the mesh bag and retrieved the balls scattered around his half of the court.

Surely, he would quit now, and Shawna could tell him that he could move closer to the net next time. But instead, he returned to the baseline and continued to hit balls. Little by little, he managed to hit them closer to the net. One ball went into the net, and Shawna could see the boy talking to himself. He took the last ball from the bag, bounced on his toes, and held his serve position. He lifted his shoulders and let them fall, taking a deep breath, Shawna guessed.

His swing looked perfect and the ball sailed over the net to drop on the other side. "Yeah!" H. L. yelled, raising his arms in victory.

Shawna and Mimi applauded and cheered, and H. L. turned to look up at them. He gave them a half-wave, then gathered the tennis balls. Slinging the bag over his shoulder, he headed for the house, red-faced and looking exhausted.

Mimi nodded her head in approval. "That boy's got determination. Like his father."

"You think he would have kept trying, if that one hadn't made it over?"

"What do you think?"

Shawna pressed her lips together. "Yep, I think he would have. He just wanted to prove he could get one over. I guess this means he plans to enter the junior tournament next month."

Mimi pushed on the arms of the chair and lifted her body to a standing position. "You could take a lesson from him."

"Me?" Shawna stared up at her.

Mimi nodded. "I'm not talking about tennis. I'm talking about not giving up."

Shawna stiffened. Mimi knew about her intention to leave Hunter. Why would Hunter have confided in her, when they had agreed to keep her decision a secret until after the election?

"Hunter hasn't said anything." Mimi could read her mind. "But it's pretty obvious that you've given up on your marriage. You may still be living here, but you might as well be living in Timbuktu. At least as far as you and Hunter are concerned."

"Really. What do you know about it?" Shawna rose suddenly, towering over Mimi. "It's not easy being married to someone who is never home. When he is here, he's concerned only with his campaign." The realization of what she had said hit her, and she clamped her jaw shut. Her marriage was none of Mimi's business. She strode through the open French doors into the bedroom.

But the balcony had no other exit. Mimi would have to pass through here, too. Shawna glanced back at the opening before retreating to the bathroom and turning on the sink faucet. Even over the water running, she heard Mimi close and latch the balcony doors, then close the bedroom door. Still, Shawna waited a few minutes before coming out.

So much for a little quiet time before dinner. But, watching Hunter Lynn's intensity while he practiced had warmed her heart. She had introduced him to the sport she loved, and he seemed to be taking it seriously. He'd been out there practicing, not because she insisted, but because he wanted to get better.

She returned to her place on the loveseat and picked up her Bible. Finding Psalm Ninety again, she resumed her reading.

We are brought to an end by your anger; by your wrath we are dismayed.

You have set our iniquities before you, our secret sins

in the light of your presence.

But she couldn't concentrate on the words. She had let her disappointment with Hunter fester, and she had taken out her anger on Mimi. The woman could be infuriating, but she wanted only the best for Hunter and the boys. Shawna shouldn't blame her for that.

The bedroom door opened, startling her out of her musings. Hunter entered, looking like a lost puppy. He had already loosened his tie; now he yanked it off and threw it on the bed.

Even knowing he didn't love her, Shawna longed to reach out to him. "Tough day?"

"You could say that." He sat on the bed and took off his shoes, remaining there with his head down and shoulders drooping.

Shawna closed her Bible and laid it aside. "Anything I can do?"

"Not a thing."

Shawna rose and crossed the room to stand in front of him. "Hunter."

He looked up at her, and she saw in his green eyes a depth of despair that mirrored her own. "Nothing's going well. Not the legislation, not the campaign. Not … this." He waved his hand, indicating the room and, she knew, their relationship. "I feel like I'm failing at everything, like I'm drowning and can't get any air."

She stepped in closer and caressed his hair, pressed his head against her stomach. "Hunter," she whispered. "I do care about you. I'm still here." She felt his body tremble. She had never seen him like this. "We're friends, no matter what. When you hurt, I hurt."

Hunter placed his arms around her legs and held on, as if grabbing a lifesaving float. He muttered something, but his lips were pressed against her body and the words were lost in her clothing.

"What? I can't understand you." Shawna could hardly breathe; his embrace pressed new hope into her heart.

He pulled away and tilted his head to focus on her. The light in his eyes showed, not despair, but desire. "I don't want to lose you. You make my life complete."

Her brain flashed warning signals—this was not new territory for them—but she ignored them. She bent over and touched her lips to his. The electricity between them overrode the alarms. "I don't want to leave you, Hunter."

He pulled her closer. "Then don't. Please."

For the first time in weeks, Shawna knew the joy of loving and being loved—if only for a few moments.

Marie Wells Coutu

Chapter 29

Nate finally called the woman who had left the message on Deb's voice mail. She insisted on meeting in a public place. Even though she claimed to want to help the Hummel for Governor campaign, she told Nate she needed money. At least a hundred dollars, she said.

"If my information helps Hummel get elected, it'll be worth a lot more than that," she said. A baseball game blared in the background. He'd probably caught her in a bar when he called the number he got from Deb's cell phone. "In fact, I bet it's worth more to Governor Wilson's people right now. So, if you're not interested …"

"Depends on what information you have." People often overestimated the significance of some tidbit they provided, especially when the information was vague or couldn't be proved.

"That's not good enough." Her hoarse voice broke,

and she coughed, a cough that vibrated over the phone line. "If I'm gonna meet you, I wanna be paid for my time."

Nate shook his head, but remembered she couldn't see him. "Why should I believe you have any information? Who are you? What's your name?"

"Call me Bonnie. I used to work for Shawna Wilson's OB/GYN."

She had his attention. "Okay. How about I give you fifty for meeting with me? I'll give you another fifty if your info is good."

"It's good. Meet me on the east steps of the Parthenon at ten tomorrow morning. Bring your money." She ended the call.

Nate scratched his bristly whiskers. What was the woman's game? If she worked in health care, she would know the laws. Revealing private information would be a federal crime.

The next morning, he put on his favorite plaid flannel shirt and unplugged his phone. Scrolling through the icons, he made sure it was ready to record. Pax sat, his ears perked, waiting for Nate to signal his intentions. "Come on, boy. Let's go for a ride." The dog waved his flag-like tail while Nate attached the leash.

Arriving at Centennial Park a half-hour early, Nate pulled into a parking space next to the Parthenon. A replica of a Greek temple, now an art museum, seemed like an odd place for this meeting. But then, the whole scenario reminded him of the Deep Throat meetings in that old movie about the Watergate scandal. He led Pax up the oversized steps, where Nate perched in the shade of one of the columns. Pax settled down beside him and rested his head on his paws. A school bus pulled up and unloaded a group of high school kids, girls chattering and boys racing up the steps to the entrance.

At 9:55 a.m., a woman wearing stained blue scrubs edged along the portico from the far corner of the building. She stopped several feet away from Nate and stared at her worn sneakers. Dark hair fell over her splotchy face, bare of makeup. "You Nate?"

He stood, and so did Pax. "I am. Bonnie?"

"Yeah. That dog bite?"

"No. He's friendly."

She put her hand to her mouth and chewed a fingernail. "Got the money?"

Nate held out five ten-dollar bills. He hoped this didn't look like a drug buy.

She closed the distance between them and snatched the money. It disappeared into a pocket in her pants. How much had this story cost him already?

"You said you worked for Mrs. Wilson's doctor. What do you do?"

Bonnie—if that was her real name—acted like she might run off at any minute. She shuffled her feet. "I used to work in medical coding at Woodmont Clinic."

"Used to?"

"Yeah. I-I lost my job. Showed up high one time too

many." She stuck one hand in the pocket of her loose top and pulled out a single cigarette. "You got a light?"

Nate shook his head. "Sorry. I don't smoke. How long did you work there?"

Bonnie's eyes flickered, searching the area around them, but no one was nearby. She gritted her teeth and stuffed the cigarette back into her pocket. "Two years. Till four months ago."

"So, you were working there when Mrs. Wilson delivered the baby."

For the first time, Bonnie's face relaxed. "Yeah. Doctor Choe put her picture on the bulletin board. So sad when she died."

Pax rubbed against Nate's leg, and Nate bent to pat his head. "Can we walk?" he asked.

Bonnie shrugged, and Nate led the way across the broad ledge. "What have you got that will help Deborah Hummel?"

The woman shuffled beside him, her head down, her voice low and muffled. "Nobody can know it was me that told you. I already lost my job, but I don't wanna go to jail, too."

"You can trust me. I protect my sources."

"Guess I don't have a choice." She stopped beside one of the columns, dwarfed by its massive size. She stared out across the expanse of grass that was turning brown in anticipation of winter's approach. "I remember the day Mrs. Wilson first came to see Doctor Choe. It was my birthday. I was supposed to have the day off, but one of the receptionists got sick and asked me to cover for her."

"When's your birthday?"

"September 28. I thought it was odd. On the news, it said they just got back from their honeymoon, and she came in for a pregnancy test."

Nate felt his breath leave him. "They married on September 19. And you're sure you've got your dates right?"

She stopped, hands on hips. "I ain't stoned. It was my birthday. You don't believe me, I got nothing more to say."

He turned to face her. "I have to make sure the facts are straight, that's all. Do you know the results of the test?"

Her mouth twisted in a look of disgust. "If I didn't, I wouldn't of called. I coded it for insurance."

"And?"

"She was already twelve weeks pregnant. Dr. Choe set her due date as April 15. As she was leaving, I overheard him joking with her about it being Tax Day."

The Wilson baby had been born April 12, so she hadn't been premature at all. Since Shawna's first husband had been overseas for eighteen months, the baby was either Governor Wilson's ...or someone else's. But Daniel Moore was definitely not the father, and Shawna was pregnant when she married the governor. Did Wilson know, or was it Shawna's secret alone?

"Is there any way you can prove all this?"

Bonnie choked out a laugh. "Me? Not hardly. That's

your job. Do I get the rest of the money or not?"

No solid proof, and no way to get it, unless Shawna would admit the truth. And why would she? But Bonnie stood in front of him, her hand out, a desperate look on her face. The information was good, even without real evidence. "Okay, here." He handed her the remaining ten dollar bills.

She counted them, then stuck them in the pocket with the cigarette. She turned and leaped down the steps.

Nate watched her cross the grass, heading deeper into the park. Headed for her dealer, probably, and leaving him with the challenge of proving what he now knew to be the truth. In spite of Bonnie's drug habit, he believed her. She had confirmed what he had suspected since last fall.

But what difference did it really make?

Chapter 30

Hunter had already called for his car at the end of the day Thursday when Johnnie appeared at his open door. "Governor, we need to talk."

He had no campaign appearances this evening, but he looked forward to spending time with Shawna. Still, he motioned Johnnie in.

She sat in one of the guest chairs in front of his desk. "You're trending on Twitter, sir."

"Normally that would be a good thing, but …?"

"But not when it's negative. Questions and innuendos about your marriage are all over social media, sir. Here are a few examples." She handed him a printed list of tweets.

"*#GovWilson's a marriage of convenience? What were u hiding?*"

"*More to #TNgov's whirlwind romance than meets the eye?*"

"Was #TN1stLady torn between 2 lovers? Timeline doesn't add up."

"What else is #GovWilson hiding? Tell the #truth now."

"#GovWilson not All-American boy after all? Maybe Shawna not his 1st conquest."

His blood boiled. Thank goodness, his boys and their friends were still too young to be using social media. These comments were vicious and hurtful. And too close to the truth, except for the last one.

He looked at Johnnie. "Somebody's behind this. Is it Hummel?"

"Probably. But we can't prove it. If we can trace it back to her campaign, we'll have some leverage we can use against her."

Hunter nodded. "Good. Let me know when you find out." He handed the paper back to her.

"Until then, governor, we can't keep ignoring the issue. Shall I draft a statement declaring the rumors totally unfounded?"

"No. Find out what they can prove and what they only think they know. And we need to know where they're getting their information."

"Of course. But what about a response?"

"No response. Maybe Shawna and I should cancel our public appearances for a few days. Give it time to blow over."

"With all due respect, sir, this is the worst possible

time to do that. The election is only four weeks away, and canceling your appearances will look like you have something to hide."

"We do! I don't want my boys exposed to this, and it will certainly ruin my chances in the election. Maybe for any elected office ever."

Johnnie didn't argue. "Yes, sir. We'll do what we can for damage control, but without a statement from you ..." She rose to leave.

He held up his hand. "I understand. Do what you can behind the scenes. And cancel my appearances for this weekend. Tell them I'm sick or something." He felt sick to his stomach, so that would be the truth. "On second thought, tell them our family needs a vacation. Have Rosemary make reservations for this weekend in Gatlinburg. I will be unavailable, unless there's a true emergency."

When he arrived home, he sought out Shawna and found her in the master bedroom. He went to her, grateful their relationship seemed back on track at last.

"Hummel's going after my character." He sat on the bed next to her. "She's hiding behind social media, and putting out innuendos about us. If you have any events scheduled in the next few days, cancel them. We're taking the boys and going to the mountains for the weekend."

He hugged her. "It's not only because of the campaign, but because of us. It'll be a good time, just the four of us."

She pulled back and looked at him, curiosity wrinkling

her forehead. "What about Mimi?"

He leaned toward her, unable to resist smirking. "I think Mimi will enjoy the time off." Her lips opened in a surprised smile, inviting him to come closer, to brush his lips against her soft mouth. He did not resist. She returned his kiss, raising his hopes for a memorable weekend in the mountains.

Hunter took a deep breath of the crisp fall air. Leaves crunched under their feet as the family hiked up the trail to Rainbow Falls.

A weekend break from campaigning seemed to be the medicine he needed. And hearing Cooper and Hunter Lynn laughing restored his soul. He held out his hand to Shawna, who, without saying a word, had taken the side of the trail closest to the falling-off edge.

She placed her hand in his, and he rubbed the sharp edges of her engagement ring with his thumb. Being here in the Smoky Mountains together brought back the memories of their brief courtship. And they would make more good memories today.

The boys ran ahead, Cooper eager to see what was around the next bend or in the valley below them. Hunter Lynn stayed away from the edge, hesitant like his father.

"Cooper, not too close." Hunter's warning had little

effect. Most of the trail had no guard rails, and Cooper would spot something interesting down below and edge his way down the slope to inspect it. Every time his head disappeared below the ridge, Hunter's heart leaped into his throat. But a minute later, Coop would pop up again, crawl back onto the trail, and run to show them his latest treasure.

"Look at this rock, Shawna. It's sort of ugly, but it's cool. I thought you might like it."

Shawna took the walnut-sized rock and showed it to Hunter. Mostly white with brown streaks running through it, the odd protrusions on the stone resembled an old woman's face. "Thank you, Cooper. It's very unusual. Can I keep it?"

Cooper nodded, and Shawna tucked it into the back pocket of her jeans. Cooper finally seemed to be accepting Shawna as part of the family, even finding things to make her happy. Unfortunately, Hunter Lynn still held her at arm's length, carrying his resentment around like a bag of stones.

Hunter pulled Shawna close and, staring into the distance, put his arm around her shoulders. The trees hadn't given up their last shreds of yellow and rust-colored clothing, as if the leaves could keep them warm through the coming winter. "We should have done this weeks ago."

She tipped her head close to his. "I'm glad we're doing it now. It's a beautiful day."

When they reached Rainbow Falls, they found an almost-flat spot beside the trail. Hunter removed his backpack and unpacked a small blanket and the lunch they had picked up at the grocery store in town. Shawna spread the blanket on the ground and passed sandwiches to each person, including Trent, their shadow for the day.

After eating, the boys scampered off, eager to explore the area around the falls.

"Don't go too near the water." Hunter lay back on the blanket and closed his eyes, letting the sun and the roar of the water lull him to sleep.

"Cooper! Come down!" Shawna's yell woke him from a dreamless nap, and his heart pounded. Trent, who had been sitting on a rock nearby, ran past him. Hunter jumped to his feet and headed in the direction of shouting voices around a slight bend in the trail.

He stopped, and his breath left him. Cooper had crawled onto a tree branch that extended far out above the waterfall. The drop below him had to be a hundred feet or more. The limb, barely as big around as Cooper's leg, sagged as if it might break. Cooper had his arms and legs wrapped around the branch. His face looked as white as the foam where the water rushed over the rocks.

Hunter Lynn stood at the base of the tree, one arm wrapped around the stubby trunk. The tree's angled shape created a tempting ramp for an adventurous boy who liked to climb, and smaller branches provided footholds every few feet. Shawna stood next to Hunter Lynn, gesturing to Cooper. She spoke calmly now. "It's okay, Cooper. You can crawl down the same way you crawled up. You can do it."

Trent stopped beside her and put his hand on Hunter Lynn's shoulder. He spoke quietly. "What happened?"

Hunter Lynn shrugged. "He said he wanted to get a better look at the falls. I told him he'd get in trouble."

"I came looking for them and found him out there." Shawna turned to Hunter as he stepped up behind them. "Apparently, he got that far, then got scared and froze. He won't move, and that branch doesn't look too sturdy."

No, it didn't. Hunter peeked at the pool at the bottom of the falls. Shallow. Sprinkled with boulders of various sizes. The chance of survival if his son fell seemed minuscule. They had to persuade Cooper to back his way down.

Keeping Trent between him and the edge of the bank, Hunter called out. "Cooper, Dad's here. You're fine. Just scoot along the branch and work your way back to us."

Crying, Cooper shook his head vigorously. "I-I can't. The branch moves. I'm afraid to let go."

Trent turned and faced Hunter. "I'll go out and bring him in, sir."

Shawna joined them. "Shouldn't we try to get a rope, in case …" She swallowed but didn't finish the sentence.

"I'm not sure there's time. The boy's going to get tired, and his arms will give out. We need to get him down soon." Trent began to remove his belt. "Maybe I can get him to grab hold of this as he works his way off the limb."

Hunter's stomach swirled and his head pounded.

285

Cooper didn't know any of the security detail very well. To him, they were simply men who hung around and didn't say much. "No. I have to go."

H. L. let go of the tree trunk and grabbed him around the legs. "No, Dad. Don't go out there."

Trent looked shocked. "Sir, I don't think that's a good idea. I'm responsible for your safety, and—"

"Shawna, you're my witness. I'm ordering Trent to stay here, and he is not responsible for anything that happens. Got it?"

Shawna touched his shoulder. "Are you sure?"

He nodded. As much as he dreaded going out on that limb, chancing Cooper falling onto the rocks below was unthinkable. "Cooper trusts me. I can talk him into coming to me. I'm not sure anyone else could persuade him." He hoped he didn't freeze up when he got out on that branch like Cooper had. He bent down to hug Hunter Lynn. "It will be all right, son. I have to get Cooper down. I'd do the same for you if I had to."

Not sure how it would help, he took Trent's belt and looped it around his neck. He wished for Indiana Jones's fearlessness as he tested his footing on the rugged tree trunk and shimmied up to the first branch. The limb bent with his weight. He paused there, summoning his courage. One look at Cooper and he forgot about the turmoil in his stomach. He had to save his son.

"Hang on, Coop. I'm coming for you." Hunter pulled himself up to the next branch. From there, he could grab hold of the branch Cooper was on. He prayed it would support his additional weight.

As he maneuvered his body onto the base of the smaller bough, his movement caused the entire limb to shudder. "Dad!" Cooper screamed.

"Hold on, buddy. Hold on tight!"

Hunter wrapped his arms around the branch until the shaking settled to a slight vibration, then he began to edge further out toward his son, talking to him softly as he moved. Concentrating on Cooper helped to take his mind off the chasm below. He tried to keep his eyes focused on the branch as he wriggled his way along. The limb bent more, creaking from the weight, until Cooper's head was lower than his feet. Cooper whimpered, and Hunter's pulse drowned out the roar of the waterfall. He still had a yard to go before he would even be able to touch his son's shoes. He had to work out a way to use the belt.

"Listen to me now, son. I don't think the branch will support us both. I need you to close your eyes and take three slow, deep breaths." He waited, watching to see if his son did as he asked. He couldn't see his face from here, but he saw the little chest expand and shrink three times. "Ready?"

Cooper moved his head slightly in a nod.

"Okay. Now, loosen your right arm and scoot your body back toward me a little ways. Cooper waited, then his feet inched toward Hunter. "Good. Bring your left arm down and do it again. Slowly. There's no hurry."

Gradually, the boy moved backward along the tree limb until his feet were right in front of Hunter's head. "All right. I'm right here. Now we're going the rest of the way together."

"I'm sorry, Dad." Hunter could barely hear the whisper above the throbbing in his ears.

"Don't worry about that right now. We can do this." He hoped his own doubts didn't reveal themselves in his voice. Holding onto the limb with one arm, he removed the belt from around his neck. He pushed the belt all the way through the buckle until it made a small noose at one end. "I've got a belt here, and I'm going to swing it. I want you to catch it as it swings by your head."

On the third rotation, Cooper caught the buckle end of the belt. "Good job. Now put your hand through that loop and pull it as tight around your wrist as you can."

Hunter kept his arm fully extended, holding onto the other end. Cooper did as he was told. "Got it, Dad."

"I've got the other end, so you're safe now. We just have to back on down the tree the way we came." The belt provided no real safety, but he prayed it would give Cooper back the confidence he'd lost when he panicked. Hunter wrapped his end around his fist two times. Good thing Cooper wasn't taller. "The belt's not very long, so we have to move together. Ready, buddy?"

"I think so."

"Good. We can do this. Right side first." Without looking down, Hunter slithered his foot backward, tugging gently with his right hand. He felt Cooper moving in sync with him. The air stilled, the birds ceased to chirp. Even the water flowing over the falls seemed to stop in mid-air. He focused on only one small movement at a time. After what seemed hours, he felt hands on his own belt.

Trent helped him out of the tree, while Shawna grabbed Cooper and pulled him away from the ravine. Hunter's legs quivered and he collapsed onto the ground. Cooper turned and dropped into his arms. "Thanks, Dad. You rescued me."

Hunter's heart rate might take hours to return to normal, but he squeezed the boy until he giggled. "You rescued yourself, buddy. All I did was help you believe you could."

"I'm proud of you both." Shawna reached a hand out to Hunter Lynn. "And we're grateful you're both okay, aren't we, H. L.?"

His older son took her hand. "Yeah. That was pretty scary."

Hunter laughed. "I agree. Let's not have any more adventures like that for a really long time. You have got to listen to what Shawna tells you, so you don't get into that sort of fix."

"I will. I promise." Cooper put his arms around Hunter's neck. "She's a good mom, and you're a great dad."

Hunter looked up at Shawna. Her hand covered her mouth and her eyes shone with unshed tears. The entire adventure had been terrifying, but Cooper had turned it into a memorable moment by referring to her as "mom."

Chapter 31

"Well, that's almost as good news as the poll numbers I got this morning. Thank you, Nate."

Nate pulled the phone from his ear and stared at it. He had told Deb about his conversation with Bonnie. But he didn't agree about it being good news. "It's not exactly proof, Deb. It's only one person's word."

"Yes, yes. I know that. But it's enough to raise doubts. The suspicions have already been voiced by a few people. This just confirms it."

"I won't run a story based on hearsay." He tossed an old tennis ball across the living room, and Pax grabbed it in his mouth.

"Of course not. But some things don't require proof."

He didn't like the mischievous tone of her voice. "What are you saying?"

"Nothing for you to worry about, Nate. When you get

your proof, you can still run your story." As he reached for the drool-covered ball Pax brought back to him, he could hear the sound of typing over the phone. "You'll only be confirming what the Twitter-verse already knows by then."

She was planning to use social media to spread more rumors. "That's not a good idea. It can be traced back to you, and that could backfire."

Her musical laugh rang of desperation. "Nathaniel, I've got people to do this for me. No traces. This is too important not to let voters know."

Too important for her campaign, maybe. Otherwise, he was beginning to think the entire affair had little or no bearing on the election. Pax sat at his feet, wagging his tail. Nate threw the ball again. "Are you sure you're not letting this election cloud your judgment, Deb?"

"Are you letting your friendship with Shawna cloud yours, Nate?"

He chose not to answer. "I've gotta go. But I'm asking you to hold off on using this information."

"You will continue digging for proof, right?"

He sighed. "I will. But putting anything out now will make it more difficult to get to the truth."

"Do what you can, and I'll do what I have to. That's the way it works, Nate." She clicked off.

Nate tossed the phone on his desk, and reached for Pax. He rubbed the dog's back with both hands, wishing he had never started working on this story. If only Shawna and Hunter hadn't created the situation in the first place. Then he wouldn't be caught in the middle, having to choose which of his friends he would betray.

"Something's wrong with Mimi."

Hunter Lynn met Shawna at the bottom of the stairs when she returned from a Fit Kids meeting downtown. His wide eyes pleaded for help, and Shawna's pulse kicked into high gear.

She forced herself to stay calm. "Tell me what happened, H. L."

"We got home from school and couldn't find her. She was upstairs in bed, which she never is. She looks awful. And she's been upchucking. Ick."

More words than Hunter Lynn normally used in a week. But this was no time to think about that. Shawna didn't know much about medicine, but she did remember that nausea could be a symptom of either a heart attack or a stroke. But it also could be something simpler, like food poisoning or the flu. "Is she still in her room?"

"Yeah. Coop stayed with her."

Shawna ran up the stairs, with H. L. close behind her.

When she reached the suite on the third floor, the sound of retching came from the bathroom. Mimi, wearing a flowered cotton nightgown, was on her knees on the tile floor. She flushed the toilet and attempted to stand.

"Oh, my goodness!" Shawna rushed to her side and helped her up. "Can you walk?"

"Just help me back to bed." Instead of her typical commands, this soft statement was more of a plea.

Shawna put her arm around the shorter woman and walked with her into the bedroom, where Cooper sat slumped on a chair by the bed. Hunter Lynn stood in the doorway, as if he couldn't decide whether to come in or run away.

After helping Mimi lie down, Shawna touched the woman's forehead. No fever. "When did this start? How bad is it?"

"About one o'clock. I lost my lunch. Drank a little water, but couldn't even keep that down." She dropped her head onto the pillow and groaned.

"I brought her some crackers a while ago." Cooper pointed to the bedside table, where a small plate with half a dozen saltines sat next to a glass of water. "She ate a couple, but ..." He shook his head and wrinkled his nose.

Mimi smiled. "You're a good helper, buddy."

Shawna tried to think what to ask. "Mimi, do you have any pain?"

"My stomach hurts."

"Do you want me to call the doctor?"

Her head moved back and forth once. "No. It's either the flu or something I ate. I'll be fine in a day or two." She tugged the blanket up to her neck and closed her eyes.

Standing by the bed, Shawna said a quick prayer that

they were doing the right thing by waiting. "Come on, boys, we'll let Mimi rest awhile."

Shawna eased the bedroom door shut. How strange it felt to pray for Mimi. They hadn't exactly become like mother and daughter, or even friends. Mostly they tolerated each other. But she couldn't imagine this family without Mimi's steadfast presence and quiet faith. If ever there was a reason to start to pray again, it would be for Mimi.

She shooed the boys to their room to do homework. "If you need help, I'll be in the office. Don't bother Mimi, okay?"

Subdued, both boys nodded and slouched into their room.

At her desk, Shawna booted up the computer and searched for information on vomiting. She read through the warning signs that would warrant emergency attention, such as chest pain, confusion, fever, or clammy skin. Thankfully, Mimi had none of them. She would ask Jean-Claude to make gelatin for later, after Mimi's stomach settled.

"Shawna?" Cooper peeked through the door she had left ajar. "Can you help me with my spelling?"

She thought her smile would reach her toes. Finally, one of the boys had asked for her help with homework. "Of course I will, Coop. Come here."

He ran to her and held out a sheet of paper. "The test is tomorrow."

"All right, let's see how well you do." She spent the

next fifteen minutes reading the words to him and listening to him spell them as he shifted from foot to foot and hopped around her chair. He mixed up the "i" and "e" in "their," but who didn't in first grade? After he spelled it correctly three times in a row, she handed the paper back to him. "I think you've got it, mister."

Suddenly still, he took the spelling list. "Is Mimi gonna be all right?"

From her chair, she reached for him and pulled him into an embrace. "You're worried about her?"

His head, resting on her shoulder, moved up and down.

"You've had a stomach bug before, right?"

Another nod.

"I'm pretty sure that's all it is. She should be back to normal in a couple of days."

"But what if she's not?"

Shawna's stomach twisted. She put her arms on his shoulders and moved him so she could look him in the eye. "Tell you what. Let's pray for her tonight. If she's no better in the morning, we'll call the doctor. Sound good?"

Cooper pursed his lips. "Okay." He squeezed his eyes shut for a minute. When he finished his prayer, he nodded, gave her a quick hug, then ran out of the office.

If only she had that kind of simple faith in the power of prayer. Instead, it seemed like a barrier kept her prayers from reaching God. But maybe this time would be different.

An hour later, Shawna checked on Mimi and found her

still asleep. But when she returned after supper, Mimi was sitting up in bed and munching on a cracker.

"You're awake," Shawna said. "Good! How do you feel?"

"Better." Mimi held up the cracker. "This is my second one. So far, so good."

Shawna dropped into the wingback chair by the bed where Cooper sat earlier. "Can I get you anything else? More water, or some gelatin?"

"Not yet. How are the boys?"

"Worried about you. Would you like them to come up?"

Mimi held up a hand. "Better not, in case this wasn't something I ate. I wouldn't want them to get sick—or you, either. You better leave me to myself."

The next morning, Shawna brought Mimi a tray with gelatin and more crackers. "It's not exactly breakfast food, but until you know you can keep it down, I thought this would be best."

"I didn't expect room service!" Mimi sat up and took the tray. "But I am pretty weak."

Shawna plumped the pillow behind Mimi's back. "You take it easy today. Whatever you need, I'll get for you."

Mimi dug the spoon into the red Jell-O. "Why are you doing this, Shawna? You could have asked Jean-Claude to bring this up."

"Nonsense." Shawna picked up the empty water glass

from the bedside table and headed for the door. "We're all family. Why wouldn't I take care of you? You'd do the same for me." She held up the glass. "I'll be back with more water."

She returned five minutes later with a clean glass and a pitcher of cold water. She filled the glass and set both on the table within Mimi's reach. "Would you like anything else?"

Her mouth full, Mimi didn't answer immediately. Then she put down the spoon and stared into the nearly empty bowl. "I've not treated you like family. I can see you love the boys as much as I do. Well, almost." She looked up and smiled.

"I do, Mimi. They're good boys. You've done a wonderful job helping to raise them."

Mimi motioned for silence. "They'll warm up to you, too. Especially when they see how much Hunter loves you."

Without replying, Shawna reached to take the tray. Mimi must have a fever to talk to her like this. No doubt she'd be back to her usual cranky self in another day or two.

Chapter 32

Nate jiggled his left foot as he sat in the governor's reception area scrolling through the news on his tablet. He looked up when the outer door opened, but a courier entered, not the governor or one of his chief aides.

He had been sitting there, hoping for a few minutes with someone who would comment on the premarital relationship between Shawna and the governor. The receptionist said she expected Mark Newton, the governor's communications director, to arrive soon. He checked the time in the bottom corner of the screen. He'd give it five more minutes. If Mark didn't show up by then, Nate would change tactics.

The courier left, and the telephone on the receptionist's desk rang. Nate tried to ignore the conversation, but he heard his name mentioned. The receptionist hung up and smiled at him.

"Mr. Matthews, Mark is on his way here. He should be here in less than ten minutes, if you can wait. He said he could give you a few minutes."

"I'll wait." What was ten more minutes, after waiting an hour?

When Newton breezed through the door, Nate put down his tablet and stood to greet him. The man saw him and crossed to him right away. "Nate, sorry you had to wait so long. I didn't know you were coming by today."

"Kind of a spur-of-the-moment thing. I'm hoping to get a comment from the governor on something I'm working on."

Newton held up a hand. "Just a minute, okay?" He turned to the receptionist. "Amy, did I miss anything else?"

He got a negative answer, then gave his attention to Nate. "I hope it's the education technology bill you're working on. We could use some positive press on that. It's an important piece of legislation."

Nate shook his head. "Maybe another time." He looked around. The receptionist appeared to be engrossed in her work, but that didn't mean she wasn't listening. "Can we go someplace to talk?"

"Sure. We can walk over to my office." Newton headed for the door and held it open for Nate. They headed across the spacious concourse toward a large room that housed several of the governor's staff. "What are you working on?"

Nate halted, putting a hand out to stop Newton. He

wanted more privacy than the warren of cubicles that included Newton's office would provide. This hallway was open but nearly vacant. He kept his voice low. "I've got a source who says Mrs. Wilson was already pregnant when she married Governor Wilson. I'd like to know how the governor responds to that."

Newton laughed. "Seriously? You don't have anything more newsworthy than that? This isn't the fifties." He started to walk away. "Call me when you're working on a real story."

"The thing is, Mark, it calls into question the governor's integrity and morality." Nate's response got Newton's attention. "In the middle of his reelection campaign, the voters are likely to care. Especially since Mrs. Wilson's first husband was serving in Afghanistan at the time."

Newton squinted his eyes. "If you're implying what it sounds like you're implying, I don't think the accusation deserves a response. It sounds like a smear campaign."

Nate held up his tablet. "Like I said, I have a good source. And I'll be talking to other people who may be able to confirm it. But I'd like to get the governor's response. I'll give you some time to check with him; give me a call if he wants to comment."

"Sure, I'll do that."

Nate shuffled toward the broad staircase and started down, confident Newton would not be calling him anytime soon.

Hunter couldn't seem to escape reminders about the rumors spreading all over social media. He expected backlash if the truth ever came out, but he hadn't expected so many people to be upset without even knowing the facts.

Of course, Hummel was to blame. Her campaign people had to be stirring up the rumors and keeping the discussion going. She was the only one who could benefit from turning suspicions into scandal.

"Your poll numbers dropped ten points overnight," Johnnie had reported this morning. "We need to respond."

"Respond how? By admitting the truth? How do you think that will play in Pulaski?"

She squirmed. "I understand your concern, Governor, but really, ignoring it won't make the problem go away."

"Look, I love Shawna. I married her because I love her, not because I got her pregnant. But people won't understand that."

"No, I don't suppose they will." Johnnie crossed her legs and leaned toward him. "You need to stay on your toes, sir. Be ready to play offense or defense. We could put out a statement denying everything, accusing Hummel of mudslinging. Or have Mrs. Wilson make a statement."

"I won't put her through that. That's all there is to it."

But that wasn't the end of it. Now, here was Newton

sitting in the same chair in his office, telling him much the same thing. He held a sheaf of print-outs of messages copied from Facebook, Twitter, and Instagram. More people were asking such questions as "When will the governor start telling the truth?" and "Did Shawna cheat on her soldier husband?"

It was beginning to feel like reading the tabloids in the grocery store checkout line.

Newton cleared his throat. "Governor, Nate Matthews says he's got a source who confirms Mrs. Wilson's actual due date. Matthews is looking for a comment from you."

Hunter wanted to spit. What facts could Matthews have? Medical records were private, and that was the only thing that would prove when Shawna's pregnancy was confirmed. Who else would have known?

Shawna herself. She and Matthews were friends. They had played tennis together recently. And Shawna had wanted him to drop out of the campaign. But would she ruin her own reputation so that she could hurt his chances of reelection?

The thought that she might have confessed to her reporter friend made his head hurt. He wanted to change the subject. "Give me some good news, Mark. Where are we with the cancer research facility incentive package?"

"I think we've about got that wrapped up, sir. House and Senate leadership have both given their nod of approval, so I think we can safely say it will pass next session."

Hunter stood, walked to the window, and admired the golf-course lushness of the capitol lawn. He watched one of the groundskeepers scouring the grass for pieces of litter. Hunter turned back to Newton. "Should we call a special session this fall, in case the election causes a lot of turnover in the legislature?"

"Something to consider." Mark tapped his pen against the yellow legal pad he held. "Right now, I'd say the project has bipartisan support, so we should be okay, but I'll keep my ear to the ground, see what others think."

"Good. Anything else urgent? If not, I'm going to take a walk." He nodded to the window.

Mark checked his pad. "No, sir. Nothing else we need to deal with today."

Ten minutes later, Hunter strolled across the grass toward the worker he had seen. The man wore a yellow safety vest over a denim shirt and jeans. Muscular and tanned, he appeared to be in his thirties or forties. The man stopped when he saw Hunter approach and rested one hand on the bag slung over his shoulder.

"Governor?" The man nodded. "Anything wrong?"

Hunter flicked his hand. "Not at all. I simply wanted to thank you for keeping the grounds looking so good." He offered his hand, and the man took it. "I'm always glad to meet a fellow public servant who takes his job seriously."

The employee shifted his feet, seeming embarrassed. "Thank you, sir. I do try."

"You have a family?"

The man answered with a huge smile. "Yessir, I have four daughters. My wife and I both work two jobs to keep them in clothes. But they're great girls."

"I'm sure they are." Hunter made a mental note to check on what a groundskeeper's salary might be. "Well, they should be proud of you, too. Keep up the good work."

As Hunter headed back to the sidewalk, he noticed a man with a dog cutting across the grass toward him. He glanced back at Curtis, who nodded and moved to intercept the figure.

Then Hunter recognized him. The reporter, Nate Matthews. Just what he needed, to be ambushed when Mark wasn't around. But he couldn't avoid him. "It's all right, Curtis."

Curtis stepped aside and Nate approached. "Governor. Looks like you're enjoying this beautiful weather. Mind if I join you?"

Hunter kept walking. "Depends, Matthews. What's on your mind?"

Nate took the spot beside him as Hunter reached the sidewalk and turned back toward the capitol. The golden retriever sniffed at Hunter's legs, and Nate tugged on the leash to pull the dog into step beside him.

"Not much. I needed to take a break and think. I imagine that's what you're doing, too."

Hunter cast a sideways look at him. "I came out to thank the groundskeeper for his work. You want to talk about my legislative initiatives or my campaign platform, fine. But I'm not answering any questions about my personal life."

Nate grunted. "I didn't expect you to. I'm waiting for Mark to give me that statement I asked for."

They walked in silence until they reached the base of the capitol building. Hunter started up the steps, then turned back to pet the dog. "Nice dog, Matthews. He doesn't ask questions."

Nate shrugged. "I do have a non-personal and non-political question to ask you, Governor."

Non-personal and non-political. Odd for a reporter to ask him that sort of question. He nodded. "Go ahead. But I don't promise to give you an answer."

Looking at Hunter intently, Nate stroked his scraggly whiskers. "There's this guy I know. He's a well-paid state employee, but it seems he got over his head with gambling debts."

Hunter glanced at Curtis, who waited nearby, and shrugged. "So?"

"His habit got out of hand. His wife didn't know he had mortgaged their house, and now he owes so much, he can't pay. He's being foreclosed on."

"I'm sorry to hear that, but what's your question? Did he embezzle any state money?" Hunter looked at his watch, hoping Matthews would take the hint and hurry this up.

"No, sir, but he has three children, and the whole family will be homeless. He's too embarrassed to tell them. I wondered what you would recommend he do."

Hunter brushed his hand through the air. "Well, the man has to start by telling his wife." He climbed two steps, then stopped. "And he needs to get help for his gambling addiction before things get any worse. I believe state benefits will pay for counseling."

"I'll pass that on to him. The man is really embarrassed about the situation."

As the reporter and his dog turned and strolled back the way they had come, Hunter continued into the capitol. Matthews had not accomplished anything by telling him about that man. The answer to the problem was too obvious. Did he think the governor could stop a foreclosure?

Hunter shook his head. Investigative reporter or not, the story seemed pointless, maybe even fabricated. If the story was true, the man's secrecy had gotten him into a drastic situation. Honesty wouldn't get him out, but it would go a long way to restore his family's trust.

Was that Matthews' point? Was he implying that Hunter and Shawna needed to confess their secret? If they did so, the consequences could be devastating.

Chapter 33

"Were you playing tennis with Matthews again?"

Hunter's question stopped Shawna as she passed the dining room. She turned and saw him sitting alone at the table, a pot of coffee and a cup in front of him. What was he doing home before five o'clock?

The tone of his voice made her wary, and she stopped in the doorway. "I was. Is that okay?"

"I don't like you getting so chummy with him."

Shawna crossed to the table and stood opposite him. "Nate's been my friend for years."

Hunter looked at her, his face clouded with doubt. Then a flicker of something else, as if he'd remembered something. "Want some coffee?" he asked.

She shook her head. "I could use some water, though. I'll be right back."

She went through the door into the kitchen. Jean-

Claude, in his white apron and chef's hat, stood at the stove adding spices to a large pot. He was humming something that sounded like a song from *Fiddler on the Roof.*

"Hello, Jean-Claude. How are you today?"

He turned abruptly. "Mrs. Wilson! I am wonderful. And you?"

The aroma of onions and beef led her to guess they would be having stew for dinner. "Fine. Dinner smells delicious."

"*Merci.* It will be. Can I do something for you, *Madame?*"

Shawna loved the way he mixed a little French with his almost perfect English. She walked to the cabinet and took out a glass. "Thanks, but I only came for some water." She filled the glass from the refrigerator dispenser, then turned to him. "Have a good weekend, Jean-Claude."

"*Oui.* And *bonne chance* in your tennis tournament."

She returned to the dining room, sat across from Hunter, and took a drink.

Hunter sighed. "I know you and Nate were friends in college. But you're spending a lot of time with him lately. Are you sure you can trust him?"

Shawna didn't like the implication. "What do you mean?"

"He's been snooping around asking questions about our ... relationship. He told Mark he had a source who could prove when you got pregnant."

Shawna glanced at her hand that held the glass. She set

down the glass to pick at the chipped polish on her thumb. Fragments of hardened gel littered her lap. She was so tired of the knots in her stomach, the worry that someone would discover the truth. When Hannah Lea died, she had thought that would be the end of the suspicions, but social media had kept it alive. And now Nate had discovered—or guessed—the truth. "Maybe it's a bluff."

"Or maybe you decided you would get me out of the race, one way or another."

Shawna's skin felt as cold as Hunter's voice. She didn't want him out of the race. Not anymore, not since she realized how much it meant to him.

"What's that supposed to mean?"

"You wanted me to drop out of the election. Since I won't do that, did you decide to work with Matthews to make sure I lose?"

"You don't trust me? You think I can't keep a secret?"

Hunter drained his coffee cup and glared at her. "Oh, I know you can keep a secret. But I'm not sure if you're keeping our secret—or one of your own."

"Right. I'm going to confess that I cheated on Daniel while he was in Afghanistan getting killed. And have the whole state of Tennessee hate me?"

Hunter rose, throwing his chair off balance in his rush. The chair rocked, but settled on four feet without tipping. "One way or another, you may get what you wanted. You wanted me out of the campaign, and when this comes out, my chances of winning will be less than nil."

Shawna stood, meeting him on equal terms. "No, Hunter. I didn't say anything. I wouldn't. Especially now, so close to the election. I know how important it is to you to finish the job. I don't know where Nate's getting his information, but it's not from me."

Hunter met her stare and held it, his eyes flashing a mixture of hurt and defeat. Then he turned and left the room. She heard the outside door close and wondered where he would go.

Had her friend deceived her? Had Nate been trying to see what information he could pry out of her while they played tennis? She hadn't thought he was that low.

And they were seeded against each other in the Bluegrass Classic on Saturday. She'd have to withdraw.

Or maybe she would hit him over the head with her racket instead.

Dense fog hid the distant houses from view Saturday morning as Hunter ran through the neighboring streets with Curtis.

Curtis seemed preoccupied this morning. Probably thinking about his coursework again.

Fine with Hunter. After the argument with Shawna, he'd gone back to his office at the capitol. Even when he returned home after midnight and crawled into bed, doubts about Shawna had kept him awake. She had spent a lot of time with Nate Matthews lately. Like she said, that didn't mean she had actually provided any information. Maybe the reporter had fooled her, hoping to get his story.

If he couldn't trust his own wife, who could he trust? He should give her the benefit of the doubt. She didn't have as much to lose as he did, but if their secret was exposed, every military family in the state would hate her, even though he was the one to blame. Why did she insist on playing with fire by spending time with Matthews?

A red pickup truck passed them in a hurry and turned into the driveway in front of them, slowing to cross a short wooden bridge over the creek that ran along the road. Hunter and Curtis moved into the middle of the road to go around the vehicle. Headlights from the trail car lit the way for them.

Hunter looked at Curtis, who was frowning. "It's all right, Curtis. That driver was in a hurry, but no harm done."

"No, sir. You're safe." But his eyes remained narrowed, in the look of someone questioning the motives of another.

"Something bothering you this morning?"

Curtis turned his head sharply and skipped a step. "Why do you ask, Governor?"

"You seem like you're in a different world today, that's all."

They ran a few more steps before the trooper answered. "To tell the truth, I'm thinkin' about my mother.

Praying for her, I guess you could say."

Hunter's heart pounded, and he stopped. "Is she sick? Why didn't you say so? You should go see her."

"No, sir." Curtis faced Hunter and motioned for him to continue running. "I saw her last weekend, and we put her in a nursing home."

Reluctantly, Hunter nodded and began to jog again. "How bad is she?"

"Her mind is going." Curtis sidestepped around a fireplug. "She can't live alone anymore, but she's in a safe place now. My brother and three of my sisters all live close by, so they'll take turns visiting her."

As they rounded a curve, the sun pierced through the mist for a split second. Hunter squinted against the sudden brightness, but the fog closed in again. "Glad you've got a big family, huh?"

Curtis nodded. "Yes, I'm grateful for them." A patch of leaves, still wet from last night's rain, littered the street ahead. Curtis reached his hand out for Hunter's arm to steady him. "Watch out, sir. These leaves could be slick."

The odor of decay filled Hunter's nostrils as the two men ran through the debris. "I was in college when my grandmother went in the nursing home. My dad was an only child, and he visited her almost every day. One time when I went with him, he washed her feet."

They reached the school and cut across the grass. A breeze blew across their faces, and wisps of fog began to scatter.

314

"Your dad washed his mother's feet? Did you go to one of those foot-washing churches?"

Hunter chuckled. "Not at all. I told him the staff would do that for her. I've never forgotten his answer. He said she took care of him all her life, and caring for her now was a privilege. He told me any act of service done out of duty is temporary, but when done out of love, it has eternal value."

At the curb, Curtis stopped before crossing the street. "I like that bit about service, Governor. OK if I use that in a sermon?"

"Sure." Hunter grinned. "My dad's probably looking down on us now and smiling to think you'll be quoting him."

When the trail car caught up, they started across the street. Curtis nodded. "And the next time I go home to see my mother, I might wash her feet."

Chapter 34

Despite the balmy October day, Nate thought winter had arrived in middle Tennessee when he shook hands with Shawna before their tennis match began.

Obviously, she had been told about the story he was working on. He knew she would be upset, but he hadn't expected the ice queen to show up today.

Her first serve rocketed toward his head, forcing him to jump aside as it went out-of-bounds. "Love-fifteen," the umpire said. The audience applauded, but Nate wondered if they were cheering the force of her shot rather than his skill.

She wouldn't make that mistake again. He prepared for her next serve, and when it came, he managed to smash it right back to her. Her face contorted as she got into position and slammed the ball back to him. He backstroked the ball across the net, landing it three feet in front of her.

She managed to hit it on the bounce—right into the net.

"Love-thirty." The crowd roared this time.

At this rate, the match would be a blowout. But Shawna would never let that happen. She would settle down after the first game, no doubt.

Nate took the next two points, and the umpire called, "Game over. Matthews."

Shawna managed to score the first two points in the next game, but seemed to lose her focus, and Nate won again.

While on the sidelines wiping his face with a towel, Nate looked across the court at Shawna. Her shoulders were heaving. She sat down and held the white towel over her face. After taking several deep breaths, she dropped the towel and picked up her racket. She did not look his way.

Shawna regained her control, and the score seesawed, with her finally making game point. Nate took the fourth game, and they alternated wins for the next four games. After Nate beat her once more to win the set, he followed Shawna off the court for a short rest.

"Shawna." Out of sight of the audience, he caught her elbow and spun her around to face him. "What is wrong with you today? You're playing like a beginner. Are you mad at me?"

Perspiration dripped from her temples and she dabbed her face with a white towel, avoiding his eyes. "Do I have reason to be mad at you? You're not only trying to ruin my husband's career, you're also going to ruin my marriage?"

She pulled her arm away and continued toward the locker rooms.

Nate's stomach flipped. "What do you mean, ruin your marriage?"

Shawna pivoted and stepped close to him. "That's right. Hunter thinks I'm your source. And I thought we were friends."

He held his hands up in surrender mode. "We are friends."

"Really. Do you betray all your friends, or only the ones where it's politically convenient?"

Nate recoiled, but he knew he had no defense. "I'm sorry, Shawna. It's my job."

"Were you on the job when you started playing tennis with me? Trying to get information from me without raising suspicions? That's how you investigative reporters work, isn't it?"

She stalked away, and Nate let her go this time.

Shawna grabbed a water bottle and sucked it dry, then hurled it into the green recycle container in the locker room.

She would prefer to swallow the towel hanging around her neck than go back on the court to finish the match against Nate. But she would not quit. The entire audience had paid dearly to watch quality tennis. She couldn't—wouldn't—disappoint the fans.

Nor did she want Cooper and Hunter Lynn to think she was a quitter. They were in the stands with Hunter and Mimi, cheering for her. She had to set a good example.

Wiping her face with the towel, she closed her eyes and took a deep breath. She could do this. She had to beat Nate—a beginner compared with her competitive experience—or be humiliated among followers of the sport. Not to mention her family.

She stretched to limber her muscles, then held her head high and strode back to the court. She didn't look Nate's way until they were both back in position and she got ready to receive. This time, she managed to control her anger and play with the skill honed from years of practice. She grunted when the ball landed just out of Nate's reach, and she gloated inwardly when she converted her breaking point to win the game.

She took the set in eight games, allowing Nate only two wins. The taste of victory within reach brought back the thrill of winning a national championship. She'd never been vindictive, but today, the thought of beating this Judas friend gave her an unfamiliar sort of pleasure.

Before starting the next set, Shawna wandered over to the stands where Hunter and the rest of the family sat on the first row. She leaned against the fence. "Hey, there. What do you think?" She aimed the question at Hunter, who had been out running when she left this morning.

"You're gonna beat him, Shawna!" Cooper jumped up and down with his typical exuberance.

Hunter Lynn, as usual, was more reserved and said nothing.

Hunter nodded. "Good match, so far. What was going on with you in that first set?"

"I let my anger at him take over. I should know better, but ..." She shrugged. "Got it under control now."

"Then you should win. He's clearly overmatched, when you're playing your best."

"Now do you believe that I didn't tell him anything?"

"Didn't tell him what?" Cooper leaned over against Hunter. "What's she talking about, Dad?"

Before Hunter could answer, Mimi stood. "Not now, Coop. Shawna's got to get back to the game." She turned to Shawna. "Go show him, Shawna. It's Billie Jean against Bobby all over again."

The two boys turned to Mimi, a quizzical look on both faces. Even Hunter looked confused. As a member of the college team, Shawna had learned about the iconic 1973 match that was billed as the "Battle of the Sexes." But she had no interest in proving which gender played better tennis. Only in defeating the so-called friend who planned to betray her.

She returned to the court with more determination than she'd had in the NCAA national championship match her senior year at Murray State. Unfortunately, that had been more than a decade ago. But she still had several years of experience on Nate. And she wasn't carrying a metal rod in her leg.

It turned out none of that mattered. Somehow, he managed to win the first game of the set. She beat him handily in three of the next four games. But Nate wouldn't give up, and they traded victories for the next seven games. That forced a tiebreak game.

Leading Nate thirty to fifteen, Shawna turned her foot and stumbled. She couldn't recover in time to return Nate's serve, so he won the point. She asked for a timeout and sat down to rub her ankle.

Nate watched her, knitting his eyebrows together. Perhaps he really did care. Still, running the story as he had threatened would hurt Hunter. And it would offend all military spouses.

She shook her head and stood, testing the ankle. She felt a slight twinge but nothing she hadn't endured before. She nodded to the official and took her place on the court.

Crouching into position, she bounced on her toes and got ready. Her ankle rebelled at the pressure, but she could ignore it.

But Nate took advantage of her injury with a drop shot. The sharp pain shooting up her leg slowed her down and she couldn't react in time to reach the ball.

"Forty-thirty," the umpire called.

"Come on, Shawna. You can do it." She heard Cooper's high yell above the smattering of applause from the stands.

She swallowed the lump in her throat along with the pain and forced herself to counter Nate stroke-for-stroke, finally hitting one that he couldn't get to.

"Deuce." The announcer's calm voice contrasted with the throbbing in her leg. She needed to repeat that last rally two more times to win the game, set, and match.

The rhythm of hitting the ball, swinging the racket, switching between forehand and backstroke when necessary, had become second nature to her. When she was "in the zone," all her troubles faded—her mother's death, frustration with her older sisters, anxiety over a chemistry exam, a broken heart. Tennis had been her sanctuary. She had been able to shut out the world.

That's what she needed to do now, but Nate managed to take the next point. "Advantage Matthews." He only needed one more point to win the match.

The fire in her ankle refused to die down to a simmer. She readied for Nate's next serve, knowing this could be her last chance. As she ran forward to swing at the ball, her ankle gave way and she batted the ball into the net. Shawna went down on her hands and knees, and the crowd moaned in unison with her.

"Game, set, match to Matthews." The announcer droned out the scores of the three sets they had played and the crowd applauded, politely, as if they had witnessed a chess match.

Nate rushed to her side. "Are you all right, Shawna?" He knelt beside her. "Do you need a stretcher?"

"No, it's only my ankle. Just help me up." She took the arm he offered and pulled herself up on the good leg. "Congratulations, Nate. You beat me." She couldn't infuse her voice with the fury she had felt early in the match. Perhaps she was in too much pain, or perhaps her anger at him had cooled as the competition heated up.

"Only because you got hurt, Shawna. You should have won that match."

"Well, I didn't. You played better today. Come on, help me over there to pose for photos." She leaned on him and hobbled toward the sidelines where reporters waited. "I guess we both have a bad leg now, don't we?"

After the obligatory pictures for the newspaper, Nate helped Shawna over to the fence where Hunter, the boys, and Mimi waited.

"What can I do, Shawna?" Hunter's voice conveyed concern, all evidence of anger at her gone. "Shall we go to the ER?"

No hospital. "I think it's just a strain. I'll ice it at home, and it should be fine in a couple of days."

The officials let the family through the gate. Hunter stepped between her and Nate and put his arm around her waist. "I've got her, Matthews."

"Of course, Governor." Nate stepped away. "I hope it's not serious, Shawna. Good game."

Shawna watched him stroll off the court, swinging his racket at motes in the air. She hated that her injury had stolen the attention from his victory. He had been the better player today, injury or no injury. If she had played her best game, the injury would not have been a factor.

Cooper edged up to her and hugged her waist. "Sorry you lost, Shawna, but it's okay. You'll win next time." The same words she had directed to him and Hunter Lynn during their junior competition.

She bent over and squeezed his shoulders. "Thanks, buddy. I'm sorry I disappointed you all."

To her surprise, Hunter Lynn spoke up. "You played tough, even after you hurt your foot."

"That's right." Hunter leaned over and kissed her hair. "We're proud of you."

Chapter 35

"Mrs. Wilson, you have visitors." Crystal interrupted Shawna with a knock on her office door. She had been reviewing materials for a Fit Kids Task Force meeting that afternoon. "I told them you were busy but they said they only need a few minutes."

She didn't even want to meet with the task force today, much less strangers. She sighed. "Who is it?"

"Dan and Charisse Moore."

Her breath left her. Daniel's parents, her former in-laws, here? She hadn't seen or heard from them since Daniel's funeral. She probably should have contacted them, at least let them know she was getting married again. For them to come to Nashville and appear at her office with no notice, they must be angry with her. Had they heard the rumors about the pregnancy? She couldn't admit the truth to them, that she had been unfaithful to their son while he was away fighting overseas. Dying for his country and family.

Crystal started to leave. "I'll tell them you don't have time today. Should I ask if they can come back tomorrow?"

"No." She couldn't send Charisse and Dan away. They had been wonderful in-laws, even friends. She would simply lie, deny the rumors were true. "I mean, I'll see them now."

Shawna rose and walked to the window, a twinge in her ankle reminding her of the loss to Nate five days ago. Through the rain beating against the glass, she could see the Greek Revival columns of the state capitol. She stared at the window of Hunter's office. She might get a glimpse of him, but he was probably busy in meetings. She turned when the door behind her opened.

Crystal showed the couple in, then quietly closed the door.

Charisse glanced around the spacious office, her eyes gleaming. She stepped forward and stopped.

Shawna crossed the room in three strides, opening her arms. "What a surprise!"

She embraced Charisse, who had aged ten years in the past year. Her formerly dark hair was now streaked with gray, and the wire-frame glasses she always wore could not hide the dark circles under her eyes. But her smile was as radiant as ever. "Look at you, a governor's wife. And this office is lovely."

Dan, a tall man with thin gray hair fringing his head,

stepped forward. His shoulders seemed more stooped than they had been when she last saw him. He gave Shawna a more reserved hug, like she might break if he squeezed too tightly.

"Come in, have a seat." She led them to the open seating area and gestured to a tapestry-upholstered sofa. She took the club chair. "What brings you to Nashville?"

"Oh, we're taking a little holiday." Charisse reached for Dan's hand. "We hadn't been to Nashville in years, and we wanted to go to the Opry."

"You should have told me you were coming. I could have arranged to show you around." She waved her hand. "Unfortunately, I'm tied up today. How long will you be in town?"

"We didn't want to put you out," Charisse said. "We took one of the bus tours yesterday and saw all the stars' houses. It was a lot of fun."

Dan leaned forward. "We're leaving in the morning. This rain'll knock the rest of the leaves off the trees, so we got to get home to rake 'em, you know."

There would be a thick blanket of leaves on the tree-filled lawn around their two-story western Kentucky farmhouse. Shawna had loved the home from the first time Daniel had taken her there to meet his parents and sister. "How is Annette?"

Charisse beamed. "She's getting married next summer." Her smile faded. "Of course, planning the wedding makes her sad, since her brother won't be there.

But her young man is splendid, and he brought joy back to her life."

"That's wonderful." Shawna reached across and squeezed Charisse's hand. "Do give her my best wishes. And how are the two of you bearing up?"

Dan looked at her intently. "We're enduring. God helps us get through each day."

Their faith had been important to them, and she was glad to know they still counted on it. She was slowly finding her own way back. "It is one day at a time, isn't it?"

"That's all we're given." He nodded. "Probably best that way."

"Shawna, we—" Charisse fumbled in the oversized blue-and-gold-striped bag she carried. "We were going through some of Daniel's things, and we thought you might like this." She held out an object loosely wrapped in white tissue paper.

Curious, Shawna stretched out her arm, and Charisse placed the item in her hand. Shawna removed the paper to reveal a crudely carved wooden cross.

"He carved it in Boy Scouts. I think it was his first project for the Woodcarving Merit Badge," Dan said.

Shawna fingered the reddish-brown carving, about the size of her hand. She caught a whiff of the calming aroma of cedar. The sides were not perfectly straight, but the piece had been sanded smooth. She felt grooves on the back and turned it over, expecting to see Daniel's initials. Instead, she saw a crown etched into the wood. She looked at

Charisse and Dan.

Charisse had tears in her eyes. "He said it reminded him that Jesus exchanged his crown for the cross, and that someday we will exchange our cross for a crown."

Dan reached for his wife's hand. "Even at thirteen, when he made that, Daniel had a lot of insight. And now he has his crown."

The room grew warm, and Shawna had trouble breathing. Her first husband had been not only intelligent, but wise beyond his years. She wished she had faith as strong as his had been. As strong as her own had once been. She wrapped her fingers around the cross and knew she would cherish it forever. "Thank you. This means a lot to me."

Charisse's brow wrinkled. "I don't know how to say this, but—"

"We've heard the rumors." Dan always got right to the point. Shawna's heart thudded.

Charisse leaned over and patted her hand. "We're so sorry you lost the baby, dear. I know that must be hard for you, so soon after losing Daniel."

Dan sat up straight. "The marriage was pretty sudden. We were real surprised."

Charisse cast a sharp glance at him. "Those rumors don't matter to us. We're not looking for answers. Daniel deserved to know the truth, of course. But as long as you were honest with Daniel, he would forgive you, and so would we."

A lump in Shawna's throat threatened to choke her.

Dan clasped his hands together between his knees. "It is not up to us to be your judge. That is God's role. We pray that you find your peace with God."

"That's right." Charisse pulled a tissue from her purse and dabbed at her eyes. "Sometimes you have to sacrifice what you think is most important in order to gain peace with God and other people."

What did Shawna think was most important? Her marriage to Hunter? Her reputation? Her pride? She didn't like the idea of sacrificing any of it.

"We need to be going." Dan unfolded himself from the sofa, then offered a hand to Charisse to help her stand. "You should know, a reporter has been leaving messages for us, but we haven't talked to him. And we don't want you to tell us anything, so that we will have nothing to tell him."

The Moores didn't want to know whether Shawna had betrayed their son. So, they could protect her. She blinked back tears. No wonder Daniel had been a wonderful man, coming from such a fine family.

Shawna stood, holding the cross in one hand. "Thank you. For bringing this to me. And for understanding." She walked to the door with them. "Next time you plan a trip to Nashville, let me know. I'll make time to visit with you."

"Thank you, dear." Charisse hugged her. "Try to find happiness. And trust God for your future."

Shawna closed the door behind them and, leaning

against it, pressed the small cross to her chest.

Chapter 36

"Hey, Nate. It's Mark Newton from the governor's office. I got your message."

"Yeah, hang on, Newton. Let me get off the road." Nate turned his car to the right, into a shopping center parking lot. After pulling into an empty space, he shifted into park and cracked the windows open. Pax, on the front seat, poked his nose through the passenger window.

Nate picked up his cell. He hated talking over the car's microphone. "Okay, thanks for getting back to me so soon." Never mind that it had been yesterday when he'd left the message.

"Of course, Nate. You know you're my favorite reporter. What can I do for you?"

"That story I've been working on? I asked for a comment a couple weeks ago."

Newton groaned. "You gotta give me more than that,

Nate. You're always working on several stories at once, aren't you? Was it on the governor's education bill?"

He knew exactly what story Nate meant. "Still trying to avoid the question? I've got a source who says she knows Mrs. Wilson was already pregnant when she returned from her honeymoon." While he waited for Newton's answer, Nate watched a woman push her cart, loaded with groceries and a small child, across the parking lot to a beat-up Subaru station wagon. Pax huffed a low "woof" at the pair. About the time the woman beeped open her car door, Nate heard a deep sigh over the phone.

"Matthews, that story got tired weeks ago. The governor didn't comment because there's nothing to say. It's speculation, fueled by the Internet, fueled by—I suspect—Deborah Hummel. You and she are old friends, aren't you?"

Nate refused the bait. He picked up his notepad. "Shall I say the governor refused to comment, or do you want to ask him again before the story runs on Sunday?"

Silence on the other end.

"You still there, Newton?"

"Yeah. I can't believe you're going with a story loaded with suspicions and innuendos, but no real facts. Even you wouldn't stoop that low. And surely your editor won't run with it."

Drops of sweat broke out on Nate's forehead. Newton was partially right. His story so far consisted of unsubstantiated statements from "Bonnie" and the maid at

Lake Barkley, coupled with suspicions and timeline calculations. Nothing that would prove adultery or a cover-up. He hoped to pressure a confession with his threat, although his editor was prepared to publish the story as "allegations." Only because so much had been said on social media already that it could not be ignored.

"Actually, the story will run." His voice sounded gruffer than usual, even to him. "The only question is whether or not it includes either a denial or confirmation from the governor. Or from the first lady."

Newton growled. "I'll ask. But don't hold your breath." He ended the call.

Nate opened the car door and got out, grabbing Pax's leash and letting him out. He slammed the door closed and banged his palm against it. If only the Wilsons would give him a statement. He'd gone too far to kill the story now. Even if Shawna Wilson had cheated on her husband, would it help anyone to reveal it? Or would it only open up wounds for other jilted military spouses?

He walked around the car once. The Subaru mother had finally loaded her purchases and her kid into her car. She turned over the ignition a couple of times before the engine started, and she drove off. Nate shook his head and he and Pax climbed back into his car. Maybe Newton would come through with a statement from the governor before his deadline.

Or perhaps some major event over the weekend would knock Nate's story off page one.

Less than two weeks until the election.

After the boys were in bed, Hunter tried listening to Shawna telling him about the visit from her former in-laws, but the election kept creeping into his mind.

The announcement that the cancer research facility would be coming to the Nashville metro area after all had boosted his poll numbers by a couple of points, but the Twittersphere persisted in raising questions about his character.

Had he made the right choice in not debating his opponent? He felt the differences in policy issues had been made clear, and a debate would have been nothing more than a dirt-throwing contest. But some pundits claimed he feared a face-off.

He shook his head. Too late to worry about that now. Johnnie had agreed to the strategy at the time, and he trusted her judgment.

"Hunter?"

Uh-oh. "What? I'm sorry, Shawna. I've got a lot on my mind."

Her face fell. "I said it was thoughtful of the Moores to come see me."

"Yes. Yes, it was. How are they doing?"

"They've aged, but otherwise, fine, I think." She

paused. "They said they would forgive me, even if I was unfaithful to Daniel, but they weren't asking."

"You don't think they were trying to find out the truth? Maybe so they could tell the press?"

"No!" The thought had not occurred to her. "They just wanted me to know. They didn't give me a chance to confess or to deny the rumors."

"Good." He studied her. "It must have been awkward to see them again."

She grimaced. "A little. But they're good people. They didn't make me feel uncomfortable. Now, tell me what's on your mind tonight."

"The election, of course. It's going to be close. I'm not sure—"

Hunter's cell phone buzzed. He pulled it out of his pocket and checked the screen, then looked at Shawna and shrugged. "It's Johnnie. I'd better take it."

She nodded, and he put the phone to his ear. "Johnnie. What is it?"

"Governor, Mark Newton is on hold. Let me conference him in."

Not good. Both of them calling could only mean bad news. He rose and moved into the bedroom so he wouldn't disturb Shawna.

Newton came on the line. "Governor, I'm sorry we had to bother you. But Nate Matthews called me. That story I told you about a couple weeks ago? They're planning to run it Sunday in *The Tennessean*. He's looking for a comment or an interview with you."

Hunter's heart thumped and he sank onto the side of the bed. "He's going with it?"

"Yes, sir. He says he's got facts, but he won't share his sources."

"Governor?" Johnnie's voice sounded hoarse. She seemed to move the phone away to clear her throat. "We need to draft a statement. We can't keep passing the ball."

"You're right, Johnnie. It's time to confess. But I need to talk to Shawna first. Can we put him off until tomorrow?"

Both Johnnie and Newton were silent for a moment. Then Newton said, "He wants to know your response by nine Saturday night."

"Sir, if you confess, it will kill your career." Johnnie sounded almost frantic. "Maybe we can explain away or discredit these so-called facts."

That sounded enticing, if impossible. But that was no longer an option.

"I'm tired of keeping this secret. I want my peace back. Hiding the truth was a mistake. Whatever the outcome, I want to be honest from now on."

When Hunter returned to the living room after taking the phone call, he collapsed onto the couch and took both of Shawna's hands in his. Looking down at their clasped hands, he said, "When we married and said, 'For better or worse,' I meant it. I hope you did, too, because we are about to face the 'worse.' *The Tennessean* is running a story on Sunday. Apparently, your friend Nate has enough facts to confirm that we had an affair while Daniel was overseas, before he was killed. Matthews has asked for a comment."

It sounded so much worse when spoken aloud. She should be relieved that the truth would be revealed at last, but the knot in her stomach had turned into a knotted mess. What was that little rhyme her mother used to say? *What a tangled web we weave, when first we practice to deceive.*

It *was* a tangled web. "What are you going to say?"

"I don't know. I want to tell the truth. The whole story. I'm tired of this deceit. But I hate to think what it will do to you." He stared down the hall. "And to the boys."

"It won't help your campaign."

"No, it won't. Johnnie says it'll ruin my career, and she's probably right. But I'm willing to take what I deserve, but you and the boys shouldn't have to deal with the fallout."

"I am as much at fault as you are. I could have said, 'No,' but I didn't. I was lonely, too. So, I deserve whatever backlash comes my way. It will embarrass my sisters, but they'll get over it." She smiled ruefully. "I hope."

He leaned close and kissed her. "At least you know how Daniel's parents will react. They already suspected, so

I guess it won't be as hard on them."

"Oh, I'm sure it will still be difficult. They'll be hounded by the media for comments, and Daniel's picture will probably be shown over and over, which will make it that much harder."

Shawna tugged at her ear. "I think we should tell the boys and Mimi the truth before the article comes out."

"I agree. But ..." Hunter stared at the dark television screen.

"What?"

"I think the people need to hear from us directly, too, instead of the story being filtered through the newspaper article. I'd like to go on *Tennessee This Week* with our confession."

"Our confession? You want me to appear with you?" Admitting to the affair was hard enough, but answering questions on a live talk show might take more courage than she could summon.

Hunter looked her in the eyes, his lazy eye drooping more than usual. "Shawna, I'm asking you to stand beside me. I may not be governor after the end of the year, but as long as you will still have me, I can endure anything."

"If that's what you want, then it's settled. We'll tell the boys and Mimi tomorrow, and go on the show Sunday morning." She patted his hand. "It won't be easy, but we can do it." She could see a glimmer of hope that their relationship could survive even this.

"I'll ask Mark to see if the show will give us a few

minutes."

Just as he reached to pick up his cell phone from the table, it buzzed with a sound resembling a school fire alarm.

Chapter 37

The alarm sound meant that Colonel Vince Johnson, head of the State Highway Patrol, was calling. He only called Hunter's cell phone in an emergency.

"Yes, Colonel?"

"Governor, sorry to bother you. But I thought you should know about a developing situation in Memphis. Maybe you heard about the police shooting there earlier today?"

Hunter stood and paced to the windows, looking out over the darkened grounds. He had been too distracted to watch the news. "Tell me about it."

Johnson hesitated. "Much the same as other places. White policeman, black kid. Officer says the kid had a gun. The black community is protesting, and it looks like it could get violent." The colonel was African-American himself, and Hunter could tell he was trying to provide a non-biased report.

"*Did* the kid have a gun?"

"That's part of the investigation, sir. Which is getting more difficult by the minute."

Hunter sighed. This could be a tinderbox in a city like Memphis. "Okay, what resources are available?"

"The city's riot squad is on the scene, and we've sent a handful of troopers to help out. But the crowd is growing. The boy's mother was on the six o'clock news, and now people are coming in from all over the tristate area. Close to five hundred people already. They're crammed into the intersection where it happened, blocking a main thoroughfare and spilling into the side streets. Sir, I think we're going to need National Guard support."

"All right, Colonel." Hunter thought a moment. "I'll talk to my people and get back to you. Can you contain the situation tonight?"

"Let's hope so, sir."

He hung up and picked up the remote control. "I need to see what's happening in Memphis." He explained what Johnson had told him as he flipped channels. Finally, he found one that had a live broadcast from the scene.

A mob of people had gathered in the street, chanting and carrying crudely lettered signs. The camera cut away to an earlier interview with the dead boy's mother. "He was a good boy. He din't mess with drugs or guns or none of that stuff. If he did, he'd a got a lashing from me, I tell you that."

346

Shawna stared at the TV screen, her face as pained as the days after Hannah Lea died. Hunter hoped she wasn't going back into that valley of depression; it had taken weeks for her to emerge from it.

He called several of his key advisors to get their take on what was happening. When he spoke with the State National Guard Adjutant General, he requested troops be sent to Memphis first thing tomorrow. Then he arranged a flight to Memphis for Johnson and himself in the morning. When he hung up from the last call, he moved next to Shawna and put his arm around her. The TV announcer droned on about the situation, then cut to a commercial for new cars.

Shawna drew back and looked at him. "You're going?"

He nodded.

"I want to come with you."

"Not a good idea. I have no idea what the situation will be when we get there. It could escalate into a real dangerous situation."

Her jaw was set. "If you're going, I'm going with you."

As the helicopter charged toward Memphis the next morning, Shawna kept her eyes on the fields and streams rushing by beneath them. She loved to watch the changing checkerboard patterns as they flew.

Clouds decorated the gray sky with the threat of rain. Hunter sat in the middle of the chopper, checking the weather forecast on his phone. "Maybe a thunderstorm will disperse the protesters."

"That would also leave us grounded in Memphis overnight, wouldn't it?"

He winked at her. "Wouldn't be such a bad thing, would it?"

She smiled. "Not at all. But what about the talk show tomorrow morning?"

He shrugged. "Johnnie can arrange a remote connection, if necessary."

"I suppose." She leaned her head against the seat back and closed her eyes. Critters seemed to be crawling around her intestines, and watching the landscape flash by aggravated the feeling. Flying didn't usually bother her. Must be nervousness about the possible danger. She took a few deep breaths.

"You okay?" Hunter's voice indicated he had moved beside her.

Without opening her eyes, she nodded. "I'll be fine. Just a little queasy."

"Rough ride. I know the pilot's doing the best he can. But that's why I hate these things."

She reached for his hand, and he clasped his fingers around hers. "I'm sure he is," she said, eyes still closed.

"It's the weather, not the pilot."

Shawna squeezed Hunter's hand before changing the subject. "I want to talk to her. I want to meet the boy's mother." She didn't know where the family lived or what their everyday life was like. Did the dead boy pick flowers for his mother, play sports, have a girlfriend? All she knew was that she and the woman shared the pain of losing a child. Her little girl had not had the chance to giggle, to wear frilly dresses, to go on her first date. Neither child would be sleeping at home tonight. She wanted this mom to know that she understood.

"Why would you want to do that?" Hunter's grip tightened until her hand hurt. "It's a bad idea. It could be dangerous. And it won't win any votes among law enforcement. Only among blacks—maybe."

She pulled her hand free. "This isn't about your campaign, Hunter. And it's not about a race war. It's about a mother losing her child. I know how that feels. I'm going to see her."

"You can see her from inside the command center. But you don't need to meet her."

She did need to meet her. She wasn't sure how, but she would find a way to talk with the woman.

"We'll be landing in ten minutes." At the sound of

Colonel Johnson's voice, Shawna's eyes fluttered open. She must have dozed off. The colonel had taken the seat opposite the row where she and Hunter sat.

"I arranged for a trooper to meet us at the airport and take us downtown." Johnson scratched his chin. "The local police have set up a mobile command center. You'll be safe enough there, but it could get dicey getting to it. When we get out of the car, we'll need to move fast and stay together."

Hunter leaned forward as far as his seat belt would allow. "What's the mood today?"

Johnson tapped his fingers on his armrest. "No better. The crowd's growing, being it's a Saturday and people are off work. Anything at all could light the match that will start a fire, and then we'll have a full-fledged crisis on our hands."

"Did the National Guard units arrive?"

"Yes sir, two units out. They were in place at oh-seven-hundred, just as protesters started arriving. They got some jeers but no trouble yet."

"What do the protesters want?"

"Same as other places where there's been riots, I reckon. They want to be treated fairly, not judged by the color of their skin."

Hunter grimaced. "Doesn't that work both ways? Simply because the police officer was white doesn't mean he killed the boy without cause."

Colonel Johnson nodded. "Yes sir. Sometimes I think

it's the uniform they don't like, and it wouldn't matter if the officer was purple. There's no respect for authority."

Shawna's stomach churned as the chopper dropped suddenly and headed for the helipad. "Was the shooting justified?"

The colonel turned to her. "We're reviewing the facts, at the city's request, ma'am. It's too early to say, yet."

"Is the boy's mother there again today?"

"From the reports I'm getting, she is. She's done more interviews this morning."

When the highway patrol SUV drew within a few blocks of the central business district, traffic bogged to a standstill. Their driver put on his siren, and cars moved to the right ahead of them. He edged the SUV through the maze of stopped cars until he reached the location of the protest.

Five streets came together, creating an unusually large star-shaped intersection where the protesters had gathered, spilling from the sidewalks onto the pavement and blocking traffic. The crowd, mostly black but with a few white faces sprinkled in, chanted "We want justice. We want justice." Many of them held signs proclaiming "Black Lives Matter" and "Justice for Jarvis."

The trooper maneuvered the SUV slowly through the crowd, pulsing his siren and tapping his horn every few feet. The mob started to move aside but as the vehicle passed them, they shouted and pounded on the windows and roof. Shawna held her breath until they reached the line of National Guard troops holding the protesters back from the mobile command center.

An officer in the police car escort spoke to a soldier, and the line opened to allow them to pass into the cleared space beyond. Blocking off one of the streets was a white converted bus with the Memphis Police Department logo painted on one side. Beyond the bus, at the end of the block, Shawna saw more soldiers holding back a smattering of other protesters. The situation was far worse than she had expected. How would she ever reach the boy's mother?

A trooper named Chip was traveling with them, and he joined Johnson, their driver, and two police officers in creating a shield as they escorted Hunter and Shawna into the command center. The chants from the crowd behind them changed from "Justice for Jarvis" to something she couldn't quite understand, but she caught the words *governor* and *change*.

Inside the bus, the chants faded and the air conditioning was a refreshing change from the warm outside air, heavy with the pending storm. Two Memphis police officers in shirtsleeves grabbed for their jackets and stood to greet them. One, who wore five stars on the collar of his white shirt, introduced himself as Perry Anderson, Memphis Police Director.

"Governor, we appreciate your coming." He attempted to wiggle into his dark blue uniform jacket. "The National Guard has been a great help. I'm hoping that storm coming our way will cool things down, and these people will go home before they do anything stupid."

Six video monitors were stacked along one wall, and Shawna studied them, looking for the woman who had been on TV last evening. Director Anderson pointed out the three screens carrying feed from security cameras on nearby buildings or light poles. "This camera is on top of the bus. And, as you can tell, the other two are monitoring local TV stations. Two are broadcasting live from over there." He pointed to a shopping center parking lot to the north of the intersection. "This one's doing continuous broadcast, and the other one is interrupting regular programming about once an hour or if something else happens."

One monitor showed footage from minutes earlier when Hunter and Shawna had arrived, followed by a stand-up with the reporter in front of the crowd of protesters. "The governor and his party are now inside the command center. We'll try to learn what, if anything, he plans to do to diffuse the situation here. As soon as we have more, we will update you. Now back to your program." The picture changed to a commercial for laundry soap.

Shawna pointed to one of the other monitors. "Is that the boy's mother, there in front?" The woman held a framed photo and was surrounded by three women and two men carrying signs. Her face looked like an old washboard. Shawna couldn't see her eyes clearly on the television screen but she guessed they would look vacant. The woman's shoulders drooped and she shook her head as one of her companions whispered something in her ear.

Hunter, Colonel Johnson, and Director Anderson had taken seats at the far end of the bus and were engaged in deep conversation. The other police officer had sat down in front of the monitors and plugged a headphone back into his ear. No one would notice if she left now.

She swallowed the lump in her throat and moved to the front of the bus. She pulled open the door, and hobbled down the steps. The thick air hit her with a fierce intensity.

"Ma'am?"

She had forgotten that Chip waited outside the bus. She didn't stop but angled toward the section of the protesters where she believed she'd find the mother. "It's all right, Chip." She spoke over her shoulder. "I'm going over there to talk to the boy's mother."

He moved to her side, alert to potential danger from all sides. "I'm not sure that's a good idea, Mrs. Wilson."

She glanced over at him. "You sound like the governor now. But don't worry, I'll be fine."

"Yes, ma'am, but I'm going with you."

Of course, he was. She sighed but kept walking. "If you insist. Just don't try to stop me."

He stayed right beside her as they crossed the open space to the line of citizen soldiers facing the crowd. As they approached, the crowd grew silent. Then someone deep in the crowd shouted, "Go home, honky. We don't want you here."

She ignored the jeers that followed that comment and

looked between two soldiers directly at the mother. She stepped forward, between the soldiers, into the crowd. She could feel Chip's presence right beside her.

The mother and those closest to her had grown silent, watching her like a pack of dogs eyeing one bone. Like waves rolling away from a lakeshore, quiet spread throughout the entire crowd, until the chanting stopped. Bodies seemed to press together as those farthest away tried to see what was happening.

Shawna stopped in front of the boy's mother and looked into the woman's eyes. "I am so sorry this happened. I know how much hurt you must be feeling."

The woman standing next to the boy's mother crossed her arms. "What you know about us?"

The mother narrowed her eyes. "What're you doing here? You're the gov'nor's wife. He don't care about my son. He gon' back the cops, like white men always do."

"No, he won't. He wants to know what really happened. But I'm not here for him. I'm here for you. I'm a mother too."

The woman next to the mother scowled. "You're a white woman, wife of the gov'nor. How you know what we feel?"

The woman was right. Shawna's life bore no resemblance to theirs. She had never felt the sting of prejudice or the closed doors of discrimination. Nor the hopelessness of poverty so evident in this neighborhood.

"Underneath our skin color, we are the same," she said

to the boy's mother, her voice cracking. "We're mothers with hopes and dreams for our children."

Jarvis' mother seemed to soften. "You lost your baby, didn't you? It's not the same …I had eighteen years to get to know my Jarvis. You didn't really know your baby."

True, Hannah had not been here long enough to develop a personality. But that didn't ease the loss. She squinted her eyes, forcing back tears. "I wish I could have seen her grow up. I'm sure you wanted the same thing."

The woman beside Jarvis' mother pressed forward, inches from Shawna's face. "Jarvis was a good boy. He didn't deserve to die. My sister tried to raise him right."

Shawna took a half-step to the side and spoke directly to Jarvis's mother. "I want you to know I care. That's why I'm here. Tell me about your son."

The mother's hard face softened. "He were a good boy. Smart. Till lately. He got bored and dropped out of school but I didn't know it. He never tell me who he was hanging with or where he was going. Secrets. That's what got him killed. But that cop coulda talked to him instead of shootin' him."

A high school dropout. Smart but bored. Would Hunter's education technology proposal have helped him, kept him in school, maybe kept him out of trouble? That was Hunter's hope. No way to know, of course, but it was too late for this boy. And this mother. "Do you have other children?"

The woman nodded. "Two younger ones. They looked

up to him."

"Maybe Jarvis's death will help them realize how important it is to stay in school."

"I shouldn't have to lose my son to prove that, should I?"

Shawna reached out her hands. "No, and I'm sorry this happened. But we can pray that good will come out of it. Can't we?"

The woman looked at Shawna's outstretched hands, then at her, and grasped her hands. "Maybe you do understand. But that don't bring back my boy."

Shawna hugged the woman, aware of cameras clicking. Then Chip guided her by her elbow back through the crowd that had closed around them. The reporter she had seen on TV a few minutes ago chased after her, holding out a microphone and followed by a cameraman. "Mrs. Wilson, what did you say to the mother of this boy killed by the police?"

Shawna ignored the question and kept walking. Raindrops spattered her head and arms.

Another reporter and camera team ran up from her right. "Are you supporting this protest? Will you be joining them?" She shook her head. She had not come here to become part of a media circus. A large drop of rain plopped on the back of her neck. She walked faster.

The first reporter ran to keep up with her. "How do you respond to the reports that you were pregnant with the governor's child before your soldier-husband died?" She stuck the microphone in front of Shawna's face, but Chip reached out his hand and pushed the reporter away.

Chapter 38

TVs on every wall of the restaurant, all tuned to different channels, showed live coverage of the Memphis protest. Almost as if the media expected—even hoped—the protest would turn into riots.

Nate thought he might be getting too cynical to stay in journalism. And that in itself told a story. He'd chosen reporting as a career because of his cynicism about politics. And here he was, considering a career change—to politics.

"Nate?" Across the table, Deb waited for his answer.

His story about Governor and Mrs. Wilson, or rather, about the allegations about them, would release tomorrow morning. At five a.m., around the time the print edition hit the streets, the story would be posted on the Internet. Then there would be no retracting it. Once it appeared on the Internet, it had to be true, or so most people thought.

"I don't know, Deb. I've spent my whole life as a

reporter. I like digging up the facts that politicians try to hide, not being the one doing the hiding."

Deb's polls had been climbing, and she had convinced herself Nate's story would push her to the top. She was already planning for her administration, and she wanted Nate to be her communications director.

"You're kidding, right? You've got the personality for it, like nobody else I know. You're persistent. You don't care what anybody else thinks. You know how to deal with reporters, and how to make the facts say what you want them to."

"Ouch." Nate winced. Did Deb really consider him that low? "You make me sound less than objective. Not a high commendation for a journalist."

Deb laughed. She held her water glass and moved it around. "Oh, come now. We both know journalism is not objective. Hasn't been since before you graduated, never mind what your professors told you."

He had to admit the truth of her statement—if only to himself. Every reporter he knew had an avowed philosophy, a pet cause, or a preferred candidate, and they always played to their favorites. Including him, as he had done with the Wilson story, pursuing it because Deborah asked him to.

On the other hand, the governor was a public figure, and Shawna had become one when she married him. She had cheated on her first husband and deserved whatever bad publicity happened as a result. Even if Wilson lost the election and they had to live on a college professor's meager salary, it wouldn't be punishment enough. Or so he told himself.

Deb leaned forward, her face reddening as she glared over his shoulder. Nate read the curse word forming on her lips. He turned to see what had upset her.

On the television set above the bar, he saw a close-up of Shawna Wilson talking to an African-American woman. The camera zoomed out, and Nate recognized the Memphis neighborhood where a protest had started yesterday.

When he read the captioning at the bottom of the screen, he understood Deb's reaction.

First Lady Shawna Wilson spoke with the mother of slain teenager...

"Wilson's capitalizing on this tragedy." Deb threw her napkin over her plate of chicken bones. "And he's using his wife to do it. That is so sneaky."

"Wish you'd thought of it first?" Showing compassion to a grieving mother couldn't hurt Deb's campaign.

She glared at him. "As a matter-of-fact. If only I had a PR guy advising me who could come up with such ideas." She dug a credit card out of her purse and waved it at the waiter as he passed. The waiter made a quick turn, took the card, and hurried off.

Nate held out his hands in surrender. "Can't say that would be me. Compassion is not my first response."

Deb leaned over and hissed, "I'm not asking you to be compassionate. Just come up with things I can do to get on the news. I know you could do that."

He folded his napkin neatly and laid it next to his plate. "I need time to think about your offer, Deb. Can I have a week?"

The waiter returned with the check in a black vinyl folder. Deb stuck the card back in her purse and signed the charge slip. "Okay, I'll wait one week, as long as the answer is 'yes.' When I win the election, I want to hit the ground running."

"What were you thinking? That mob could have erupted!"

Hunter gathered Shawna into his arms the moment she reached the top of the bus steps. His rapid heartbeat began to calm as he held her close and felt her shivering.

"I know. But I had to meet her." She seemed to melt into him, tension leaving her body as she took several deep breaths.

He brushed raindrops off her face. Leading her toward one of the chairs, he helped her into it, then sat next to her. He moved a loose strand of hair off her forehead. "I was so afraid for you, darling. But I've never been more proud of you, either."

She smiled, that half-smile that reminded him of his mother. "When I was talking to her, it was like no one else was around. I wasn't scared until we started walking back and I heard the crowd yelling. Then those reporters!" She shook her head.

He rose and offered his hand to Chip. "Thank you for getting her back safely."

Chip returned the handshake. "Only doing my job, sir. But you're welcome."

Hunter wanted to take Shawna home where he could protect her. He turned toward her. "We need to get out of here. That reporter doing the live broadcast speculated that you were joining the protest."

He'd heard the reporter's last question. A media firestorm would hit after Matthews' article was published. Would it be released online tonight? He and Shawna needed to talk to the boys, tell them the truth, and prepare them for what they would hear and the possible backlash.

"Colonel, what more can I do to help you here?"

Johnson focused on the video screens, which showed that the dark clouds had finally burst open. The deluge was soaking the people and they were running for cover. "Governor, I think this rain is going to cool things down here. With any luck, tempers will die down and we won't have any violence."

"I hope you're right. My wife and I need to get back to Nashville. Since the chopper can't fly in this, can you arrange for a car to take us?"

"Yes, sir. You can use the one that met us when we landed."

Hunter turned to the Memphis Police Director. "I'd appreciate it if you'd keep me posted. We'll leave the Guard units on standby for a week or so until we see how things shake out."

Anderson offered his hand. "We appreciate that, Governor. Good luck with the election, by the way."

"Thank you. It will be interesting to see what happens after tomorrow."

"Tomorrow?"

He didn't want to take the time to explain at this moment. "Do you get *Tennessee This Week* on TV here?"

"Sure do. Why?"

"You might want to watch it tomorrow morning, if you're not needed here."

The man nodded. "Will do. Have a safe trip home."

In the car, Hunter longed for privacy so he and Shawna could talk. He reached over and grasped her hand, looking into her eyes with tenderness. She returned his smile and squeezed his hand.

"We need to talk when we get home." Hunter leaned his head back to rest, knowing he would have to wait three hours to be alone with Shawna.

Sometime during the day—when he watched Shawna cross the street, into that angry mob, to talk with the slain boy's mother—he knew they had made the right decision. They needed to start with a clean slate, if they were going to spend the rest of their lives together. He understood now how important that was to him.

But how could he demonstrate to Shawna that she was a vital part of his life? When Dad washed his mother's feet, he had said, *An act of service done in love has eternal value.* Maybe that was his answer.

As soon as they got home, they greeted Mimi and the boys. Then he said, "Shawna and I need a little time to talk before dinner."

He took her hand and led her into their bedroom, to the loveseat by the French doors. "Wait here, will you? I want to do something for you."

He left the room, and went to ask Mimi for help in locating the supplies he needed. When he had gathered everything, he opened the bedroom door but didn't go in. "Shawna, close your eyes for a couple minutes."

"Okay." The way she dragged out the last syllable conveyed confusion and curiosity. And maybe a tinge of concern.

He edged into the room, hiding what Mimi had provided behind his back until he could see that Shawna's eyes were really closed. Then he shut the door and hurried into the bathroom, where he rolled up his shirtsleeves. After filling the plastic washtub with warm water, he called to her. "Eyes still closed?"

"Yes, but I'll fall asleep if you don't hurry up."

Cautious not to splash water onto the carpet, he carried the yellow tub into the bedroom and set it on the floor at her feet. He returned to the bathroom for the other items. As he knelt in front of her, his stomach twisted. She might think he'd gone crazy, but for the first time in months, he could see clearly. "Okay, you can look now."

Slowly opening her eyes, she took in his position and the tub of water. She raised her eyebrows. "What—what's going on?"

Hunter reached for her feet and slowly, tenderly, removed her sandals and set them to one side. "I am so proud of what you did today, how you talked to that boy's mother. You weren't afraid, but only cared about how she felt." He lifted first her right foot, then her left one, and placed each one into the water.

Shawna didn't resist. "Ahhh, that feels good. But ... I did what I felt I had to do. Why are you doing this for me?"

Fearful of how she might react, he avoided her eyes and began adding the bath salts Mimi had given him to the washtub. Stirring with his fingers, he focused on the water swirling around her slender ankles. The fragile thread of connection might break if he looked directly at her. "Because you deserve it, darling. From the first moment we met, I have failed to be the man I should have been for you. The man I want to be."

He submerged both his hands in the water, eager to show her his penitence. He caressed one foot, massaging it from the heel to the toes, softly at first, then more firmly, rubbing away the fatigue. "Shawna." He chanced an inspection of her face. "I've been distant these last few months because I didn't want to admit that I was at fault."

A look of surprise flashed in her eyes, replaced

instantly by a question. Her lips parted but she kept quiet.

"I know I've made mistakes. At times, I've felt trapped by our secret. And I suppose I expected you to act like Lynn. But you're not Lynn."

The words he had to say constricted his throat. He swallowed hard, forcing the blockage down so the truth could be freed at last. "That time I persuaded you to come to my room—our first night together—I was wrong. I sinned against you and against God. I've never been that kind of man. But you were so beautiful and smart, and I had been alone for so long."

She opened her mouth to say something, but he held up a hand. "Let me finish."

He gently placed her foot back in the water, then he took her right foot in his hands, repeating the massage as he spoke. "Being lonely doesn't excuse my behavior. Even after you told me you were married, I couldn't stop myself. I wanted you—all of you, for myself. I ignored what I knew to be right, and pulled you into the pit with me."

Shawna sighed, a moan escaping from deep inside. Her eyes closed. She couldn't look at him, no doubt wishing she had not married him. Or maybe she thought he regretted marrying her.

Hunter lifted his shoulders then dropped them. The marriage was the one thing he did not regret. He only regretted the way their relationship had begun. And the distance he had put between them since Hannah died.

He picked up a clean white towel and arranged it over

his knees. Then he lifted her right foot from the water. Placing it on the towel, he began to wipe it dry, slowly, lovingly. The way he wanted to care for her spirit. "As a husband, I have put my campaign ahead of you, neglected you, expected you to support me. But I haven't taken care of you and your needs. This is my way of starting over. My pledge that I will love you and serve you for the rest of my life."

His throat sounded hoarse with the fullness of his emotions, as he saw tears slipping out of her closed eyes. He lifted her other foot and moved the tub of water to one side. He whispered as he dried her other foot, praying that her heart would hear his clearly. "Although we didn't honor God in the beginning of our relationship, I want us to honor him from now on."

He studied her perfect foot, red polish glittering on her toenails, then he reached for the bottle of lotion. He hated to mention this next part, but it was necessary. "Shawna, even if Nate wasn't running the story in tomorrow's paper, it's time we stop denying the truth. We should be transparent about our mistakes."

Even as he said it, he wanted to retract the words. "*My* mistakes. I'm responsible."

Her mouth dropped open. "No, it wasn't—"

"Shhh." He applied the vanilla-scented lotion to the foot he was holding, and rubbed the white cream over her heel, between her toes, up her leg. As he massaged her calf, he realized this was the ankle she had strained a week ago.

He stroked the muscles with extra care. "You would never have been unfaithful to Daniel if I hadn't pressured you. Now, don't misunderstand. I regret how we got together, especially my part in it. But I do not regret the outcome. I am honored to be your husband, and I pray that you'll allow me to show you how much I love you. Every day for as long as we live."

She reached out and put a hand on each side of his head, caressing his face. Her tears were flowing now, and she took a halting breath. "Thank you." She wiped at her eyes, and her shoulders shook with the intensity of restrained sobs. "It wasn't all your fault. I was lonely, too. I could have walked away, but I didn't."

He gazed into her hazel eyes. They reflected his own guilt, mixed with determination. "It doesn't matter anymore. We simply have to make it right."

She slid off the chair onto her knees in front of him. Hunter pulled her close, breathed in her flowery sweetness as she clung to him. "Shawna, I am sorry for the shame and hatred that are sure to be aimed at you after tomorrow. I wish I could protect you from that."

Her eyes gleamed with a light he hadn't seen there in months, but concern wrinkled her forehead. "Are you sure it can't wait until after the election? Maybe I can get Nate to—"

He put a finger to her lips. "No. Now is the time. It will probably mean the end of my political career, but that's okay. I'll go back to teaching. It's more important that we have no more secrets."

Shawna rested her damp cheek on his shoulder and murmured into his neck, her breath kissing his skin. "At least we can face whatever happens together."

Chapter 39

Cooper's eyes got big as saucers when they told the boys about the baby. "I didn't think you could make a baby unless you were married."

Shawna decided to let Hunter handle that one, since she wasn't prepared to explain the facts of life to a young boy.

"Dork." Hunter Lynn reached out and punched Cooper's arm. "Lots of people that aren't married have babies. You saw Jeremy's sister the other day, right?"

Jeremy was one of Hunter Lynn's classmates whose high-school-aged sister had gotten pregnant. "Yeah, I saw her."

"Well, did she look old enough to be married, dummy?"

Hunter held up his hand. "That's enough. Hunter Lynn, there's no need to call your brother names. Cooper,

God intended that a man and woman marry before they have babies, but sometimes people make mistakes. And Shawna and I made a mistake and spent too much time together alone."

Shawna loved the way Hunter explained things so patiently to his sons. "Yes, and even worse, I was married to someone else at the time. You know I've mentioned Daniel, my first husband who died?"

Both boys nodded.

"Well, he was a soldier and he was fighting overseas when I met your father. I was lonely, and your dad was nice." She smiled at Hunter.

"The important thing is, boys, that after Daniel was killed, Shawna and I knew we loved each other, so we decided to get married. The problem is, we were ashamed of what we had done and didn't want anyone to know about our mistake."

"Does that mean you had to lie about the baby?" Cooper's innocent questions seemed to get right to the heart of the matter.

"Yes, Cooper." Shawna had to swallow the lump in her throat. "In order to keep the secret, we lied. And that was wrong. We were afraid that if people knew the truth, they wouldn't like your dad anymore, and wouldn't want him to be governor. But we should have trusted God."

Hunter Lynn dropped his head and sat quietly. Shawna said softly, "What is it, H. L.?"

The boy jerked his head up, apparently surprised she

had noticed. "I was just thinking. If Hannah Lea was a mistake, is that why she died? Was God punishing you?"

Shawna collapsed against the back of the couch. She had no answer for him.

Hunter leaned forward and looked at his son. "Honestly, we don't know why Hannah Lea died. But we do know that God loves us. We have asked Him to forgive us, and He has."

Shawna squeezed his hand. "Now we realize that God doesn't want us to keep secrets. He will take care of us whether your dad gets reelected or not. It's more important that we be honest."

"Right. That's why we wanted to tell you boys." Hunter nodded in Mimi's direction. "And Mimi. There will be an article in tomorrow's newspaper, and Shawna and I are going on TV in the morning to tell our story."

"The thing is," Shawna said, "some people will be really upset. We may get hateful letters, and you boys may hear nasty comments at school. We're sorry you have to go through this because of us, but we want you to be prepared."

Hunter Lynn squirmed in his seat, but Cooper grinned. "We can tell 'em that God forgives them for being mean to us."

Hunter reached out and tousled his son's hair. "That's right. And you can pray for them."

Cooper gave a firm nod. "I will."

Mimi had been sitting in a chair to one side listening,

but not saying a word. Now she spoke up. "God will honor your decision to tell the truth. I'll be praying for you."

Shawna looked at her. "We were hoping you and the boys would come to the TV station with us in the morning. We have to be there pretty early, though."

Mimi nodded. "I can pray as well there as I can here in my room."

Hunter was perspiring under the studio lights. The producers of *Tennessee This Week* had canceled the scheduled guests in order to give Hunter and Shawna the entire half hour.

After a brief introduction, host Davis Jefferson started the interview by holding up the morning newspaper with the headline, "Governor Accused of Cover-Up: Affair Results in Pregnancy." With the size of the type and the way the headline was worded, the paper could have been a tabloid in the grocery store checkout lane.

"Governor, this is a pretty scathing article. Are you and your wife here to deny these allegations?"

Hunter swallowed hard. "No, we are here to tell the full story. We've been through a tough time since our baby died. It didn't look like our marriage would survive, but we are working through our problems and we're now committed to building a strong family."

"Shawna, this can't be easy for you. If this story is true, it casts doubt on your whole marriage."

Hunter knew from Shawna's tightened jaw that the statement irked her. But she paused before answering. "For a time, I felt that way. Now I realize that it wasn't how or when I got pregnant that drove a wedge between us, it was that we had this huge secret. There was more to our relationship from the beginning than just physical attraction. And, despite some ups and downs this past year, we have grown closer, and are committed to each other."

Hunter leaned forward. "Maybe we should start at the beginning and tell the whole story, for those viewers who haven't read the newspaper."

"Excellent idea, Governor," the host said. "But first, isn't it true that you asked to appear on the program today because the story is out, so you might as well confess it all?"

That's why he hated the news business. They always twisted things to make them sound as negative as possible. "No. We're here because we no longer want to keep this secret that we've held for the past year. The people of Tennessee deserve to know the truth."

"Are you saying the newspaper story is not true?"

"We're saying it's not the full truth, and we want people to hear the truth directly from us."

The host leaned back and crossed his arms. "So, what exactly is the truth?"

Shawna met his challenge. "It's no secret that I was

married to a soldier. The truth is that I met Hunter—Governor Wilson—while my first husband was serving our country in Afghanistan. I betrayed my husband, and in a sense, I betrayed every soldier who has to be away from home while serving his country."

The host snickered. "Lots of people have affairs. Are you condemning everyone who has ever been unfaithful?"

"That is not for us to judge," Hunter said. "God has convicted us that we were wrong to act on our feelings, but we have sought and received his forgiveness."

"Unfortunately, my husband was killed before I could confess to him and ask for his forgiveness." Shawna's voice cracked, but she kept going. "I can only trust that he would give it. I loved him, and I love Hunter. But starting a marriage with a shared lie was not the best foundation."

The host waved the newspaper. "So, this article is accurate. You were already pregnant with Hunter's baby when you received word that your husband had been killed in action?"

"Yes. And at the time, we felt it was best for our families and Hunter's career if we kept that a secret. Now we realize that was the wrong decision, that what we were really thinking of was self-preservation, not what was right or wrong."

The host gave a sympathetic nod and leaned toward Shawna. "What was it like to lose your baby, after losing your first husband and then marrying Governor Wilson so suddenly?"

"I was angry—with God, with myself, and with Hunter. But the real problem was that I had sinned. And now that I've found and accepted God's forgiveness, and Hunter and I have forgiven each other, we hope and pray that our story might help someone else to find that forgiveness and healing."

The host's demeanor changed to defensive. "Are you saying that God punished you by taking your baby?"

Marie Wells Coutu

Chapter 40

Nate sipped coffee from his favorite cup, the one with the words, *"Old reporters never die, they just miss their deadlines."*

The Sunday *Tennessean* rested on his lap, rustled by the morning breeze. He liked his morning routine, reading the newspaper while sitting on his seventh-floor apartment balcony with Pax resting beside him. Especially when he had a page one byline. From here, he could see the state capitol across the expanse of lawn. Brown and gold leaves clung to the trees, unwilling to let go and reveal the bare limbs that would be exposed all winter.

People all over town would be reading today's headline and changing their minds about their beloved governor and his wife. Never mind the below-the-fold story about how the couple's visit to Memphis ended the protests there. He'd probably lose Shawna's friendship after this, but that was his penance for being an investigative reporter.

His cell phone vibrated in his pocket. He pulled it out and glanced at the screen. Deborah Hummel. He tapped the screen. "Hey, Deb. You've seen the paper?"

"I have. But are you watching *Tennessee This Week*?" Her voice sounded tense, rushed.

"Not yet. But I'm guessing I need to." He set his cup on the small white table next to his matching plastic chair and stood, stuffing the newspaper under his arm. He slipped through the open sliding door and picked up the TV remote. "Who's on?"

Her disgust was unmistakable. "Who do you think? They're apologizing for deceiving the public. At least you got the scoop. Forced them into confessing."

Nate punched the button on the remote, then navigated to the right channel. Host Davis Jefferson turned to Shawna Wilson. "Are you saying that God was punishing you by taking your baby?"

The close-up of Shawna showed her closing her eyes briefly, a flicker of pain crossing her face.

"Okay, Deb. I've got it on now. I'll call you back when it's over." Nate dropped onto the sofa to watch the program. Too bad he hadn't recorded the whole show.

He had to admit the couple seemed sincere, even when Shawna talked about her first husband. He wondered what she would have done if her husband had not been killed. Would she have ditched him in favor of the prestigious governor? Most soldiers' wives did that, after all.

But somehow, watching Shawna on television and knowing her, Nate didn't think she would have done so.

Shawna touched Hunter's arm, letting him know that she wanted to answer the question.

She reached in her pocket and slipped the wooden cross onto her lap, keeping it hidden in her hand. "I struggled with that, at first. I thought Hannah had suffered because I had been unfaithful to my first husband."

She glanced at Hunter, who gave her a slight nod, encouraging her to continue. "It took a while for me to remember something I've known most of my life—that God loves us. He doesn't cause this sort of tragedy as punishment, although he does allow terrible things to happen. We usually don't understand why. Job, in the Old Testament, didn't understand. But God can use a situation like this one to draw us closer to him."

When she stopped speaking, Hunter leaned forward and looked straight at Jefferson. "You see, Davis, we realize that we can't handle life on our own. We need God to give us strength and comfort in terrible times, as well as in the good times. I've certainly needed his strength throughout my career."

Jefferson's friendly demeanor disappeared as he went

on the attack. "Two decades ago, a presidential candidate and his wife went on TV together. They famously confessed that he had an affair and she had forgiven him. Based on what happened later, it's widely believed that was a calculated political move with little to do with honesty. Isn't that what's going on here? With the election less than two weeks away, your numbers in the polls are not as strong as they were four years ago. Aren't you doing this to gain an edge in the election?"

Hunter didn't take the bait. "It's understandable that you and the voters may think that. And that my opponent may use this against me. But my wife and I want to show other couples that there is hope for a troubled marriage. What happens with my campaign is not a factor. I will continue to serve to the best of my ability, but I will not again dishonor my faith."

Jefferson had a glint in his eye. "You're saying that you will never again do anything wrong? Sin, as you call it?"

"If I said that, I'd be lying." Hunter met Jefferson's gaze. "Which is a sin. What I'm saying is that I—" He reached for Shawna's hand. "We—covenant before God and before the people of Tennessee to not intentionally do anything wrong."

The host frowned. "Many of my viewers don't believe that public figures like you, Governor, should be talking about God so publicly. Isn't religion a private thing?"

"My faith is personal, Davis, but it can't be private.

It's too much a part of who I am."

Shawna's heart beat faster. "It's why Hunter is such a good governor—because he cares about people. And he cares about people because of his faith."

Jefferson looked down at his notes. "If what you say is true, and your god has forgiven you, why did you think it necessary to keep this secret in the first place?"

Hunter held his hands in front of him, palms together. "It's like two faces on a coin. On one side, we have this modern belief that people should not have boundaries. That sex before marriage is acceptable, and no one should claim that it's wrong."

He turned his hands over. "On the other hand, people don't want their leaders to have flaws. Therefore, a governor should not do this thing that they claim is not wrong." He separated his hands and held them open, palms up. "It can't be both ways."

The host started to interrupt but Hunter held up a hand. "I want to continue to serve the great people of this state to the best of my ability as governor. This whole episode does not negate my qualifications to do that. But it is important that I be open and honest, and let the voters decide."

"So, what's ahead, if you lose the election?"

A few months ago, Shawna would have been thrilled to consider that possibility. Now, she couldn't imagine such an outcome. But the two of them had discussed the prospect and were prepared for any future.

Hunter smiled. "Why don't we wait and see what

happens?"

By the time the show ended and Nate called Deb back, she had moved into defensive mode.

"People won't believe that baloney, will they? Clearly, they only did this because of your story. I'm preparing a statement calling for him to withdraw from the race."

Nate's hand holding the phone tingled. "On what basis?"

Her voice sounded like ice. "He's lied about this … relationship … for over a year. What else has he been lying to the people of Tennessee about? If we can't trust our governor, who can we trust?" She paused and Nate heard paper rustling. "Yes, that's good. Hang on. I have to write that down."

After a minute with sounds of a pen or pencil scratching on paper, she came back. "Got it. Anything else you think I should say, Nate?"

He certainly wouldn't say what she had written down. But she was too excited to listen to his advice. Still, he had to try. "To be honest, you ought to take the high road. Say how refreshing it is for an elected official to admit to his mistakes in spite of the potential consequences."

Silence. Probably deciding whether to withdraw her job offer now or later. Which was fine with Nate. "Sure, it's refreshing. But that doesn't negate the fact that he lied. This race is a shoo-in for me, now."

"Glad you're so excited about someone else's troubles."

"For crying out loud, Nate. When you say things like that, I'm not sure whose side you're on. But, listen, I've gotta finish this statement and send it out while it's hot. Bye."

Nate stared at the phone in his hand. Pax nuzzled his leg, and he bent over to press his face into the dog's fur. He, too, wondered whose side he was on. And what had happened to his idealistic, but ethical, friend Deborah?

Nate always thought that, as a reporter, he stood on the side of truth. But it seemed that sometimes truth didn't matter as much as compassion and forgiveness.

When at last the red lights on the cameras shut off, tension drained out of Shawna's body. She felt as if she had just played at Wimbledon and wouldn't know the results for ten days.

"You did great, sweetheart." Hunter stood and offered his hand to help her up.

She took it, feeling so weak she wasn't sure she could make it back to the green room. "I'm so proud of you. Whether you win the election or not, I think you're a winner."

They turned as Davis Jefferson approached them and held out his hand. "Governor, First Lady. This was … an *interesting* discussion. Good luck with the election."

After he left, Hunter chuckled. "Bet when he got up this morning, he didn't expect to hear so much about God today."

"Maybe he *needed* to hear it." Shawna smiled. "At any rate, we needed to say it. Let's go see what the family thought."

They headed for the green room where Mimi and the boys had watched the program on a monitor. When they entered, Cooper ran to Hunter and hugged him around his legs. Hunter Lynn hung back but he gave them a smile.

"You did great." Cooper looked up at Hunter and Shawna. "That man was mean, wasn't he?"

Shawna loved that Cooper would defend his dad against any criticism. She hoped H. L. would also be able to make the best of the awkward situation.

Hunter laughed and squatted down next to Cooper. "That man's job is to ask tough questions, so he was simply doing his job."

Cooper crossed his arms. "Well, I'm going to pray that he won't be so mean all the time."

Hunter Lynn snickered. "Coop thinks praying is the answer to everything."

Hunter held out one arm to Hunter Lynn. "It pretty much is, son. Now how about a group hug?"

Hunter Lynn stepped forward into Hunter's embrace. Hunter rose into a half-crouch and reached for Shawna. She moved in close, drawing Mimi into their circle.

"At least it's over." Mimi allowed the group hug but stepped back quickly. "And you know you did the right thing, no matter what happens. But I'm believing you're going to win this election."

Hunter looked at Shawna, his eyes glowing with affection. "We'll see, Mimi. Whatever happens, we'll get through it together."

A tap-tap sounded on the door, and it opened right away. Johnnie entered waving her iPad. "You're a hit! Social media's going crazy, and it's mostly positive."

Hunter let out a loud sigh of relief. "What are the negative comments?"

Johnnie looked at him hesitantly. He nodded. "Not about you, Governor. A few people are criticizing Shawna for being unfaithful to her husband while he was fighting for freedom, but other people are defending her. Saying that always happens during war, and that she doesn't have to be punished for the rest of her life."

Shawna pressed her lips together. That was good news, indeed, now that she knew she had been forgiven by God. She put an arm around Hunter's waist.

Johnnie looked up from her iPad. "I guess I was wrong. Telling your story was the right thing to do. You did well." She hesitated. "Both of you."

Shawna knew that compliment did not come easy for

Johnnie. Maybe Shawna hadn't played at Wimbledon today, but she had won a championship contest, after all.

Epilogue

Election Day

Shawna and Hunter went to their polling place shortly after lunch. As they were leaving the school after voting, Shawna suggested a visit to the cemetery.

"Of course," Hunter said. "Let's stop and get some fresh flowers."

Trent, their driver for the day, stopped outside Shawna's favorite flower shop. Shawna climbed out and, without waiting for Curtis to get out of the front passenger seat, ran into the store. She breathed in the sweet aroma of flowers and greenery. A country music radio station played in the background.

Curtis followed her inside and stepped up beside her. In a low voice, he said, "We'd appreciate it if you would stop running off like that, ma'am. You make it hard for us to do our job."

He was right. She turned to him and put a hand on his arm. "I'm sorry, Curtis. I don't mean to be difficult. I'm just not security-conscious when it comes to myself. I'll try to be more considerate." She gave him her brightest smile.

He nodded. "Thank you, ma'am." As he moved away, the radio deejay announced the next song—Lynn Wilson singing *No Secrets, No More.*

Shawna had not heard the song since the benefit concert, but now the words seemed meant for her and Hunter. They had found trust and contentment by confessing their failure, and the public response had been encouraging. Whether that translated into victory no longer seemed to matter.

The store owner approached, and Shawna purchased a dozen white roses. She held the paper-wrapped bouquet to her nose and inhaled, the faint fragrance a reminder of the emptiness she'd felt after her baby died. That blackness no longer called to her. Shining daylight on her relationship with Hunter had chased away the shadows cast by their secret.

Hunter took her hand as they walked from the drive to Hannah Lea's grave. The grass on top of the grave had finally begun to spread; by spring, the bare patch would return to green like the surrounding area.

But November had not yet released its hold on autumn. Sunlight warmed Shawna's back, providing comfort and hope that she had missed for most of the summer.

She knelt beside the granite stone and used bottled

water from the SUV to fill the vases on each side of the headstone. Dividing the roses between the two, she arranged them as if in preparation for a contest. When she had finished, she stood and took Hunter's hand again.

"Well," Hunter said, "Hannah Lea, I hope you are proud of us. We finally told the world the truth about you. It may keep me from being reelected governor, but we did the right thing. I love your mother, and she and your brothers mean more to me than any job ever will."

Shawna spoke in a low, reverent voice. "You may have been an accident in our timetable, but you were not an accident in God's plans. We admit the pregnancy was a mistake, little one, but don't think that we don't love you. We only wish you could have stayed with us longer."

She stopped and held her breath. Should she say what was on her heart? Was Hunter ready to hear it, or would he still think it was too soon? She let out a long breath. "We'll be sure to tell your new brother or sister all about you, when he or she gets old enough."

"What?"

Shawna turned, relishing the shocked look on Hunter's face. "That's right. Looks like we're back in the baby-building business."

"No kidding." He didn't smile.

"Hunter? Are you okay with this?"

He took Shawna in his arms and rested his chin on the top of her head. "Okay? Don't you know that's the best news I could get today?"

Warmth spread through Shawna's body, content in Hunter's genuine love. "I do think we should keep this between us for a few weeks."

"What? Another secret?"

She looked up to see him grinning. "Not for long. I just don't want to steal the spotlight from the election."

They stood there a few more minutes, then Shawna thought of one more thing to say. She turned back to look at the gravestone. "By the way, Hannah, don't pay attention to what your daddy says. He has a good chance of winning today."

Hunter laughed. "Your mom has more faith in me than I do. If you have any pull from up there, this might be a good time to use it."

Shawna squeezed Hunter's hand and smiled at him. "Ready when you are. Would you like to stop by Lynn's grave?"

"You don't mind?"

She lifted his hand to her mouth and kissed it. "You will always have a place in your heart for your first wife, the mother of your sons, just as you do for Hannah. As I will for Daniel. We can and should cherish their memories."

Hunter took her in his arms and expressed his thanks with a long, tender kiss.

After a brief stop at Lynn's burial site, Trent drove them downtown to the Omni, where Hunter would thank campaign volunteers at a post-election party. In a suite upstairs, Mimi waited with the boys, no doubt riveted to the multiple TV sets that had been brought in.

But all three sets were dark.

"You're here!" Cooper took a flying leap at both of them at once, nearly knocking Shawna over.

Hunter reached out a hand to steady her. "Easy, sport," he said. "She's not as tough as you and me. Now, come give her a gentle hug."

Cooper moved to her, spread his arms wide, then wrapped them loosely around her. "Sorry, Mom. I was excited."

Mom. He called her "Mom." She bent over and squeezed him tight, looking over his shoulder up at Hunter. Had he noticed? He must have, since his grin had spread from ear to ear.

"Okay, that's enough of that. What's the news?" Hunter looked at Johnnie, who stood waiting to be acknowledged, an iPad in her hand.

"Not too good." She shook her head. "The exit polls have you running neck and neck. We had hoped to have more of a lead by now."

"I'm a winner today, no matter what." Hunter grinned at Shawna. "But what's with the TVs? I thought you'd be watching the coverage."

Mimi came in from the kitchen with a tray of soft drinks. "I turned them off. The boys wanted to play video games, which of course we don't have here, and the election coverage won't really start until later. So, we've been playing the Game of Life."

Hunter nodded. "Sounds like a good way to pass the time."

Johnnie excused herself to check on arrangements for the volunteers.

"Dad," Hunter Lynn said. "Will you be my partner, so we don't have to start over?"

"Sure, H. L., if it's okay with Cooper." Hunter sat at the dining table next to his oldest son.

Cooper took Shawna's hand and pulled her to the opposite side of the table. "Mom can be my partner, then."

As Mimi took her seat, she laughed. "And I suppose you'll all gang up on me. I don't have a chance."

An hour later, the game was interrupted by a rapid knock on the door. Trent opened it to admit Johnnie.

"Congratulations, Governor. We did it!" She stopped short, eyeing the piles of money and cards in front of Hunter and H. L. She looked around the room. "You haven't turned the TVs back on?"

Hunter leaned back and laughed. "We were having too much fun to worry about the election. Why?" He stood and moved towards the TV sets, turning them on one by one.

"The networks have declared you the winner. And Hummel is giving her concession speech right now." Johnnie grinned from ear to ear. Sure enough, all three televisions showed Deborah Hummel at a microphone.

"Woohoo!" Cooper jumped up and ran to give his dad, then Johnnie, a high five, while the others shouted congratulations. Mimi applauded. "I knew you'd win."

Shawna sprung from her chair and hugged Hunter, then gave high fives to Cooper and Johnnie. A few months ago, she had hoped her husband would drop out—or lose. But now, on the first of many election nights they would share together, the victory caused warmth to spread from her feet to the top of her head.

She turned to Hunter Lynn, still sitting at the table, and held up her hand, which he slapped half-heartedly. "Aren't you happy for your dad, H. L.?"

He shrugged. "I guess so. But it's no big deal. He's already governor."

The top government figure in the state of Tennessee and his son thought it was no big deal. Would he feel the same if Hunter ran for Senator ... or President, some day? There would be no opportunity tonight, but she would have a talk with H. L. in the next few days, explain why his dad cared about the election.

Johnnie clapped her hands to get everyone's attention. "Y'all, we need to get ready for the celebration. Your people are down there waiting for your victory dance."

Shawna checked her hair and makeup, then she and Mimi helped the boys put on sports jackets and ties. Meanwhile, Hunter went into the bedroom for a few minutes to review the speech he had prepared. When he came out, working his arms into his suit coat, he went to Shawna and put his arms around her. He whispered into her ear, "Your announcement is still the best news of the day."

She tipped her head to look at him. "I think it's a tie." She grinned at him as he leaned in to kiss her.

Johnnie waited by the door with the trooper. "C'mon, team, we need to get going."

Hunter's cell phone, left on the table next to the Life board, rang. Johnnie gave Hunter a warning look.

But Mimi picked it up and answered. She listened, then held the phone against her stomach. "It's the chairman of the national party."

Hunter took the phone and touched a button. "Good evening, Paul. You're on speaker phone. My family is with me, as well as my campaign manager."

"Greetings, Governor, and everyone else. I'll keep this short so you can get on with your celebration. But I wanted to call with my congratulations."

The tone in his voice indicated his call had another purpose. On a day with key elections all over the country, a call from national headquarters had to be significant. Shawna's heart pounded and she held her breath.

"We've been watching your campaign down there with great interest. We'd like you to consider putting your name in the hat for the presidential nomination in two years."

Eyebrows raised, Hunter looked at Shawna. She returned his gaze, hoping her closed-mouth smile conveyed her unconditional support. But Hunter shook his head. "Thanks, maybe in the election after that. I need time to finish what I've started here in Tennessee. I want to fulfill my commitment to the people of this state, and to my family."

"How about vice president, then? As a stepping stone?" The man sounded like he was unaccustomed to being told "no."

"Mmm. Too soon to say. That would depend on the candidate, and whether I've accomplished my goals here. Ask me in eighteen months or so. Now, if you'll excuse me, I have supporters waiting to celebrate with me."

Johnnie shepherded the entire group out of the room and downstairs to the ballroom. As they made their way through the crowded halls, one young woman in a blue t-shirt with a "Four More for Hunter" slogan put her hand on Hunter's arm. The badge around her neck identified her as a campaign volunteer. "Governor, thank you."

He stopped. "It's all of you volunteers that deserve my thanks for your support and hard work."

The woman shook her head. She looked at Shawna, who had stopped next to Hunter. "The two of you saved my marriage. My husband had left me, but he saw you on that talk show. He came home and we decided to give it another chance. We even went to church together Sunday."

Hunter's face showed that he was moved. He cleared his throat. "Hearing your story means a lot to me. Thank you for telling us." They continued through the door into the ballroom.

As they prepared to go onstage, Hunter motioned to Mimi, who was standing at the back of the group. "Mimi, come on. I want you on stage, too. You're part of our family."

Hunter took Shawna's hand. She turned to take the hand of Hunter Lynn. He scooted to the back of the line and took Mimi's hand instead. Not everything could be perfect, even on a night of celebration.

Grinning, Cooper eagerly grabbed Shawna's and Mimi's hands, and Hunter led them on stage, with H. L. bringing up the rear. The crowd erupted in applause and hoots and whistles. The family raised their hands in a victory salute.

But to Shawna, the biggest victory was symbolized by Hunter's hand clasped around hers.

Acknowledgements

Writing is not a solo journey. So many people have provided assistance and encouragement as I worked on this book, as well as the first two in the series.

I am especially grateful to Amanda Kerns, Office of the First Lady of Tennessee, for providing insight into the daily life and duties of the governor's wife. Lt. Bill Miller of the Tennessee State Patrol answered as many questions as he could, regarding the security details of the governor's family.

Thanks, also, to Lisaann Dupont for answering my questions about Ryman Auditorium. My friends, Vince Riley and Marti Heape, shared pertinent experiences with me, and fellow ACFW member Darby Kern provided general information about security and the police.

Speaking of ACFW (American Christian Fiction Writers), I would not be published if it were not for all I have learned through that organization and its conferences.

It goes without saying—but I will say it anyway—that I am thankful to have the support of dear friends: Angela Arndt, my encouragement partner who understands because she is a writer, too; Crystal Allen, one of my first readers who is always asking for the next book; many members of the Master's Blend Life Group in Fort Myers, who pray for me (and buy my books); and Jerri Menges, who provides valuable editing services and isn't afraid to offer criticism, even though she is also a friend.

Last, but most important, is my husband Ed, who has been my biggest supporter and greatest fan since I began this publishing journey. Thanks for traveling this road with me.

A Second Chance

The Secret Heart *was inspired by the life of Bathsheba and her relationship with King David as recounted in 2 Samuel 11:1-12:24. The following is a dramatic recreation of that story.*

Until my baby died, the quicksand kept pulling me down.

One step at a time, I was sucked into the mire deeper and deeper.

I knew the king was in his palace that day. Maybe I wanted to punish him for staying safely in Jerusalem while my husband, Uriah, and the rest of the army faced the enemy on the battlefield.

I knew King David could see the roof of my house from his palace balcony, where he liked to walk, but that day I chose to bathe on the roof in broad daylight.

That was my first step into the quagmire. But I didn't expect what happened next. One of the king's servants appeared at my door, saying my presence was requested at the palace.

How could I refuse? He was not only the king, he was my husband's supreme commander. And perhaps I was lonely. Whatever the reason, I went to the king and willingly gave myself to him.

Can a woman love two men at the same time? I believe I did. My love for my husband did not dim—we planned to share a life together, and I longed for his return so we could begin that life. But David was here now. He was immediate and touchable, and he made me feel beautiful and loved again.

We enjoyed being together and the loneliness faded away. Spending time among the riches of the palace, and drawing the attention of the most popular and powerful man in Israel, brought new excitement to my hum-drum life.

Until I learned I was pregnant.

Since my husband had been away at war, everyone would know that I had been unfaithful. Uriah could have me stoned for adultery.

When I revealed the situation to David, the color fled from his face. Soldiers would no longer want to fight for a king who slept with the wife of one of his commanders, while the army slept on the ground miles from home. He devised a plan and sent for Uriah, but when David told him to go home and spend time with me, he refused to even sleep in the house. "How can I enjoy any comforts while my men are on the front lines?" he asked me. Nothing I did could seduce him to lay with me.

Then David arranged for Uriah to be caught in the middle of the line of battle, ensuring that he would be killed. When the word of his death reached me, I grieved. The life we had planned together ended on a dusty battlefield, and I wasn't there to hold his hand, to kiss him one last time, to say good-bye. Was this my punishment for breaking my marriage vows?

But guilt and relief made a tasteless stew in my belly. I thanked God for giving me—and the king—a way out of our predicament.

How wrong I was!

David and I married and soon we celebrated the birth of our son. Life seemed to be all I ever wanted it to be. David wanted an heir to the throne, and he believed our son would be king one day.

When the baby became ill, David begged God to heal him but nothing helped. Not his prayers. Not sacrifices. Not the herbs and spices of the healers. After our son died, I thought the heartbreak would kill us, too.

That's when God showed me the sins we had committed against Him. I confessed my transgressions to God and knew the cleansing power of His forgiveness.

It took David awhile, but after he went to see the priest, he changed. He returned with a peace about him that he had not shown since we met. He even wrote this beautiful song that says, "Create in me a clean heart, O God, and renew a right spirit within me."

Maybe you've heard it, but no one can sing it like David can. His voice resonates with his passion and love for the Lord.

God pulled us out of the mighty mess we walked into with such stubbornness. He rescued us and gave us another chance. He also gave us another son.

See, he's sleeping now. We named him Solomon. And our God has promised me that he will be a great king, and that through one of his children, all the people of the world will be saved.

God is a God of second chances, and I am so grateful.

Questions for Thought and Discussion

This story is loosely based on Bathsheba and King David, but the Bible says little about Bathsheba's life after their marriage. Do you think her emotions and attitudes might have been similar to Shawna's? In what ways might they have been different?

Why did Shawna and Hunter's secret affect their marriage? What could they have changed at the beginning to make a difference in their relationship?

Why did both Shawna and Hunter feel at times that they had betrayed their first spouse? Were these feelings an accurate assessment of the situation?

Since Hunter was afraid of heights, how was he able to overcome that fear to save Cooper? Have you ever had to conquer a strong fear in order to accomplish something important?

What were the undercurrents in Mimi's relationship with Shawna? Can you think of a time when you had to deal with a similar situation? Is there anything Shawna could have done to improve the relationship?

Did anything surprise you about the visit from Shawna's former in-laws, Dan and Charisse? Why? Did they remind you of anyone you know?

How did Nate Matthews' past experiences influence his actions? How do our own histories and our decisions affect our lives, even years later?

About the Author

Marie Wells Coutu claims she has been writing all her life. Through story, she hopes to inspire women to find God's purpose for their lives regardless of where they've been or what they've done.

A writer and editor for newspapers, magazines, nonfiction books, and government agencies, she has edited devotionals and other books published by the Billy Graham Evangelistic Association. A member of American Christian Fiction Writers, she is a past president of Carolina Christian Writers.

The Secret Heart is the third book in the Mended Vessels series. The first, For Such a Moment, was her debut novel and won the Books of Hope Contest. Thirsting for More, the second book in the series, was a finalist in the 2016 Selah Awards Contest and a semi-finalist in the Royal Palm Literary Awards sponsored by Florida Writers Association.

Marie retired after 15 years with the Billy Graham Evangelistic Association, and she and her husband now divide their time between Florida and Iowa. You can learn more about Marie and her novels on her Facebook page (Author Marie Wells Coutu), at her website (MarieWellsCoutu.com), or follow her on Twitter (@mwcoutu).

Also by the Author

Available in print and e-book at Amazon

When Wendy's family faces financial hardship, she must find a way to see Mrs. V and Sam again—but will she lose David forever in the process?

When Wendy's stepfather loses his job, she needs more personal and urgent help—the financial kind. The family's plan to visit Alaska on vacation is headed down the sewer like a hard Louisiana rain. How will Wendy ever see Mrs. V or Sam again?

An opportunity arrives in the form of tutoring Melissa, one of the Sticks, and Wendy's money problems appear to be solved. Until the arrangement takes a turn that gets Wendy into trouble like never before.

In the final months of ninth grade, she might lose everything she counted on for the future.

Write Integrity Press

Romance Collection

Capture the Magic!

**Thank you
for reading our books!**

**Look for other books
published by**

Write Integrity Press
www.WriteIntegrity.com

66945760R00227

Made in the USA
Charleston, SC
31 January 2017